INTO DARKNESS

For all Content Inquiries, please visit my website:

Dedication

Rely on yourself before anyone else, and when you're tired, paint your face and set your warrior free.

PROLOGUE

"I forgive you," he whispers as he drops his chin to his chest, the blood loss making him weak.

I chuckle dryly, then reach out and grab a handful of his hair, lifting his face so his eyes meet mine. At that moment, a dry flake of Tommy's blood floats off my face and lands on his cheek.

"Thank you. I'm going to need it." I jam my forefinger into the gunshot wound at his shoulder and revel in his scream, his blood pumping out around my fingers and down my arm like a warm, soothing bath. "I doubt my mother forgave you for taking her from me." I grab his chin, smearing it with his blood and forcing him to look at me. "We were all each other had." Rage coats every syllable I spit out between clenched teeth.

"She… knew it… was going to happen." He's panting, and his leg wound is losing a lot of blood. I can't have him dying too soon though, because I'm just getting started. I look around his office and find a fancy-looking Burberry scarf wrapped around a wooden coat stand. That'll do. I apply the makeshift tourniquet around his leg and look into his eyes, wanting to claim every ounce of pain he portrays. "Thank you, my daughter."

I laugh and slap him hard across the face, the sound bouncing room like a cacophony of mocking laughter. Finally, the meek mask he's been wearing up until now drops, and his eyes become cold. This is the real Raphael who runs the Eastside Rampage. "There you are, Father." I grin sadistically. "It's finally nice to meet you."

"My son will come looking for me," he says between blood-coated teeth, his voice filled with scorn.

"Carm?" I put my bloodied finger to my nose, tapping lightly as I look to the ceiling in thought. "I killed him." The words tumble out of me with complete nonchalance as I shrug, my gaze finding his once more.

The alarm in his eyes sends me into another round of manic laughter. "Your mother would not want this," he pants out as his eyelids grow heavy.

Just the mention of her from his mouth sends me into a red void, and what little restraint I had on my anger is suddenly gone. I punch him in the face, and his nose buckles under my knuckles as his pain-filled yell awakens a hunger inside me.

"We're going to have so much fun," I say as I reach out and tweak his crushed nose.

His answering whine of agony makes me giggle.

9

Chapter One

"Hello, twin."

His voice still echoes in my head as I'm walking down the dirt road, the crunching of gravel under my feet the only sound out here. Pressing my hand to my chest, I let the slow rhythmic beat of my heart convince me I'm still living, even if I'm nothing more than an empty void. It shocked me when his turquoise-blue eyes met mine, but that was it. No excitement, no fear, no nothing. For a girl who's had very little family her entire life and learns she now has a half-brother and a twin brother, you'd think I'd be overwhelmed. I should be full of happiness or *something*.

Now that I think about it, I didn't even ask him his name. Did our mother name him? Or was he taken right at birth? My father said he was with me for the first six months of my life, so that should mean my twin was too, right? So what happened? Did my father separate us right away or did someone do it after he went to jail? That sounds more like something he would do to punish my mother because she never once mentioned a brother, let alone a twin. Nothing was ever said, and if I ever brought up anything about family, she would lose it.

There's been too many secrets she kept from me, and I'm beginning to wonder how the fuck she slept at night. How did she look at me and not feel some sort of guilt about keeping an entire family from me? My aunt and uncle, and now a twin brother too. This woman had a double life, and I was part of that false persona. If I had a handle on my emotions, if I even had the capacity to feel something right now, I would be livid.

The breeze catches on my ponytail and blows my hair across my face. The one thing I really love about Canada is how the air is always so fresh. It has a floral blend mixed with the scent of freshly mowed lawns. I don't miss the car exhaust and garbage from the overcrowded New York streets. Up here in Muskoka though, the air is crisp. It has just a slight touch of pine and fresh lake water. I fill my lungs up and try to inhale some contentment.

Still nothing.

The therapist my parents found, for my sanity, says I have locked away my humanity to protect myself. It's PTSD at its finest. I don't care, and I tell her as much weekly, which only affirms her prognosis. There's a laundry list of drugs she wants to put me on to help me cope with what I've been through, but I absolutely refuse. I've dabbled with marijuana but nothing chemical. I've seen what people become on that shit. I've beaten people who have wasted their whole lives for it. So, I basically tell her where she can shove those drugs each time we talk. I don't care what she or anyone else says. What she nor my parents know is, I won't be going back for any more appointments. This darkness I've succumbed to is cold, and it feels like I'm finally where I belong. If I need to pull myself out, I will do it without the help of prescription drugs.

This therapist is constantly trying to coax me into opening up about what happened while I was being held prisoner in the Rampage compound. I keep to the story of being drugged and waking up covered in blood and not remembering a single thing. She doesn't believe me though, I know that. I can see it in her eyes, yet I don't fucking care.

The new parents have patience because the girl they brought home no longer exists. If they had trepidations then, well, I could laugh at what they must feel now. They still treat me the same with love and attention, but they're afraid of what I'm becoming. It's in the timid way they look at me when they think I don't notice, or the trepidation in their voices when they start a conversation. It's clear they're wondering about what's going on inside my head.

When I learned of my mobster sperm donor burning our home to kill my mother, it damaged me, but I've always been a little on the dark side. Before the revelation, I flirted with the darkness, teasing it when I needed a little boost but also staying firmly on the other side. Until the day that man confessed to killing her, then I took the plunge into the inky abyss.

With the death of my mother, my aunt and uncle took me into their home and lives, and I am loved beyond anything I ever dreamed of. They provide me with everything I need. After the adoption, I formally started calling my aunt and uncle, Ma and Dad. I used to want them to be proud of having me, of fulfilling their need for a family, but after I was taken, I lost that version of myself.

After I was forced into that vehicle with my murderous father, and then all the events that unfolded afterward, my life has been turned upside down. When I close my eyes, blood coats the back of my eyelids, the tangy iron invades my nose, and the sound of screaming fills my ears. I was gone for nearly nine days—two hundred and eight hours—give or take a few minutes, and for the last half a day, I succumbed to that deep darkness inside of me.

I go through the motions of my day-to-day life since I've been back. It's been mostly locking myself up in my bedroom and then sneaking out to Vin's every night. He's my light in an ocean of black, and for that short amount of time I'm connected to him, I can submerge myself into warmth and love.

I've dealt with this numbness a few times before when I needed to tune my humanity out, but I have never been stuck in it for this long. When I fight, I let myself become numb with no emotions to cloud my judgment, but I can usually bring myself out of it after a few hours. This time though, I think I stayed in for too long. I had let that inky-black, evil part of my soul devour me so I could seek my vengeance. Revenge is sweet. I don't care what people say, it really is sweet. Regardless of the price I'm paying currently.

The only other time I'm not living in a numb void is during my nightmares. I guess they aren't nightmares really, more like vivid memories, but they scare me when I wake up because I can't believe how far I had gone. I can't believe I sank so low into the dark pool. I'm not saying my father didn't deserve it, he fucking did, and to be completely honest, I'd do it again in a heartbeat for my mother and for Tommy.

I haven't really processed Tommy's death yet because I've compartmentalized him away for now. If I linger too long on thoughts of him, the familiar rage swirls deep in my stomach and the red seeps into my vision. Carm says Tommy's foster parents found him in his room at home and the police deemed it a suicide. Dumbasses. There would have been blood if he shot himself, but his blood wasn't in his room because it had pooled inside that ring in the compound. Luckily for Carm and his nepotism, the position his daddy left him is a powerful one. That's how it is when you own the police like Carm now does, he can make anything the truth. He told me the home isn't having a funeral, just burying him at the local cemetery. When I'm ready to visit, I'll ask for more information.

Anger, raw and debilitating, has become a constant emotion besides apathy. I can no longer control it, and once I'm triggered, it's like a fucking tsunami. Luckily for everyone, it's been laying pretty dormant lately, and I have had little to provoke it. My parents are sweet and patient, my therapist reads the cues I project, and Vin is so in tune to me that I'm sure he can sense what lies just beneath.

The gravel along the road jabs into the soles of my shoes, and the extra weight on the waistband of my shorts is annoying, the metal against my lower back cooling. Carm was adamant I carry a gun on me at all times to protect myself. At first, I refused him. The last time I had a gun was when I'd lost myself—no, gave myself over—to the darkness. The night I used *four* bullets. Carm insists I *pack heat*, saying he and the twin are here for a while and that he also wants me to train to shoot. *Whatever.*

Apparently, someone by the name of Jennifer Talia is looking for me and I can't place why her name sounds so familiar. According to Carm, she's pissed I killed Raph. *Boo-hoo, bitch.* I wouldn't change a single thing I did, no matter who the fuck is after me. That man who kidnapped me, drugged me, and forced me to kill for his entertainment. The man who killed my mother and Tommy, and stole my twin brother.

Carm promises to text my phone from his burner to stay in touch, but I couldn't care less either way. He may prove useful to me though because I will need eyes and ears in New York. If this woman comes for me or my family, I will take her out first. If I can commit patricide, I can do just about anything. For now, I just need to keep it together, continue to control the need to assuage the darkness growing inside of me, and just be a normal teenager.

Adri and Travis are on their way here and I haven't seen them since before the kidnapping. I can't be the old Ember who drank and partied because I need a firm grip on my anger, but I can fake it. I'll pretend to drink and to laugh, even if it slowly kills me more on the inside.

Texting them these past few weeks has been tough. I don't have any desire to keep up with their day-to-day lives when I don't even care about myself. I still care about their well-being, of course, and I would still take out anyone who threatened them. They're my family now too, but I can't muster the feelings for their everyday activities. Trust me, Travis and Adri have difficulties every fucking day. Those two will either crash and burn or end up married at eighteen with a kid on the way.

In a few hours, I will be turning seventeen and it's so

anticlimactic. I've been looking forward to this day, and now that it's here, it's nothing special. I may be turning seventeen, but I already feel like I'm twenty-five. I look at other teenagers around me like Travis and Adri and ascertain that their life experiences just don't line up with mine. Our lives are so different, even if the outside looks the same. I just can't compare them. How would they ever understand what I'm going through? I can't imagine sitting them down and telling them everything I went through, the lives my father forced me to take and the torture I inflicted on him for it. Adri wouldn't look at me the same, and Travis—superstar baseball player Travis—who has lived in a mansion on the hill his entire life, would never understand.

I purposely left Vin out of that because he also hasn't had the greatest life. His father never wanted him, and his mother struggled to raise him. He witnessed her pain when he found out he actually had a half brother who his father adored. So he has some experience with the anger living inside of me, and his soul has a darkness similar to mine. That's why he doesn't push and doesn't have any expectations from me. He gets it… he gets all of it. My anger, my apathy, and most of all the walls I've built. As long as I love him, he is content.

And I really fucking love him.

17

C.A. RENE

Vin

She's not here.

The cabin is completely empty, and she's not down by the water either. My heart rate increases and practically jumps out of my chest. My mouth goes dry, and I have a lump lodged in my throat, making it difficult to breathe. I leave for twenty minutes, and her ass is missing. Where would she go? Did someone take her again?

I dump the groceries on the table, not caring if the ice cream melts, and run back out to my Hummer. Anxiety rushes through me with the need to find her before anything else happens to her. She's already filled with so much turmoil and ready to snap. Worried for her safety and the weight she'd no doubt be piling on if she hurt others, I jump into the vehicle and open my glove box, seeing the gleam of metal tucked inside, and then close it again. I'm not taking any chances, and if I find her with anyone, I'm shooting first and asking questions later. A gun isn't foreign to me, and I've had enough experience with them.

Why the fuck did I leave her alone? The cops have found nothing in her still very open case and she could be in danger. I'm so fucking stupid! I slam my palm against the steering wheel and let out a few colorful curses as I drive. Why didn't I make her come with me? What if she was being followed again? I didn't exactly look out for a tail on our way here.

I turn left at the end of the driveway since I came in on the right. She must've gone this way toward the public beach because I didn't see her on my way back here. The back of my Hummer fishtails as I gas it out onto the gravel road with haste. My heart is racing like I don't have a lot of time, my intuition screaming that something is wrong.

"Fuck!" I scream out, the sound bouncing around my head.

Ember means the world to me, and she's become part of my family. Just her and my mom, no one else matters. Sure, I have a dad, but he was too busy playing house at college with another woman while my mother was raising me when she was just barely out of high school herself. To rub salt in the wound, he never acknowledged me. Despite that, my mother gave me his last name to ensure I had a choice to chase him down later. I have a half brother, Travis, who is the apple of our father's eye, and I resent him for every single thing he possesses. His life was simple and filled with privilege, while mine was hard and filled with anger. I don't blame my mother for the childhood I had because she was the best mother a kid could ever ask for. She did her best while Travis had dinner at a fancy table with both happy parents each night, and they tucked him into bed with a book and a kiss. *Fucking dipshit.*

Then Ember came along and brightened things up. She brought with her the sun to my clouds. The one spot of color in my life of black and white. Yeah, I sound like a fucking poet right now, but it's the truth. She saved me. I was drowning in a pit of self-loathing and hatred, and she broke through and dragged me out. So now, I'm going to save her right back. She seems lost, and the anger is building like a torrent inside of her. It pours from her eyes like a tidal wave, ready to devour everything in its path. Sometimes when she zones out, I can see the flashes of pain and sadness that come over her. She has it locked up so tight and one day it'll explode. The look is familiar because I was there, and it's only a matter of time until she's lost for good. I would never let that happen though, not if I can help it.

I just wish I knew more about what happened to her because then I can determine her trigger. We all have one.

Mine?

Travis Greene. He knows it too.

Before Ember, he was my fucking punching bag, and depending on the day, he'd fight me back too. But most of the time he'd take it, and that made me livid. Like a display of pity or shame. He knew the conditions I grew up in and that they were because of his father. So, he would just take it like a beating was the most natural thing to him, like he deserved it, and that would make me hate myself even more. It was a vicious circle with no end in sight. Not until her. She bridged the gaping chasm and slowly sealed up the missing parts of my soul.

Now I just wait for what happens next, watching her for any signs of an impending explosion, and if that happens, hopefully I'll be with her to soften the blow for the poor bastard or take it myself. Either way, she'll always have me, no matter what.

I worry my tongue ring between my teeth, the metal ball providing the diversion I need. When I'm agitated or angry, I try to distract myself by playing with it. If I let my mind wander, it flips through too many scenarios, which causes me to be anxious or angry. More often than not, it's anger. Last year, or about eight months ago to be exact, was the last time I punched Travis in the face and the last time I let my anger dictate my actions. It's still there, raging beneath the surface of my skin, but I've learned to stop reacting to it without careful thought of the repercussions. I was immersed in my rage that day, and the anger burning inside me had reached its peak. It doesn't fucking help that he's in my space every day either. I have to look into his smug, privileged-ass face day after day only to be reminded of the hardships I went through. Things he couldn't even imagine. How could I not beat the fucking shit out of him? I had options, other schools I could transfer to, but my mother went to Precious Blood and it's the best school in our area. I'd be a fool to leave its benefits behind.

That day was the first time I regretted it afterward. He's always been mouthy and never held back when we would fight. Some of the shit he said deserved my wrath, but that time he didn't hit me back, and when I was done, he walked away from me without saying a word. I hated him even more for taking the beating and not retaliating in some way because I wanted him to prove me right by acting smug, but he never did. So, after that, I decided I wouldn't hit him again unless provoked, and not just by his fucking face, but actually physically provoked.

Seeing him and not releasing the anger makes me antsy, like I have this energy inside me that has nowhere to go, then the anger becomes too much. The gym helps, but I find distractions are better. So I got the tongue ring and fucked girls constantly. I'm ashamed to admit it, but Marlana was a go-to for me for the longest time. Then, a few months before Ember showed up, I decided I had had enough. She wasn't a long-term thing for me, and if I'm being completely honest, I always knew that. Even if she saw me as her endgame. My ambitions for my future didn't have her in them, and I grew the fuck up. Plus, she was pestering me constantly about not kissing her in public or that I was too distant and it became a topic of contention for us. I have never been a people person. Expressing any emotion was hard unless it was violence or anger. I sealed myself off from forming any type of relationship, including friendships because life taught me that nothing is permanent. Everyone leaves. That was nothing but a defense mechanism and Ember blew it all apart.

Now I want to love her, and I want everyone to witness it because I want them to know she's mine. She's the one I've chosen. Most importantly, I want her to trust in our love. Yet, as if pulled from my very nightmares, she just naturally becomes close to the two people I want nothing to do with, but I can't deny her, and when she asks me to make the effort, I do it. Family means so much to her and that's what they are to her. It makes me want to help her find her father and to become a part of her family too. So if that means playing nice with my prick brother, then that's what I have to do.

A female figure walks in the distance toward me as I round a bend in the road. It's her, I can recognize the gait and her hair blowing in the breeze. I pull over to the side and jump out of the vehicle. She's walking so slowly, as if her shoulders are burdened with everything she's been through, each step like a leaden weight in front of the other. It really makes me think she remembers what happened to her and it isn't good.

I jog toward her as her head jerks up at the noise. Yeah, my girl is antsy about anyone approaching. Ember has always been sensitive to her surroundings, but lately it's become much more. She's always tense, like she's prepared to fight any time.

She stops to look into my face as I approach her. "I wanted to go for a jog," she says, her eyes narrowing on me, waiting for the reprimand for scaring the shit out of me. I let it go though because I don't want to add to her stress.

"Leave a note next time." I reach out and brush her ponytail back over her shoulder, my fingers lingering on the soft skin of her cheek.

"You scared, baby?" she teases, a small smile coating her mouth but not quite meeting her eyes. Eyes filled with demons.

"Yes, Em. I am," I admit to her, and her eyes drop to the ground, her mouth tilting downward.

She exhales and her shoulders slump a bit. I can't be soft with her though because my girl is like a wolf and can sniff that weak shit out. "Okay," she mutters and kicks at the gravel.

"Let's head back. My ice cream is melting," I grunt out before turning to look at the Hummer over my shoulder and then back at her.

"After you." She gestures toward the vehicle, her eyes finally flicking back up to meet mine.

We head to the Hummer with her shuffling along behind me. I want this weekend to be good for her. I'm hoping she gets some of her spark back to help her to move on from whatever it was she went through. We get in and buckle up as she squirms a bit in her seat. "Everything okay?"

"Yeah, running on gravel is different. My lower back is a little sore." She winces as she adjusts again, then looks out the window.

I turn the Hummer around and head back to the cottage as we sit in silence. This is the way it's been since she came back. It's not uncomfortable, but I miss her voice. I don't know what to do to make her open up to me. How can I make her trust me enough to unload all her fears? She has to believe I'm her long-term, that I'm not going anywhere, but I don't have all the time in the world to prove it. I want our lives together to start now without wasting any more time. What else can I do to show her I'm not going anywhere?

"Thanks for bringing me here," she whispers, her gaze still out the window.

"You like it?" I quickly glance at her before looking back out to the road.

"Yeah, it's calming." Her reflection in the window shows a small smile on her mouth as her eyes scan the trees.

"That's why we got this place a few years ago. Ma thought it would help calm me." I drum my fingers along the steering wheel.

"Did it?" She turns back to look at me, curiosity burning in her turquoise eyes.

"While I was here, yeah, but when I went back home, it was all forgotten."

"Mmm," she replies in thought, her eyes turning back to the window.

We pull up to the cottage and I hurry out of the Hummer, hoping I can save the ice cream before it becomes a puddle in the middle of the kitchen. Then I need to prepare dinner for our *guests*. My teeth clench with the effort to hold everything in and not rock the boat on already tumultuous waters.

"I'm going to shower!" Ember calls out as she heads up the stairs on her way to our bedroom.

"Okay." I listen to her take the stairs one step at a time, slow and methodical. She no longer has a pep in her step.

My phone pings on the counter with a message, the screen lighting up with Adri's name. I can deal with her... most of the time. I hold little animosity toward her, but I had resentment for a while. Adri was my best friend too, and she always chose Travis. She loved him from the beginning, but I existed too. Now that she and Ember have this strong bond, I have to move on from that.

Adrianna: We're turning onto the road. Be there in 5.

Me: Cool.

Time to temper my emotions and think about what Ember needs, and right now, she needs her closest friends. As much as I want to hate Travis forever, there is a logical part of me that understands we're family. Blood doesn't change, no matter how tainted it is. It's going to take a fuck ton of time though before I can look at him and not want to break his nose.

The front door opens and Adri's voice drifts toward me. "No, Travis, you're being unreasonable."

"Whatever." Travis sounds bored, but there's a ripple of tension beneath that single word.

Those two and their constant bickering. Fuck, I'm so happy that Ember and I just mesh. We don't fucking bicker. If we have a problem, we tell the other what the fuck is up, then done, end of story.

"Hey, Vin," Adri says, coming into the kitchen. Her maroon and highlighted pink hair is gathered on top of her head in a messy bun and she's dressed in a tank and jean shorts.

"'Sup," Travis adds as he leans against the doorframe of the kitchen. He looks around the cottage, taking it all in. I hope he recognizes just how hard my mother worked for this without the help of his deadbeat father.

I nod my head in reply before focusing on preparing the food in front of me. "The rooms are up the stairs. Pick whichever ones you want. Doesn't matter."

"Okay, cool," Adri murmurs. I listen to her heading toward the stairs, her steps quick and light. Such a contrast to my girl's.

"How is she?"

"Different," I mutter as I stop what I'm doing to look at Travis.

He's lingering behind, his tone low as he watches Adri walk away. Then he shakes his head before turning to look at me. "How so?" His green eyes remind me of our father and I swallow down the urge to punch him in the face. It's irrational because we have the same eyes. The same eyes I look into every time I face a mirror, making me want to shatter every reflection.

"Quieter, emotionless." It's hard to have him here, but I'm hoping it'll be worth it for Ember.

"Fuck." He exhales, lifting his hat to run his hand over his hair before placing it back. I nod and continue to mix the burger patty meat. "Need some help?"

"Nah, I'm good." I keep my focus on the bowl in front of me as I say, "You can go on up and get situated."

I watch through my periphery as he nods before heading out of the kitchen, then I drop my hands to the countertop to exhale slowly. It's so fucking hard, listening to his voice and being around him. It's like nails on a chalkboard sometimes. Compared to last year though, I've come a long way.

Then the room shifts as I work on my breathing, sensing her before I even hear her.

It's been this way since the first day I saw her walking through that gym. The hair stood up on my arms, and when Shay muttered, "That's her." I felt it. I had turned to look at her and my eyes landed on the nicest ass I had ever seen. I wanted her even then. It was like my heart recognized she was meant for me.

"The shower here is sick." Her tenor has my cock instantly hardening as her scent washes over me in waves of vanilla.

"Yeah, all those jets," I agree as I take her in. Her damp hair glistens and her dewy skin shines under the kitchen lights. "I'll press your pussy into one tonight."

She comes to stand beside me and looks me in the eyes, heat clouding her features with lust. "How about my ass?" she rasps as heat and humor swirl in her eyes. "I found coconut oil in the cabinet."

We haven't gone there yet, but with how we've been going, it's only a matter of time. "Done."

"That's what I'm talking about," she quips as she lightly punches my arm.

I wrap my arm around her waist and tug her close, keeping my burger-coated fingers from touching her. "You treat me like I'm just one of your boys again and I'll be spanking that ass before I fuck it."

"That a threat?" She quirks her brow as I turn on the sink and wash my hands. "Because it's sounding mighty tempting." I tip my head back and groan. She's so fucking seductive and frustrating at the same damn time. I turn back to her after drying my hands, tossing the towel to the counter. "So, they're here, huh?" she says into my chest as I gather her close, her words muffled by my shirt.

"Yeah, upstairs picking rooms, or fucking. I don't know." I press my face into her vanilla-scented hair and inhale her essence.

"I liked our alone time." She pulls back to look up at me, mischief twinkling in her eyes.

"Well, we've had a ton of alone time and they miss you." I flick her nose.

"I know."

"Ember!" Adri bellows as she runs down the stairs. Ember stiffens beside me and cringes at the sound. A total one-eighty to how she used to greet Adri.

"Babe, you're a soldier," I whisper.

Chapter Two

"Ember!" Adri's loud squeal rips through my ears like a personal assault on my brain. I turn around slowly as she barrels toward me, the smile on her face wide.

"Babe, you're a soldier," Vin says into my ear. It's similar to what Carm used to say to me in that underground hell and it does nothing to quell my quaking insides. I shake the thought away and fully face Adri.

"Hey." I plaster on what must look like the biggest, fakest grin.

"Oh my God! I'm so happy to see you!" She's still squealing, the sound like nails on a chalkboard.

"Me too." I'm still holding this fucking grin, the burning of my cheek muscles heightening as I'm nodding my head.

"Are you okay? What happened?" She grabs my face with both hands, and it takes all my self-control not to knock her hands away.

"Hey, Adri. Can you… ah… help me grab the beer out of the fridge?" Vin saves me, as if sensing my energy. "We can put them in the cooler and eat down by the beach."

"Yes!" she squeals… again. "We can swim!" She runs off to do Vin's bidding, and he leans in to kiss my ear.

"She just loves you," he whispers, and I nod. I know she loves me. I love her too. Adri is my family, but right now I'm skating along on the thinnest ice. All the emotions I should be having are locked tight under a numb blanket. I just wanted some time to adapt before being thrusted into life again. Being forced to fake life right now is wearing thin on my nerves.

Vin and Adri bring the food and cooler outside as she practically skips with happiness, and I feel like the biggest asshole for not doing that with her. Although seeing Vin try to mask his irritation of having to shoulder most of the squealing is like watching an improvisation set.

"Nice," Travis says sarcastically behind me.

"What?" I continue to keep my focus on Vin and Adri outside, refusing to look my friend in the eyes for fear of what he'll find.

"You don't have to pretend with us, you know." Am I that much of an open book? Have I lost my touch?

"I'm not." I muster up the courage to look at him, finding him leaning against the wall with his arms over his chest.

"Yeah, you are. I'm not Vin, I won't let you pretend like shit is normal. That isn't my style. I recognize when someone is faking because I've done it most of my fucking life." I'm not sure how to answer him and I don't understand what he's talking about being fake. I want to throw so much into his face right now about his privileged and loving home, but what would that prove? What could he possibly have to be fake about?

"Look,"—he scrubs his hand down his face—"we're here because we want you to know we care. A lot. But don't pretend." He shoulders by me and opens the fridge to grab a beer. It takes all of my will to stop myself from turning him around and punching him in the face. Clenching my fists, I count and regulate my breathing before I look into his eyes again.

"I don't know how to be happy anymore." Did I really just say that out loud? The shock must register on my face because he suddenly relaxes and gives me a sad look.

"What did you do before? You know… when you felt too angry?" He pops the cap off his beer bottle and takes a sip, his eyes watching me closely.

"Made people bleed… profusely." The corners of my mouth rise with just the thought of violence and my stomach twists with anticipation.

"Hmm." He strokes his chin while he purses his mouth in thought. "Do that again." Shock tears through me as I stare at him, waiting for him to laugh at the absurdity of his words.

He can't be fucking serious. "Where?" I ask when I realize he's completely fucking serious, throwing my hands up in exasperation. "Whitsborough is like a Disney princess compared to New York."

"So start taking some trips back to New York. Call them business trips." He snaps his fingers with the idea before taking another drink from his bottle.

"Business trips." I snort. Did I just laugh? Kind of? The sound is nearly foreign to me now.

"Hey!" He points at me with mock surprise on his face. "Was

that a snort?"

"Fuck off." I grin and shoulder past him to the fridge.

"Travis-one, Anger-zero." This time he earns a chuckle from me and he quickly joins in.

I shake my head and grab a beer too. I'm clearly going to need it. We both lean against the counter, silently sipping our beers and watching Vin and Adri barbecue. As much as he is pushing me, I know Travis loves me and wants to help me. He and Vin have more in common than just their shared parentage. There's a small piece of me that hopes they can succeed and I can move on from everything that's happened to me.

"How annoyed do you think he is right now?" Travis asks, humor thick in his voice. "On a scale of one to ten?"

"Thirty-two."

We both chuckle and continue to drink while watching Vin and Adri.

We're all chilling on the beach, drinking beers, and digesting all the food we ate for dinner, thanks to Vin. The sun is setting over the water in shades of red and orange and I'm sitting between Vin and Travis while Adri has her head in my lap.

"Trav, let's make a fire in the pit," Vin says, getting up and dusting his pants off. "Ember, go set up some music."

Adri and I get up, both of us making our way back into the cottage. Vin showed me the iPod dock and how to turn on the exterior speakers earlier. So I pop my iPhone on the device and start scrolling through my playlists.

"Are you ever going to talk to me?" Adri asks quietly behind me. *Well, damn. Here we go.*

"I talk to you." I shrug as my finger swipes over the screen of my phone, my heart beating a mile a minute with pent-up irritation at her question.

"About what happened," she reiterates, her tone filled with annoyance which in turn pisses me off.

"I don't remember what happened." I turn around to face her as my cheeks heat with anger and my eyes narrow in on her widening ones.

"Ember, if you didn't actually remember, you'd still be the same," she counters as she crosses her arms over her chest, her own eyes narrowing in accusation.

"I was abducted," I stress as my hands curl into fists at my sides. "Of course I'm different."

"I think you remember exactly what happened and you're hiding it." The words fly from her mouth with irritation as her arms fall back to her sides.

"Adri, stop digging—"

"Was it the gang?" she cuts me off. "Maybe you can find out more from Tommy."

"Don't talk about him," I snap harshly and turn back around, forcing myself to calm down before I do something irrational to my best friend.

Her gasp fills the room and then the door opens and shuts. Thank God she left because I was about to lose it. I know she means well, but I can't have her digging around too fucking hard. I won't let anyone else become entangled with my problems. Plopping my ass onto the stool, I lay my forehead on the cool granite counter, the feeling calming my rage. I'm going to have to tell them about Tommy now, obviously. All of them because the questions will never stop and I can only avoid it for so long before I snap.

The door opens again and Vin's energy moves over me like a cooling balm. I love how my body reacts to him, how it sometimes becomes so attuned to him. "You good?" His gruff voice has my stomach fluttering with desire and erases the irritation completely as I raise my head to look at him.

"Yeah," I answer, the word muted against the granite counter.

"We can call it a night—"

"Tommy is dead," I cut him off. Band-Aid firmly ripped, Ember style.

"How?" See? He gets me. His nonchalant question is his way of not crowding me and letting me tell him when I'm ready. No need to shower me with affection or pester me with too many fucking questions.

"Shot himself." Bile begins to work its way up my throat as I swallow it back down, forcing myself to remain calm.

"Any idea why he'd want to do that?" he asks as his scent washes over me.

"Not sure, but it looks like I'm heading to New York next weekend." I lift my head to look at the iPod dock, the music forgotten in my argument with Adri.

"Cool, I'll come with you." I turn around and find him leaning against the patio door, his thick, muscular arms crossed over his wide chest and his face obscured by a baseball hat. His jaw tics with irritation, preparing for the inevitable fight, yet he's still so fucking gorgeous.

"No can do." I shake my head and give him a heated once-over.

"You're not going back to New York alone, Ember." He pushes up the rim of his hat, making sure the determination in his eyes is clear.

"I need answers. I can't do that and look after you too." I shrug as I bite my bottom lip, trying desperately to hold in the moan threatening to spill when he smiles at me.

He laughs and drops his arms to stalk toward me. "Your aunt and uncle would never agree to it without me." He has a point. "Besides, we can look for your father as well… right?"

I'm looking him in the eyes, and he's practically daring me to disagree. Vin is ignorant about my father's fate and the role I had in it, but that doesn't mean Vin isn't inside my soul. He senses some things about me without me having to say a single word.

"Fine, but you're acting like a stage five clinger." I smirk at him as he comes to stand in front of me, forcing my head to tilt back as we maintain eye contact.

"Don't care." He leans down, crowding me against the counter, his arms caging me in. "You knew what you were signing up for." True. "A few hours until the big seventeen." He kisses my neck and bites into the tender flesh softly.

"Mmm."

Birthdays have never been exciting occasions for me. We grew up poor and some years it was like any other day. That's why no one is making a big deal about my birthday today, and I'm sure Vin told them without me having to say a word. I've spoken to him about my birthdays before and he's the same way. These days aren't happy ones, per se. I just look forward to getting older and more independent.

The door slides open again, and Travis' laughter fills the space. "Are you guys done being antisocial?" he calls out, forcing us to break apart.

"Yeah, yeah," Vin answers. Then he leans down, his mouth pressing against my ear as he says, "Talk to Adri." Right, of course I have to consider the girl's feelings. I've forgotten just how sensitive Adri can be. Tamping down the annoyance at having to navigate Adri's feelings, I remind myself that she loves me and only cares about what's happening with me.

We head outside and I make my way down the beach to sit in the lawn chair beside Adri, the fire in the pit attracting my attention so I can avoid the sadness in her eyes.

"I'm sorry about earlier. I received some news this morning," I tell her, softening my tone. She doesn't answer and I don't fault her. She's pissed. "Tommy killed himself." I see her head snap around to look at me and her eyes fill with unshed tears in my periphery. "So, I'm sorry I snapped at you," I say, my eyes still on the fire.

"I know you're going through some shit, Embs, but we just want to help." Her voice is quiet and filled with the hurt I caused.

"I know."

The guys make their way down to the beach once the air has cleared and when it's obvious Adri and I won't be pulling each other's hair out. *Ball sacks.* Then we all just sit by the fire, me sipping the same beer while everyone else gets progressively more drunk.

It's creeping closer to midnight when Travis comes to stand

behind my chair. "What does the birthday girl want?"

"Nothing." I shrug. "I already have everything I need." Truer words have never been spoken. Revenge is something I crave, but that will be the gift I give myself.

"Well, I got you something anyway." He hands me a thin, rectangular-wrapped gift, the paper coated in bright colors that say Happy Birthday all over it. I hold it for a few seconds, unsure of what to do. Sure, sometimes my mother and Tommy gave me gifts when we could afford them, but I wasn't expecting anything tonight. "Rip the paper off to get to the gift," he says sarcastically.

I rip open the wrapping to find a picture frame, and when I turn it around, a picture of me and Adri at Vin's party earlier this year is staring back at me from behind the glass. We're dressed in our bikinis, with our arms wrapped around each other, and our heads tipped back with laughter. It's a sweet photo, reminding me of the girl I once was.

"Thank you," I mumble, the awkward sound of my voice not lost on me.

A sniff breaks the hold the photo has over me and I look over at Adri. "I have something too." She lifts a small gift bag and passes it to me.

I take it and smile at her. I can tell she needs reassurance— our actual friendship is still young—and I'm not doing a good job at being her friend right now. I take a peek inside the bag to find a small book, the leather on the binding a soft brown. I pull it out and on the front it says *family*. When I open it up, I quickly discover it's not a book but a photo album. She has our party pictures, selfies of us getting ready together, Vin and me dancing, Travis and me at lunch, and my favorite, a selfie of all four of us after the theater party. The ice encasing my heart cracks a little as I turn the pages.

"Thank you, Adri. This is amazing." It really is, I'm not

even pretending. It'll be a bright light during the dark moments I'll inevitably face every time I look at it.

"You're welcome. There are some empty pages we can fill up during our senior year," she explains with a small smile, her eyes still swimming with moisture.

"My gift will come later," Vin says with a wink, breaking the tension around us and making everyone laugh.

I can only imagine it includes the coconut oil I mentioned earlier.

He's decorated the room with candles, casting a warm, flickering glow throughout the space. The music playing is Niykee Heaton's "Lullaby" and a large, rectangular-wrapped gift lies on the bed.

"Go on, open it," Vin says into my ear, his body heat seeping through the thin material of my shirt as he stands behind me.

I walk to the bed and sit down beside the gift, my heart pounding with anxious energy. It looks like a picture frame, and I can only imagine it's something totally inappropriate, given he wanted us to be alone when I opened it. I pull the gift onto my lap and slowly unwrap it. The back of a canvas unveils itself and my heart pounds even harder.

"Can you hurry?" he huffs out. "Fuck, this is making me so fucking nervous."

I cock a brow at his uneasiness before flipping over the

canvas, and I'm shocked when I find my face on it. My head is tipped back, facing the sky while my eyes are closed, and my lips are slightly pursed as my brows are tense with concentration.

"That was the first time I saw your face up close." He sits down beside me, running his finger over the painting. "This was the first day of school and you were standing at the doors, looking like you wanted to be anywhere else but there."

"You've made me look like an angel when I'm anything but." My finger touches the blurring colors around my head, casting an angelic glow to my painted features.

"I don't know about angel, but this is how you look to me," he whispers, his voice filled with awe.

"I love it." I really do, and I love him so much too.

"I love you." He leans in to kiss my cheek as realization dawns on me.

"This is the painting that was in your room the first time I was over." I turn my face to look into his bright green eyes as mine widen.

"Yeah, I almost fucking lost it when you saw it. Thank God you didn't recognize yourself." He chuckles and nudges my shoulder with his own.

I place the canvas on the side table by the bed and then move to straddle my man. My knees are on either side of his waist as I run my fingers along his cheeks, and his hands automatically fall to my hips to pull me closer, rubbing me along his hardness. With one hand on his chest, I force him to lie back before dragging myself lower, taking his pants and boxers with me. I sink to my knees on the floor by the side of the bed with my hands on his knees and look at his beautiful cock standing tall in front of me, the piercing at the tip glistening with his pre-cum. Vin lifts himself onto his elbows to watch as a gorgeous smirk crosses his mouth.

"You gonna suck that shit, baby? Or stare at it?" he mocks me, saying the same thing I did to him the first night we were together after my kidnapping.

A growl escapes my mouth as I lean forward and lick the pre-cum off the tip. He moans so deeply that I can feel it in my heated core. I keep my eyes on his as the green swirls with a stormy color and his eyelids become heavy. Then I run my tongue along the underside of his cock and revel in the salty taste of his velvety skin. The noises he makes are spurring me on as I swallow him whole, his cock hitting the back of my throat. My gag is automatic, and he curses as I do it again and again. My left hand cups and massages his balls as my right hand strokes his shaft to meet my mouth. His hand grips my hair, pulling it tight to lift my mouth off of him.

I growl in frustration, and he growls right back at me. "I want to fuck you, Ember, not come in your mouth." That does it. I stand up and remove my bikini and jean shorts as he chucks his T-shirt and removes his pants from around his ankles. Then I crawl over his body, but he quickly flips us around so that he's on top with a wild grin on his face. "My turn."

He kisses slowly down my neck, flicking his tongue against my skin, and then he nibbles his way over my chest, paying extra attention to my nipples as his right hand gently skims up my thigh and his fingers dance along my soaked folds. Another growl slips from my mouth from the teasing touches, and I grab his head to drag him back up to me, bringing us face-to-face. His eyes shine with passion and love for me, sending my heart clambering into my ribs. I don't care to be eaten out right now. "I need you inside me, Vin." My need for him coats every word, and he nods in reply.

Then he hooks my left leg over his right arm and lines himself up with my opening. I wait for the pinch of discomfort as he pushes into me, but with how wet my pussy is, I open and suck him in without resistance instead.

"Oh, fuck," he breathes into my neck. "Ember, this pussy is mine."

Vin always has something filthy to say, and it never fails to make me that much wetter. My fluids gush around his cock as he pounds into me, lifting my leg higher and hitting deeper. His piercing drags along my walls, making me clench around him, and I push a hand against his chest to switch places with him. He falls to his back, his cock now deeper inside me as I grind down on top of him. The stimulation on my clit warns me of how close I am to coming as his hands grab both of my ass cheeks, squeezing hard as he pounds me down onto him in a punishing rhythm. Stars dance around the edges of my vision as I come with a scream, tossing my head back with the effort.

"That was one." He chuckles before lifting me off of him and turning us around. "Get on all fours, baby. I want you to spread those cheeks." My lower belly ignites again with arousal, shocking me with how quickly I've recovered.

I do as I'm told though and spread my legs wide as he pushes two fingers into my pussy, pumping leisurely with a groan. I moan and hang my head, just letting myself feel what he's doing to me. He slowly slides his fingers out and up around my ass. This isn't new. Vin always loves fingering my asshole. Then the smear of something cold hits back there and instantly melts against my heated skin.

"Coconut oil," he whispers when I instinctively tighten my glutes.

We're really doing this. I breathe through my nervousness and relax as the slick noises of Vin coating himself with the oil sound from behind me. Pain isn't something I'm afraid of. These days I welcome pain because it helps me feel. So when he lines himself up against my rear hole and slowly pushes himself inside, I relish in the pain as excitement courses through me. The ring of muscle holds tight, barring his entrance, and we both groan at the feeling.

"Take a deep breath, baby," he coaxes, and I do as he says.

Finally, with another short pump, the tight ring of muscle gives way and the head of his cock is inside. The burning intensifies as he continues to push his way in and when his balls slap against my pussy, we both groan at the contact. The sensation of being filled I usually have with Vin is magnified back there, making me pant with shallow breaths. I need *more* of something, I just don't know what. As if sensing this, he begins to move slowly in and out. It's good, but I need him to pick up the pace. So I rock back to meet his thrusts, increasing my speed.

"Play with yourself," he grunts out as he starts to pound into me.

My fingers find my clit as I rub, the smooth oil and my wetness combining, along with the telltale tingling in my lower stomach. I'm about to come again. Without further warning, my orgasm flares through me and I scream out again as my pussy clenches around nothing and my ass tightens in response.

"Fuck, it's so tight," he says as he withdraws. "That was two." The smugness of his tone makes me snort as I fall to my stomach on the bed. My muscles are trembling and my thighs are sticking together with the oil and my releases. "Let's get one more." He pulls my legs wide apart and lies on my back, kissing the back of my neck before whispering, "This one is going to be rough, baby."

His hands grab my ass cheeks as he lifts my pelvis a few inches off the bed, then he plows into my pussy at full force, causing me to gasp and moan all at once. The feeling of him spreading me wide with his cock and his sack slapping my oversensitive clit is almost torture. He keeps up his attack on my pussy and I clench again. I twist my fists into the sheets, knowing this one is going to be messy. His piercing keeps hitting my G-spot, driving me closer to that edge, and finally, stars dance around the edges of my vision as I come apart, liquid gushing out and running down both of our legs.

"That's what I wanted," he moans as he comes inside me.

It's the last thing I remember as I fall to the bed, passing out before my head hits the pillow.

Chapter Three

"We're going to have so much fun," I say as I reach out and tweak his crushed nose.

His answering whine of pain makes me giggle.

Then his head falls back against the back of the chair, his eyes rolling to the ceiling. "I didn't think my child would ever do this to me."

"Why not?" I ask curiously, his statement giving me pause.

"Because, God gives us children to protect us when we grow old." He can't be fucking serious. He's smart enough to know you reap what you sow. My eyes widen with surprise as I chuckle and pull open the top drawer of his desk, finding some folders and pulling them out. "You understand business, don't you?"

Not really caring about his questions or concerns, I ignore him and start opening the folders. The top one is information on a police chief in New York and the documents inside basically say he's been bought. The next one is a senator. He's also bought. A doctor, a few lawyers, and another senator, this time a female in a sea of men.

"This is business?" I ask, waving the papers in the air as I stare him down. "Blackmailing these people to do your bidding?"

"They aren't all blackmailed, but yes, that's business." He has trouble lifting his head to speak to me, his chin nearly touching his chest. "I was going to give this to you one day, my entire empire. Do you know why, Emberlise?"

"Let's hear it, Pops." I slap the papers back on the desk and lean against it, crossing my arms over my chest.

"You are exactly like me. Ruthless, cunning, and a natural-born killer." This time when he lifts his head, his eyes shine with pride. The look makes me want to slit his throat and let him choke on his blood but that would be too easy, so I swallow down the urge.

"No." I shake my head, giving him a pitiful look. "I wasn't a natural-born killer. A fighter, yes. You created this killer, so I figure you should reap the rewards." I hold my hands to my sides and do a slow spin in front of him, showing him the residue of what exactly I am capable of now because of him.

"Our blood has always been potent. My father…" He hacks out a bloody-sounding cough before speaking once more. "He was wicked, truly. He beat my mother and all my brothers, but me? He trained me to love the look and feel of blood. Sound familiar?" His heavy breathing fills the silence as I absorb his words and lean back against the desk once more, my body tense with his declaration.

"Yep." I finally nod, there's no point in fighting the truth.

"I should've taken you. You're the one I've been needing this whole time." What sounds like a sob erupts from his chest as his head lolls forward.

I ignore his ramblings as I open the second drawer, and what's inside makes my entire face light up. I pull out a large hunting knife and hold it up. The sheath is ornately decorated with skulls, and I gasp at its beauty.

"That knife was a gift to me from your mother when we first got here to New York. She found it in an antique shop and thought I would like it. She

just didn't know how well I would use it over the years." He coughs again, a wet suction sounding from his lungs this time.

"How about we permanently paint your face like one of these pretty skulls?" I chuckle as I pull out the knife from the sheath.

His head falls back against the chair again in defeat, sending a shot of disappointment through me, and I grab a handful of his hair before making my first cut into his forehead. His grunt of pain doesn't come close to satisfying me as the blood sprays a bit at the end with a flick of the knife.

"Damn it, I got blood on her pretty face." I frown at the open folder still on my father's desk. Then I smear the drop of blood across her picture and read her name out loud, "Jennifer Тална."

Chapter Four

Ember is thrashing in bed beside me. She's already thrown the blankets to the floor and sweat is currently running off her naked body, absorbing into the bedsheet. I have only witnessed this once before when she accidentally fell asleep at my house a few weeks after she came back.

Her face crinkles in pain or disgust… I can't tell, but she makes no noise, just fights whatever her mind is torturing her with. I should wake her up because whatever is playing out in her dream is not pleasant. The last time I tried to wake her up though, she punched me so hard in the stomach that I almost threw up. I'm not really wanting a repeat.

I push up out of bed and pull on my sweatpants. There's no way in hell I'm letting her near my balls. I stand at her side of the bed as the writhing stops, but her breathing comes in quick pants. The sweat hasn't ceased as it pools between her breasts, and I give my dick a firm grip through my pants when it twitches. I just fucked the shit out of her earlier and I'm ready to go again. I've never been like this with any girl.

"Ember," I say calmly. Her brows crinkle together and her plump lips turn downward. "Em, wake up." Her head turns in my direction and her fists clench against the bed. I instinctively take a step back, my balls ascending back into my stomach. "Ember, it's me, Vin," I say a little louder.

She lets out a painful moan and sits straight up in bed, her chest heaving and her sweat flying outward. Her eyes are frantically searching the room as she tries to figure out where she is, like she's done this before, and her fists grip the sheets so hard that I'm afraid she's going to rip them.

"Em?" Her eyes close and her shoulders drop a bit, like she's relieved. I get on the bed and sit down behind her, then I wrap my arms around her waist and chest, gathering her up to me. "Where were you just now?" I whisper.

"Somewhere close to Hell," she whispers back, her voice full of anguish.

This is the most emotion I've seen her display since she's been back, and she's giving me a piece of where she was. I'm now completely certain she remembers everything that happened while she was being held and always has. My heart thumps heavily inside my chest and just the thought of her being in this much pain makes me feel like I want to kill someone.

"You're with me now. Don't let it drag you back." I kiss her temple, the sweat from her skin coating my lips.

"It drags me back every night." Her body trembles as she takes a deep breath, her chest hitching on the exhale.

"You need to talk about it." She shakes her head, so I latch on to her chin and make her look at me, her eyes a crystal-clear ocean color. "Free the demons inside because that's where your Hell is." I tap her chest and then her head. "Inside."

"How do you know that?" she asks, her eyes full of skepticism as her spine straightens.

"That's where mine are too." I run my thumb along her bottom lip as she slips her tongue across the pad, hardening my cock further.

"I can't tell you because you'll hate me." It's the most vulnerable I have ever witnessed my girl being.

Yet I laugh, loud and obnoxious, and her eyes narrow as she bares her teeth in anger. "Ember, I never had a fucking choice. I will always love you, and I don't give a fuck what you've done." She shakes her head in disbelief, but I pull her chin back to me. "It's unconditional... forever." I stare into her enormous eyes as they warm with trust. "Try me."

"You'll be in New York with me. I'm sure you'll learn it all soon enough." She's locked down and I won't be able to penetrate any further tonight, but it looks like I'm going to have to open up my soul to Ember if I ever want to see hers. I have to give her something in exchange so she knows I can handle anything she tells me. My first tremor of fear hits my chest as I decide to start from the very beginning, from when I can remember actually feeling hatred for the first time.

"The night I found out about Travis, my father paid my mother and me a visit. Well, I didn't know he was my father at the time. I was up in my room when I heard my mother yelling at someone. I remember creeping down quietly and being surprised to hear a male's voice.

"They were in the kitchen, so I crept closer and looked in. My mother sat at the kitchen table with her face in her hands and this tall man was standing over her, yelling about his son. I stood outside the doorway, confused as to why he was in my house and why my mother was crying, but then he said, 'Keep that mutt of yours away from my boy.' Being as young as I was, I didn't have a clue what he meant. A mutt is a dog, but we didn't have a dog. My mother just looked so fucking defeated, and I knew, even at that age, something was really wrong.

"He threw a piece of paper on the table and told her to 'Take the check and get out of his life by morning or he was taking the boy.' I didn't know what he meant, so I crept back upstairs and went into my mother's office. I googled 'mutt' and found out it was a mixed breed dog, not a purebred. It wasn't until a few years later that I pieced together he was talking about me."

The silence is deafening in the room, and just when I think she's fallen asleep, she speaks. "Vin, I remember everything that happened to me. I've never forgotten." I rub circles into her back as a weight lifts off my chest. I can bring her back.

"I know, baby," I murmur as I press my lips to her forehead. "I know."

I'm watching Ember as she sunbathes on the beach with Adri. She seems lighter than last night, her small smiles look more genuine, and I'm hoping her sharing what happened to her really helps bring her out of her self-imposed prison.

"Do we have a plan?" Travis asks from beside me as he drinks his beer.

"For?" I refuse to look at him, keeping my eyes on my girl with her head tipped back and her skin glowing golden under the sun.

"Figuring out what happened to her. We have to help her."

My jaw clenches with his words, the suggestive tone making me want to punch his teeth down his throat.

"You think I'm not doing that?" I turn to look into his shade-covered eyes as my hand clenches around my beer.

"I think you need help." He looks back out at the girls. "The four of us need to stick together." Just the thought of being near him on a regular basis threatens to throw me into a spiral but I tighten my restraint, reminding myself what he means to Ember.

"Fuck that," I growl out as he turns to look at me, one of his brows coasting upward over his shades.

"I know you hate me, but it's Ember." Do I hate him? I internalize every emotion I'm feeling as I quickly analyze them. No, it's not him I hate, it's his life.

"I hate your father. You just grate on every nerve I have," I admit, feeling relief at the admission but still a little weird.

"So, we're getting somewhere." He chuckles, but I say nothing and continue to drink my beer, my eyes still on his face. He's right, we are getting somewhere. I don't fucking hate him anymore because he genuinely loves Ember.

"We're going to New York next weekend to find some answers about Tommy." The words slip from my mouth as if I'm speaking to a close friend and not the person I've been treating like shit under my shoe for years. Shock slips over me but I decide to roll with it.

"Oh yeah? Adri told me what happened to Tommy." He nods as he looks out toward the water. "Where are you staying?"

"I'm leaving it all to Ember." I shrug and lean forward against the railing of the deck. "If I push too much, she'll go without me."

"Dad has a condo in the Upper East Side. You guys should use it," he offers, as if it's the most natural thing in the world for me to stay at a residence belonging to my father.

"No, thanks." My answer is quick and dismissive, hoping he leaves it at that, but I'm not so lucky.

"Look, I've been to New York plenty. Dad has a business there, so we go once every few months. You should let me come or at least take the condo." He continues to push the subject as fresh anger rolls over me with his persistence.

"Your father wouldn't be happy to have the mutt staying in his uptown condo," I grit between my teeth, each word spoken with vitriol. I refuse to look at him even though I can feel him staring at me.

"Our father has been trying to see you since that terrible fucking dinner. All he's talking about is having you take over some family business." Travis sips his beer. "He's trying to right his wrongs." I swear there's a little bit of sarcasm in his tone.

"He's still going to Hell," I snap before straightening, my body humming with agitation.

"Fucking right, but that doesn't mean you shouldn't benefit from years of neglect first." I look at him with surprise. "Look, I know what happened to you was fucking filthy, and I never wanted it to be that way." His face turns toward me as his mouth curls downward. "I don't expect us to be brothers right away, but we are brothers regardless, and it's something we should work toward. So I want to help you and I want to help Ember."

"I've hated you for years," I admit as I relax my expression, hoping to jar his fucking memory so he can stop being so nice.

"I know." He lifts the beer to his mouth again and turns back to face the girls.

"I fucking beat your ass for sport for so long," I continue, watching as his throat works on a swallow.

"I know." This time his answer is slow and hoarse, as if emotion is affecting his speech.

"And you still want a relationship with me?"

"Yes," he answers with no hesitation.

"Are you like a masochist? Into pain for fun or some shit?" At this, he bursts out laughing, the sound making it difficult to keep the grin off my face.

"Fuck, maybe I am? I'm also chasing a chick who's just so fucking impossible," he says with a chuckle as his chin juts out toward Adri.

"I'll talk to Ember about the condo. She says the gang runs Hunts Point mostly." He whistles under his breath and gives me a raised brow. "What?"

"That's a really rough area," he whispers, then clears his throat.

"That's where they found her, man. Covered in blood and holding a gun." I scrub my hand along my chin as I'm once again reminded of the life Ember lived before she met me.

"Fuck," he curses and sets his empty beer bottle on the table beside us.

"Yeah." I nod.

"No wonder she's so fucking tough," he mumbles as he shakes his head in awe. I already know just how tough she is, but even I was startled to learn exactly what neighborhoods she was running through in New York.

"The business Dad wants you to take over is in New York. He described it as export/import," he informs me, his hands out to placate me before I snap at him again. "If you had stuck around until the main dish, you would've learned more."

"I'm not interested."

After Ember came back, I agreed to dinner with my father. I was waiting to lay eyes on her and was constantly being hounded by the sperm donor. He broke down my mother before me, and she convinced me to go. To say it was explosive would be an understatement. He kept trying to push his business on me, stating it'd be generational, something I could leave for my children—a legacy, if you will. I basically told him to eat shit and die. *You're probably thinking 'a little insensitive.' You must have forgotten, he referred to me as a mutt.*

"It's up to you." He shrugs.

My eyes flick back to Ember with Adri, baking out in the sun, Ember's golden skin becoming darker and the mahogany in her hair more prominent from the sun's exposure. All I ever want to do is keep her safe and make sure she understands I'm here for good. Last night, after I told her something I had told no one else, she opened up. I need to do more of that, but just the thought of letting her in on some of my darkest moments makes me nervous.

When my mother and I moved out of Whitsborough and into Toronto, it's suffice to say my life went into a downward spiral. I had promised myself to tell no one the depths I had to go to survive because they were deep. Then my mother found out a few little things and flipped her shit. We moved back to Whitsborough within a week and she armed herself with a lawyer in case the fucker threatened to take the mutt again.

When I came back and saw Travis in all his privilege, really living the best and easiest life, I lost it. He really became my personal punching bag, but it was wrong. The real person who deserved that treatment was my douchebag father.

A laugh cuts through my thoughts from the beach and my heart hammers inside my chest. It's been a while since I've heard it and I'm so fucking glad I agreed to Adri and Travis coming here because, to be honest, I feared I was losing my girl for good.

That just cannot happen.

Ember

I'm still reeling with anger after learning about Robert and how he spoke about Vin when he was just a child. Mutt! If he wasn't already dying, I'd add him to my list. Actually, I haven't totally decided not to yet, dying or not, maybe I need to pay him a late-night visit. The more I think about this, the more I like it.

"Embs!" Adri interrupts my daydreams of a screaming Robert as he clutches his squirting throat.

"Shit." I shade my eyes with my hand to look at her. "My bad. What'd you say?"

"I was saying you look as happy as a pig in shit," Adri retorts, irritation lacing through her words. "What were you thinking about just now?"

"Honestly, that saying is just gross." I smile at her as I shake my head. "And you probably wouldn't want to know."

"You seem better today," she remarks as she readjusts her position in her lawn chair, tipping her head back toward the sun.

"I feel it." I admit with relief and settle back into my chair too. "It'll just take some time."

"Shay is having a party next weekend. Her parents are away on a trip." Adri just slips this bit of information into our conversation as if I don't hate the girl and the people she hangs out with.

My eyes pop open at the mention of Shay's name and I fight the urge to snap at my best friend. "You're still talking to her?"

"Yeah, she seems legit. Her and Marlana unfriended each other on IG and Facebook." I bite into my cheek to stop the sarcastic snort threatening to escape.

"Hmm." I don't really care. I still don't trust those bitches.

"Shay says many people keep asking for you at the gym." I try not to react to the rising anger inside of me at learning they have spoken about me.

Before the shit happened in New York, I taught two MMA classes. I talked to Andrew, and he's willing to take me back whenever I'm ready. I just don't know when that will be yet. I swallow down the rage, knowing people are talking about me, and snort. "I'm a famous bitch. Men, lock up your wives."

Adri lets out a good cackle, which makes me laugh. It feels good to let the dark anger go instead of having it fester inside of me. "Travis and Vin have been conversing for a good ten minutes now," Adri says, lowering her voice.

"I know. It's amazing, really," I murmur back, hoping we don't break whatever spell they're under. I've been waiting for this moment for a long time.

"Did Vin tell you about going to dinner at Trav's?" Adri's chair creaks as she turns in it to face me.

"He touched on it." I nod and turn to squint at her. "His father is a prick of epic proportions."

"He tried to offer Vin a business. It's too much like a payoff. Like, 'Oh, I'm so sorry for being a cunt. Here, have a business,'" she states mockingly, her eyes rolling.

"A business?" A shiver runs down my back, a feeling of foreboding.

"Yeah. I think it's in New York." She shrugs her shoulders as my stomach bottoms out.

No fucking way.

It can't be… If this motherfucker is grooming Vin to take over drug running for the Rampage, I'll lose it. That'll be the final straw on my restraint.

"Interesting," I mutter, my jaw clenched tight.

"Yeah, but Travis told me Vin raged out and his father looked like he almost shit himself." I snort and relax a bit at that because I know how intimidating my man can be.

"How's everything with Travis?" I ask, changing the subject. "I can't believe you drove for two hours alone together."

"I slept with him again last week," she moans into her hands, the shame pouring off her in thick waves. "I'm a horny idiot."

"Nah, he's hot and you care about him," I try to comfort her. The relationship she and Travis have is complicated and I can't even begin to understand it fully.

"He won't buy the cow if I give the milk for free!" she exclaims, dropping her hands from her face.

"That's bullshit," I scoff. "If he just wanted to sleep with you, he wouldn't be putting up with you this long."

"He asked me if I'd want to have a threesome," she whispers and bites her bottom lip with a wince.

"Guy or girl?"

"What?" She looks at me, mortified, her teeth releasing her

lip instantly.

I try to put myself in her shoes and imagine how I would feel if Vin approached me with the same proposition. I think I would rip his dick off and choke him with it, but Adri is not me and Travis is nothing like Vin. "What? Does he want to add a guy or a girl?"

"I didn't ask! Obviously, it'd be a girl." She crinkles her brows in thought. "Right?"

"I don't know." I shrug with indifference. "You should ask."

"Would you do it for Vin?" I could tell her I'd rip his dick off and that Vin would forever sit down to piss, but I don't want her to think it's not normal to want something more in the bedroom sometimes.

"It's hard to imagine that because Vin is so possessive. He doesn't even like me kissing you for fun," I remind her, then imagine patting myself on the back for the diplomatic answer.

"True." She nods.

"But honestly? I don't see a problem as long as your relationship with him is strong." I look at her. "And don't look at it like you're not enough."

"Yeah, that's what I have to work on." We're silent for a while, watching the waves on the beach and soaking up the sun before Adri breaks the silence. "How old were you when you lost your virginity?"

"Fourteen, and it was terrible." I chuckle. "You?"

"Last summer…" she hesitates, "with Danny."

"What?!" I quickly sit up in my chair, nearly tipping it over as I stare wide-eyed at her with shock.

"Shh!" She waves at me, then turns to look back at the guys on the deck.

"How did that happen?" I whisper harshly, making her face me once more as she cocks a suggestive eyebrow at me, and I roll my eyes. "Never mind." Then I fake a shudder. "I don't want to know."

"Travis is my second," she whispers as if the guys can hear us.

"Ladies!" Travis calls out, startling us out of our bubble of secrets. "Let's figure out lunch!"

"I need to pee first!" I scramble up out of my chair and toward the cottage.

When I get to the bathroom, my phone starts pinging, and I grab it out of my bag before heading for the toilet. I open my messages and find about ten from Carm.

Devil's Offspring: We need to talk more.

Devil's Offspring: When ur done with ur little excursion, call me.

Devil's Offspring: Happy Birthday.

Me: Thanks, I need you to get a gift for me by tmr afternoon.

Devil's Offspring: … Okay?

Me: There was a knife in our father's desk drawer. It had those skulls on it. I want it.

Devil's Offspring: Is that the one you flayed him with?

Me: Tmr afternoon.

I close my messages and stand from the toilet, pulling my shorts back on and putting the phone in the back pocket. If he wants anything to do with me, he'll come through. It is indeed the knife I used to flay some skin off my father, the blade so sharp and precise. The thought of it makes my body wrack with a shudder, and not the bad type. I actually enjoyed the shit I did to him, especially when I think about what he did to my mother and all the things I made him admit while he was under that knife. No one deserved the things I did more than him. I honestly wish I could somehow bring him back so I can do it all again.

My breathing accelerates and I have to begin counting backward to bring myself down. Thinking about causing someone pain and suffering, especially those deserving, really gets my heart pumping. Maybe becoming a vigilante wasn't such a bad fucking idea.

I leave the bedroom and head downstairs to music blaring and the scent of grilled meat filling the air. Adri is in the kitchen, bopping around to "Monster" by Lady Gaga and Travis is eyeing her from the corner, his eyes hooded with desire as he takes a swig of his beer. *Creepy fuck.* I raise an eyebrow at him as I pass by, and he shrugs with a smirk on his face. I find Vin outside at the grill, and my heart stutters when I see that he's taken off his shirt and his low-slung basketball shorts are dangerously close to his ass crack. He's wearing a backwards New York baseball cap on his head and his hair is curling around the front edges.

His back muscles bunch as he flips the steaks. "You gonna stare at me all day or come over here and kiss the cook?"

I snort and press up against his back, placing a soft kiss between his shoulder blades. He smells like coconut lotion and it takes me back to what we did last night. "The lotion on your skin reminds me of your dick in my ass."

He chokes out a laugh and lifts his arm to drag me in beside him. "I'm never sure what's going to come out of your mouth."

"I'm like a Kinder Surprise."

He chuckles again and then kisses my temple. It's a long weekend, so we don't have to be back in Whitsborough until Monday. The parents have been really accommodating and had no issues with me coming here with Vin, as long as I check in each day. Speaking of which, I should do that now.

"I'm going to call my parents," I tell him and walk off the deck toward the beach.

"Steaks will be done in ten," he says.

I dial my uncle's—Dad's—phone and wait for him to pick up. It takes about a ring and a half before his voice fills my ear. "Ember?"

"Hey," I say, trying to push some contentment into my voice. They don't deserve to deal with my demons as often as I do.

"Everything's okay?" It's become normal for him to question if I am safe and I understand why. It couldn't have been easy when I disappeared and then reappeared covered in blood.

"Yes, it's great here." Even I wince at the high-pitched squeak in my voice.

"Why do you sound like a cheerleader on crack?" he asks, making me burst out laughing and internally thanking the stars I have him in my life. It's always his humor that breaks through to me.

"Crack is whack." I chuckle. "How's everything over there?"

"We miss you. Your Ma is cleaning and I'm searching for rare wheels." He finds old cars and fixes them up. Our garage is stacked with them.

"I miss you guys too. How's Shelby?" Shelby is my Mustang

convertible and one of his rare finds.

"I gave her a wax job this morning. She's waiting for you to come home." I picture him in the garage with his shirt sleeves rolled up and working on Shelby, knowing it'll make me happy. I'm homesick for them.

"We'll take her for a spin when I get back," I promise.

"Sounds good."

"Tell Ma I love her, and I love you too."

"Will do, young lady," he says. "Do you remember my one rule?" His one rule is not to have sex in the instance I make him a Grandpa-Uncle.

"That's still a thing?" I respond teasingly.

"Just be safe." He snorts.

"See you Monday."

"Bye, Kiddo."

I hang up the phone and look over my shoulder toward the cottage, finding Adri, Travis, and Vin standing around the table as they lay out the food. As hard as it is to keep pretending to be the girl I once was, I do it for these three people and my family at home whom I've instantly formed a lifelong connection with. When I'm here at Vin's cottage, I can almost pretend that what happened to me was just a dream, that I still live the life of a carefree teenager with a rough past and a bright future.

Chapter Five

"Let's talk about my mother for a bit." I pause and swipe my finger through his blood on the blade.

"What about her? She betrayed me," he moans as his head drops to his chest.

"Why would she do that if she loved you and had your child in her belly?" It's like I'm questioning him from outside my body because I can't seem to feel a damn thing.

"Because she was a whore." He spits out a wad of blood at my feet, his face a mask of disgust. Before I can even form a thought, my fist flies out and catches him on his left eye. His head snaps to the side and the blood that was running down his face sprays all over me and his desk. "She hated what I did here and wanted to go back to her life in that shit town," he groans, giving me an answer to avoid another hit.

"That can't be right. We stayed here in New York, right under your nose." I bend down to look him in his swollen eyes, keeping my expression blank and hoping I find out everything soon so I can fucking kill him.

"*I don't know why she stayed here.*" He attempts to shrug and winces from the pain in his shoulder. "*It wasn't one of the questions I asked her the night I killed her.*"

My body becomes rigid, each muscle locking tight. He spoke to her the night he killed her, and he thinks it's a good idea to tell me this? Does this motherfucker not have one ounce of self-preservation?

"*You spoke to her?*" My voice is deadly calm.

He swallows, his Adam's apple moving against his skin, and he avoids my eyes, instead, looking over my shoulder. His slight nod sends my heart into overdrive. If I had any reservations before about torturing and murdering him, they are all fucking gone now. "*I asked her if she knew where you were.*" He chuckles dryly. "*She didn't know you were in this very place, decimating my best fighter, nearly paralyzing him for life. She told me you were working.*"

"*That was work, you bitch!*" I snarl into his face, my anger working its way to the surface and breaking the calm I've been fighting to keep in check. "*The money I made by 'decimating' your fighters helped us to survive.*"

"*She didn't know how bad you were, how far gone you were. If she did, I'm sure each time she looked at you… she would've seen me.*"

"*What else did you speak about?*" I grab his chin and force him to look at me.

"*I offered her an alternative because I didn't want to kill her.*" He jerks his head out of my hand. "*I asked her to come back into isolation. To live here like she did before, and we would raise you together.*"

"*You kept her prisoner here?*" I whisper as dread coils in my stomach. My mother and I were both prisoners to this man and the connection only further fuels my rage.

"*In the very room you were in. I couldn't let her out of my sight after the stuff she had witnessed. Your mother was weak, and she would never have a role in this business. So I kept her here. Then you were born, and I didn't want her to leave with you. But of course, she seduced a guard, and he helped her escape." He grits his teeth. That's why he kept changing my guards. He didn't want history repeating itself.*

"I see," I murmur and drag the blade of the bloody knife across my lip. "She chose death to protect me from you."

I reach out quickly and snatch his hand. He tries to fight me, but he's so weak at this point. I slam his hand down on the desk and quickly stab the knife into the desk between his thumb and forefinger, the sharp edge dangerously close to his skin. He whimpers with relief, his head falling forward.

A giggle escapes me as I pull the knife forward and slice through his thumb from below the knuckle. God, I love a sharp knife. His screams send a shiver through me, and I smile widely as the blood squirts from the tip of his nub. Then I pull his hand up and hold it between our faces, watching as the blood sprays us both.

"Let the real fun begin," I say with a toothy grin.

CHAPTER SIX

I wake up alone in bed, finding Vin's side empty. My hair is stuck to my face and I have sweat pouring down my body. I place my hand to my chest and will my heartbeat to slow. My nightmares won't release me, not until I've replayed the whole thing from start to finish. It's like my brain is forcing me to remember every detail when all I really want is to forget.

The en suite bathroom door opens and Vin struts out with a towel in his hand. A sense of calm washes over me as he moves toward me. I'm not alone. "I went to get you a towel," he says as he wipes my face.

"Thank you." My voice is hoarse and I'm still slightly out of breath as my hand drops from my chest.

"Same nightmare?" I take the towel from him and nod.

"Different, but the same," I murmur as I wipe the towel along my neck, then drop it to the floor beside the bed.

He wants me to tell him about my nightmares, the levels of depravity I succumb to each night, but I just can't. I'm afraid it'll change the way he loves me and I don't think I could handle that.

He lays down on his side of the bed and opens his arms for me to curl against his chest. The warmth of his skin seeps into my cheek, and I instantly relax as his scent ingrains itself into my brain.

"When we moved to Toronto, I was seven and we had no money. My mother refused to cash the check my father gave her, and our house was still up for sale." He takes a deep breath and pulls me in a little tighter. "So we lived in government-supported housing. It was bad. Kids ran around with no shoes or clothing and there would be really young kids—toddlers—crying without a parent in sight. Then there was the blatant drug use and gang violence.

"It exposed me to a lot at a young age and my mother was also absent. She was putting herself through business school and working as a waitress. So it's only natural the gang members on our block kept an eye out for me. They slowly gained my trust and raised me when my mother couldn't. By ten years old, I was running drugs and getting into trouble at school for fighting."

His heart rate increases under my cheek, and I run my hand from his chest to his stomach. I know what he's doing. He's showing me he can trust me by telling me things he isn't proud of, hoping I will do the same. I get it. Trust goes both ways and what he's doing is working.

"After seeing me with a few black eyes, a few of the gang members taught me how to fight, and also how to kill if it came to that."

My breath gets lodged in my throat, my hand pausing on his abs, because his life was so similar to mine. An absentee single parent and gang interference. I look up into his face and find his moss-green eyes watching me. He's grown out his facial hair and has a permanent five o'clock shadow now, making him look older than his seventeen years.

"I found out I have an older half-brother named Carmelo while I was in New York. He was the one who… ah… collected me," I confess, instantly feeling lighter.

He mulls that over and probably has about a million questions, but the thing I love the most about Vin is that he doesn't pry. He lets me be me and knows the more he pushes, the more I will back off.

"I'm guessing you know who your father is then. Unless he's your mother's child?" He's so perceptive and sometimes it's forgotten because of how quiet he is.

"I know who my father is," I confirm.

He doesn't push for more and rubs soothing circles along my back until I fall back asleep.

"Ember!" Travis yells to me from across the beach. "A courier is here with a package for you!"

"Ugh… his voice is hurting my head. I should sit on his face to shut him up," Adri moans from her chair as she grips her head in her hands.

"Stop getting so drunk and the hangovers will stop too." I snicker, standing from my chair.

Then I rush to the cottage and see a delivery man with a large orange envelope in his hands. "Emberlise Torres?" he asks me, his brow quirking toward his hairline.

Fucking Carm. "Yes, that's me," I grit out between my teeth as I hold out my hand for the envelope.

He holds out a handheld device, waiting for me to sign my name as I grip the bubble-wrapped interior. I can tell by the shape of the object that he sent me the knife.

"Emberlise Torres?" Travis asks from behind me.

I turn around after the courier leaves and look at him. He has his shirt off today and I notice he got some new tattoos on his arms. There are scripts running up both forearms and they look like literature quotes. His sandy hair has grown out a bit and is haphazardly hanging over his brow. His green eyes look at me questioningly.

"Curiosity killed the cat, Trav," I say with a *tsk*.

"All secrets come out at some point, Ember."

"I'm banking on it." My back is already turned on him as I head upstairs.

I hurry inside my room and close the door behind me. I'm so eager to see this fucking knife and sheath. Did they clean it? Will it still have his blood caked on it? The excitement is overwhelming, and I don't stop and analyze what that means about my current mental state. Instead, I rip open the envelope as the knife and ornate sheath spill out onto the bed. The colorfully painted skulls look back at me tauntingly, like we share old secrets. I guess we do. I run my finger along the sheath and over the skulls, white paint on a gilded gold background and the matching handle twinkles in the light. I pull the knife out to find that it has indeed been cleaned, meticulously so, and the edge looks like maybe it's been sharpened for me as well.

I run the serrated edge along my fingertip and hiss when it

cuts into my skin, making me smile as a bubble of blood runs down my finger. This knife was always meant to be mine.

I sheathe the blade and look inside the envelope. Just as I expected, there is a letter waiting for me.

Ember Torres,

Don't get mad, that's your name.

I found this knife tucked back into my father's drawer a few weeks ago, completely covered in blood. I knew right away from the state of his body that this is what you used. The sight of his tortured corpse had a few of my guys puking, so... well done.

Anyway, happy birthday. I am here celebrating with your twin brother, who you will have to face soon enough.

I will be seeing you next week.

Love your brother,

Carm

I rip the letter up into small pieces and then head into the bathroom to flush them down the toilet. I love how he thinks I will have to do anything. If I decide I don't want to see my twin, I won't. I have so many questions about that though, like how, when I was torturing the shit out of my father, he didn't utter a single thing about a twin. It all seems so suspect, but then I think about his face, and I know he is who Carm is saying he is. Looking at him was like looking in the mirror. Again, thinking about my twin brother leaves me struck with betrayal from my mother. She never said a damn thing about him either and there was never any evidence of his existence.

A soft knock sounds on the door, and I scramble to put the knife in my bag. No need to scare the shit out of anyone.

"Em?" Vin calls out. He had gone into town to grab some more food because all we have stockpiled here is alcohol.

"I'm here!" I answer as I straighten and turn toward the opening door.

"Everything good?" He comes in, his eyes skimming over the room.

Travis must've told him about the delivery. He has questions written all over his face, but Vin won't interrogate me and he lets me tell him as much or as little as I want. "Carm sent me a letter and I made plans to see him next weekend." Not a complete lie because I'll be in New York next weekend.

"Okay. I will get us the tickets." He pulls his phone out of his jeans pocket and begins to tap along the screen.

"Are you sure you want to get involved with this, Vin? It won't be pretty," I warn him, making his fingers stall.

"Ember, nothing about my life was ever pretty. I'm sure I can handle it, and I won't let you do it alone." He tucks his phone back into his pocket and raises an eyebrow at me. Yeah, I'm done. He's my forever person. I cross the room and jump into his arms, locking my legs around his waist. He chuckles as his hands grab my ass and pulls me in tighter. "I keep getting missed calls from my father. I think he wants to speak to me about this fucking business," he grunts out.

I already have a plan formed for that asshole and I will make sure he never bothers Vin with his illegal shit again. "We can go together this time. Make it for Thursday before we leave for New York," I suggest and kiss his cheek.

"Sounds good." His nose runs along my cheek as his lips follow behind.

"Are Adri and Travis killing each other yet?" I snicker, making him draw back and look me in the eyes.

"One can only hope. Two birds, one stone, and all of that."

The next night, I am back home and relaxing in my room, twirling my beautiful new knife in my hands. I may use it again tonight, to stain the golden handle red once more. Since my kidnapping, I've accepted the darkness inside of me, and I know exactly what I need to feed it. My stomach trembles with excitement and I can't control the smile that stretches wide across my face. I play back the phone conversation I had with Carm when I got home and commit to memory everything he meticulously taught me. My plan is concrete—foolproof.

It's midnight when I jump out of bed and dress in a pair of black leggings, paired with a black hoodie sweater. I pull my hair back tight into a bun and I sit at my fancy vanity to apply my makeup. Tonight, I'm not doing just any regular makeup. I hold the knife out in front of me as inspiration and grin. Tonight I will be a beautifully decorated skull.

When I'm finished, I turn my face to the left and right, feeling proud as the white face paint and the colorful skull makeup completely obscures my features.

This will do just fine.

Chapter Seven

The house is eerily quiet, and the only light visible is from the moon splaying across the foyer's marble floors. This house is decadent, there's no other word to describe it. The arrogant display of wealth bleeds through every fiber, from the marble floors with splashes of gold glittering throughout to the walls' textured plaster, making it look like supple velvet. The cherry on the cake is the hanging chandelier, its crystal beads sending rainbow shards across every surface.

Decadent.

The house was simple to break into, and with my disguised face and dark clothing, any images they might pull from the camera won't reveal who I am. I thumb the knife in my hoodie pocket, the cool feel of the sheath sending a jolt of excitement through me.

I memorized every detail of Travis' home from Adri, who suspected nothing when I began to question her about the layout. To the right is the staircase to go to the second level and to the left is the kitchen, dining, and however many other rooms. Straight ahead is an office and a den. The den has been made into a makeshift bedroom for dear Robert, as he is too sick to climb the stairs.

That's where I'm headed.

My feet are light as I walk across the shimmering floors toward the large double doors in front of me. The anticipation courses through my blood and I can't stop the grin that spreads across my face. This is exactly what I've been needing to release some of the numbness. I push the door open and step inside the room. It's dark, so I stand still until my eyes adjust. The sound of whirling wind and a humidifier pumping steam dulls the sound of my footsteps.

In the center of the room sits a king-sized bed and lying in the middle is the man I'm looking for. I move to the right of his bed and look down at his thin, sunken face, the skin having a gray pallor. He looks pretty fucking sick. At this point, most people would turn back around and say fuck it, the man is dying anyway. Not me. Even though the body is failing, his mind is still the evil piece of shit it's always been.

"Wake up, Robert," I say. He stirs and turns on his side, facing me, his mouth hanging open and his pale pink lips chapped. I roll my eyes and bend forward, placing my mouth near his ear. "Wake up, douchebag," I say a little louder.

He gasps and falls to his back, his eyes wide open. When they finally land on me, I can't help the grin that comes over my face once more. His fear is so palpable I can almost taste it.

"Who are you?" he asks, his voice weak and breaking as his eyes roam over my face.

"Later. Right now, you and I are going to have a little chat, and if all goes well…" I pull the knife from my pocket, leaving the sheath there. "I won't have to hurt you." He continues to take in my face and the knife I'm running along my lips. I must be a sight right now with the skull painted onto my skin. "Please keep in mind, Robert,"—I wink at him—"I really want to fucking hurt you."

He nods slightly and pushes himself into a sitting position against the headboard, the small movement leaving him out of breath. I grab the chair from his desk, setting it beside the bed before sitting down in front of him. "Any idea who I am?" I ask.

"No." He shakes his head as he coughs. "Who sent you?"

"No one. I came of my own volition." I take in the surroundings as my eyes land on a framed photo of Travis beside his bed. He's young and in a baseball uniform.

"What is it you want?" He swallows thickly, his eyes flicking from me to the door.

"I came to find out more about this business you have in New York." I lean forward to rest my elbows on the bed, letting the knife dangle from my fingertips.

"Did Ms. Talia send you?" he whispers, his fingers twitching around his bedsheet.

Hmm, there's that name again. "I told you, no one sent me."

"New York is my primary source for product distribution," he reveals.

"Ooh, fancy words for drug running." His eyes widen at my words as he looks frantically around the room. "So, you thought, *Why not give the mutt the dirty job and I'll save my legit businesses for the son I acknowledge?*" I press the knife to my cheek, the sharp edge pinching into the skin, sending tingles of pleasure over me. "Please, correct me if I'm wrong."

"Travis is weak. He would never do the things that need to be done." A fire burns in his eyes as he speaks of his son in such a disparaging way.

"Like?" I drop the knife from my cheek to let it glide over one of his hands, which is still gripping the bed sheet.

"Disposing of trash, intimidating the competition, and making sure no one is skimming," he mumbles quickly, his eyes on the blade.

"Skimming? Like what your older brother did, right? Wasn't he *disposed of* for that?" I use air quotes as the knife moves in my palm and watch him keeping his eyes on it.

"Yes." His bottom lip trembles as his voice cracks. He sounds so damn old. So damn fragile.

"And who was he skimming from? Who's the big boss?" I ask, leaning forward with my arms on the bed as I twirl the knife.

"Raphael Torres," he confesses as he swallows loudly.

"Ahh… yes, Raphael Torres. Scary guy, huh? Wouldn't want to cross him. Am I right?"

"He can be intimidating," he agrees as he sucks in a quick breath.

"I'm going to tell you a secret, just between us buds," I say, waving the knife between the both of us. "I killed Raphael Torres." I blink at him innocently as my cheeks burn with the effort to keep the grin in place.

His eyes widen again and his breathing increases. I can almost hear the pounding of his heart as I commit his look of fear to memory. It'll be something I'll look back on in the future when I need to cheer myself up. "Impossible," he whispers.

"Apparently not." I grin at him. "His blood bleeds red like yours and mine. Trust me, I saw plenty of it."

"Who are you?" he chokes out as his body begins to tremble

beneath the sheet.

"You'll find out soon enough. First, I want to discuss more about this business of yours." I wave off his questions as his fear swirls around my head.

"What about it?" His voice shakes as his body is wracked with tremors.

"When do you need a replacement by?" I bounce the knife off my knee.

"The next meeting of heads, three weeks from tomorrow." His brows come together in confusion as he shakes his head.

"This is what's going to happen. You're going to sign that business over to me and I will go to that meeting." I press the knife to my mouth. "I'm assuming you have the paperwork already drawn up for Vincent?" He nods, keeping his eyes on the knife. "Great, where are they?"

He points to his desk. "Second drawer on the right."

I head over to the desk and open the drawer. Inside, he has a few file folders. I bring them all back to the chair and open the one on top. It has a picture of Jennifer Talia—the same one I saw in my father's office—and what looks to be pages of information.

"I'm going to keep this," I say, holding up the folder.

"She will hunt you down if you did indeed kill Raphael." He has a ghost of a smile on his face as he threatens me, and I can't blame him, I would be just as excited about the prospect.

"They were married, yeah?" I ignore his jab and change the subject. I'm only here for the information I'm looking for, not idle threats.

"No, never married, but they've been working together since before he went to prison." *Interesting.*

"I see," I hum, opening the next file. This one has the paperwork I'm looking for, and this piece of shit really has Vin's name all over it.

"So, this is what's going to happen, Mr. Greene. I'm going to cross out every one of Vincent's names and write in my own, and then you're going to initial my changes. After that, you're going to call your lawyer about the changes, agreed?" I point my knife at him for emphasis.

"Yes." He noticeably swallows as he continues to eye the knife in my hand.

"Excellent. I love when things just fit into place." I start in on the paperwork and write in my name, replacing Vin's. When I'm done, I hand it over to douche supreme and tell him to begin initialing.

"Emberlise Craven…" he whispers as the papers crinkle in his shaky hands.

I gasp mockingly. "Oh no! My secret's out!"

"You're Rebecca's daughter." His eyes flick to mine and for the first time, I think he really takes in my appearance. He can't see the features I inherited from my mother, but my eyes are a sure tell.

"Ding, ding, you're smart." I chuckle. "You knew my mother, right?" He inclines his head as he goes back to initialing the paperwork. "Did you also know that Raphael killed her? Because you must've known she fled from here to New York with him, right?"

"I knew she left home to be with him, but he maintained she fled from him too once she found out about his… ah… profession."

"He was a magnificent liar, that's for sure. Since we've bonded here and I consider us buds, I'll let you in on a few more secrets. My father was Raphael Torres. A few months ago, he kidnapped me and in retaliation, I killed him with a shot to his head… after torturing him with this knife."

His skin grows impossibly paler and I'm watching him to see if he passes out. I wouldn't mind slapping his gaunt face to wake him back up. "He never spoke about you," he groans then shifts on the bed to get more comfortable.

"Did he speak about any children?"

"Just Carmelo, his heir."

"I see." The knife is against my temple now. "I must've been a dirty little secret. Keep signing those papers."

Turning back to the final folder, I open it up. It's Robert's last will and testament. *Nice.* I'm reading through all his documents and notice not a single thing is going to Sharla or Vin. He was just hoping to dump off his shady-ass, under-the-table business, and that was it. This just won't do.

"I'm going to need you to fix this up as well," I say with a few *tsks*.

"How so?" His voice wobbles as he shifts on the bed again.

"For beginners, you will leave some money to Vincent and his mother. It's the least you can do for fucking up their lives. Then I'm thinking this property you have on the Upper East Side would be convenient to own. I doubt he'll take much more than that." I hand him the folder. "Make the changes and initial." His hand shakes as he takes the folder.

Then he hands me back the original folder with the legal business documents. I go through it thoroughly and sign my name at the end. He finishes up with the will and hands that to me too. Once I am completely satisfied, I hand him his phone and tell him to call his lawyer on speaker.

"He's probably asleep," he says, his excuses finally starting to really grate on my last nerve.

"I'm sure you've woken him up before, Robert." I stick out my tongue and run the knife along it.

He hesitantly takes the phone and dials his lawyer. After a lengthy phone call where the lawyer kept asking him why he made these changes, what's motivating him, and if he's under duress, to which my knife was pressed to his throat until he answered correctly, it was done.

"Now, I'm going to give you a choice, new buddy." I stand up with the folders still firmly in my hand and pace along the foot of his bed. "I really can't have you recanting everything once I leave."

"I won't." He tries to give me a wide-eyed innocent look, but I know better than to believe a seasoned criminal like Robert.

"You will." I nod. "So, first choice, I give you my knife here and you end your life, with a written note, of course. I don't want Travis always wondering if you actually did it. Or… I'll pay a visit to Travis' room before I leave."

"What?" he asks astonishingly, his mouth gaping open. "He's told me you're his best friend."

"Even better. He'd let me in, no problem." I walk toward him, each step a dull *thud* reverberating around the room. "I might've been raised a Craven, Mr. Greene, but my blood is Torres."

He's trembling under the covers once more, his eyes closing briefly. "Where's the letter?"

"There's a good boy," I say with a chuckle and pull the letter from my pocket. "Rewrite it in your own hand."

His tears cover his cheeks as he rewrites the letter. I want to carve out their path with my knife so badly. He doesn't get to cry, because Vin cried as a child wanting a father. The thought hardens my resolve as he signs his name to the letter.

"Perfect. Now I really want this knife to be coated in your blood." I put on the latex gloves I have in my pocket.

My knife lands beside him on the bed as I instruct him to slice his wrists open. I have to hand it to him, he doesn't flinch. He takes the blade and runs it down his wrists, just as I instruct. It's a beautiful sight really, his blood pouring out of the wounds and soaking into the bed. I take back the knife with his blood on it and sit at his desk. I find the file on his computer with the security footage and download the virus Carm provided me with. Then I watch as everything deletes and the computer crashes.

My eyes catch on a letter opener on his desk. It's ornate with the devil's face on it, and it's so perfect that I want to squeal. I pick it up and walk back to Robert. He's on the brink of death as I run the letter opener along his wrists, gathering blood before wrapping his hand around it.

"Goodbye, Robert. Nice doing business with you." Then I stay at the end of the bed until his life is completely drained.

Chapter Eight

The late morning sunshine is gleaming across my face as I wake up from the best sleep I've had in weeks. I stretch out in my bed, my supple muscles feeling great after a proper rest. No nightmares plagued me last night and I know why. The darkness has curled back inside after I sated it with Robert's blood. I'm more like myself, even though I've committed murder again. I mean, I didn't exactly do it, but I definitely caused it with my coercion, and it felt so good. So deserved.

After Carm gave me detailed instructions on how to wipe any surveillance program, he made me promise to meet up with them today as payment before they leave to go back to New York. I tried to decline, because fuck, I'll see them next weekend, but he wouldn't take no for an answer. I fire off a text telling him to make it as early as possible because shit is about to hit the fan when everyone finds out about Robert. The fifties-esque diner Adri once took me to comes to mind, and I text him the address.

After my shower, I throw on a pair of light wash skinny jeans and a red off the shoulder blouse. I leave my hair to dry into its natural waves and apply a light coat of makeup. Once I am pleased with my appearance, I head downstairs to check on my parents.

Since I've been back, I've mostly kept to myself. I barely speak to them and eat most meals in my room, but today I'm feeling pretty great. They're murmuring in the kitchen so I head that way. Before I enter, I catch a snippet of their conversation.

"Can you believe he would do that?" Ma asks, her voice shaking.

"Robert was such a vain man. Maybe he couldn't stand for anyone to see him sick and weak," my dad supplies, his tone a little unsure.

"Yeah, maybe," she replies. "Should we tell Ember?"

"No, I think we should let Travis do that. They're close," he reminds her softly.

The kitchen falls silent, so I take this opportunity to enter. Both of them are sitting at the table with coffee, the smell pulling a groan of pleasure from me.

"Oh! Ember!" Ma jumps up. "How are you?" Her eyes are the size of dinner plates as she takes in my appearance and then they fill with hope.

The surprise is obvious on her face at seeing me dressed and a pang of guilt strikes my chest for my behavior lately. "I'm much better today." I smile as I kiss her cheek.

Her eyes instantly fill with tears, and she smiles at me widely as Dad gets up from his seat and moves to the coffee machine. "Here ya go, kiddo. We know how much you love it," he says, handing me a cup of coffee. I add some sugar and lean against the counter to take a sip.

"I'm going to go for a drive today, maybe stop by the gym

to see Andrew while I'm out. Do you guys need anything?" I blow onto the steaming liquid in my cup as they look at each other with pleasure.

"No, no! You go enjoy your day and the weather," Ma says as she waves me off, her smile nearly blinding. "I have to get to the office today."

After saying goodbye, I settle into Shelby and smile in contentment. I missed this car, and I missed being free. I forgot just how good the hum of Shelby's motor feels as it vibrates through my body and how easy it is to lose myself in her speed.

I pull into a parking spot and instantly spot a blacked-out sedan parked a few spaces down. Can these assholes purchase different cars? Does it always have to be a fucking blacked-out sedan? I should go over there and key it, then piss on the tires. I get out of Shelby and make my way inside, seeing them right away. They couldn't blend in here if they fucking tried. I lock eyes with the one who shared a womb with me, and again, it hits me like a ton of bricks. He really is like my reflection, and by the look in his eyes, he has a similar reaction. Someone should teach him not to be such an open book.

I head over to their booth and sit across from them. Carm looks a lot like Raphael, and I don't understand how I missed it the entire time they held me captive. His black-blue hair is slicked back, just like his father's, and the terracotta hue of his skin is bright against the ink-black of his eyes. He's dressed in a worn leather jacket with a black T-shirt underneath, looking casual when his demeanor screams anything but. I look at the other one and his dark brown hair shows the mahogany highlights under the fluorescents. His skin is a light olive color, a tad lighter than mine, but that may be because I laid in the sun all weekend. He's built just as wide as Carm, and he looks to be just as tall. His eyes are two bright turquoise orbs shining out of his face and he's sporting a slight mustache and a bit of hair on his chin.

"You either need to grow more facial hair or shave it all off. You look like a fucking douche canoe." I point at my womb partner as I break the silence.

"Shit." Carm chokes on his water as he laughs.

The smile widening on my twin's face is contagious and I give in to one of my own.

"Emmett, this is Ember. Ember, meet your twin, Emmett," Carm says, waving his hand between us.

"Emmett and Ember… cliché." I shake my head. "Did Mom name you? Or Raphael?"

"I don't have a fucking clue," he answers. His voice is smooth and deep, resonating with something inside me.

"Did you know I was your sister while I worked for you and the Rampage? While I was almost raped and killed during pickups? Or while my blood spilled for you fuckers?" I ask Carm, my voice deadly calm.

"From what I was told, you did more damage than what was done to you," he scoffs. "And no, I didn't know. I had never seen you."

"When did you find out?" I place my elbows on the table and link my hands together.

"While I was driving Raphael to pick you up." He takes a sip from his glass of water on the table and avoids my eyes altogether.

"The proper word is kidnap," I retort.

A server interrupts us to take our orders, and I nearly throw Carm's water at her in irritation. Carm orders a burger and fries with a pop as Emmett stares hard at the menu.

"The milkshakes are good here," I tell him as his eyes meet mine over the folded booklet.

"Never had one." He shrugs as his brows come together.

"What are you? An alien?" I turn to the server. "He and I will have a vanilla and chocolate swirl milkshake with funnel cakes."

She nods and collects the menus from us, then skates away. All the while, Carm has his eyes on her ass.

"What if I didn't want that?" Emmett asks, his mouth pursing and instantly reminding me of our mother. The image is like a shot to the chest and it takes everything not to let that pain exude through my features.

"Too bad. Call it twin-tuition. If you hate it, I want a DNA test done." The words flow from my mouth unencumbered as I fight to regain my composure.

Carm laughs and Emmett cracks another grin as I lean back in my seat to watch them both. Carm and Emmett are tight. I can see that.

"Is this the little brother you were worried Raphael would kill?" I ask Carm.

"Yeah, he threatened me with Emmett all the time."

"Why didn't you tell me about him?" I point at Emmett, who busies himself with his phone.

"Because Raphael said not to and I couldn't trust that you would keep that to yourself."

His answer is something I can understand. When Raphael admitted to killing my mother, I fucking lost it, and to be honest, if I knew about Emmett, I don't know that I would've kept it to myself either. The food arrives at the table, and we are all quiet as we dig in. Emmett's brows shoot up when he tries the milkshake, his eyes immediately finding mine.

"Wow, that is good," he says with obvious surprise.

"You pass, brother." I grin at him, which earns me a smile.

"So, you came all the way here for me?" I turn to Carm.

"It's not that far." He snorts with a slight shake of his head. "And we have business here."

"Right, with Robert Greene." It's not a question, and by the way his eyes widen, he confirms it.

"How do you know that?" he asks, becoming still.

"Our father. He was happy to rub it in my face when he told me about my mother. How the father of one of my best friends and boyfriend was his drug runner in Toronto." I take a mouthful of funnel cake as Carm squirms in his seat.

Then he clears his throat and shakes his head. He looks at Emmett and then back at me. "We came here to meet with him yesterday. He told us about his plans to have his son take over the business. His name is Vincent. Which one is that? Your boyfriend or best friend?"

"I'm also sure he told you he was having trouble convincing him, right?" I slurp loudly on the milkshake, making Emmett snort.

"Yeah." Carm nods, his fingers running through his hair. "He wants us to come back next week and maybe rough him up to help with the convincing."

"There are two problems with that." I lean forward and look him dead in the eyes. "One: Vincent is my boyfriend. He doesn't get touched, and if he is by any chance *convinced*, I will kill you and anyone else involved. Two: Robert Greene killed himself last night."

"Noted," Carm replies. "If he's yours, we obviously won't touch him, but Greene killing himself causes us a problem." His mouth tightens into a straight line as his hand curls on the table.

"He found a replacement and you'll meet them in a few weeks. At the meeting of heads, right?" I slurp on my milkshake again as his eyes narrow on me, my twin flicking his gaze between us curiously.

"I don't know whether to be impressed with you or worried," he grumbles, scrubbing his hand down his face.

"After seeing her fight, I think you should be impressed," Emmett says, slurping on his own milkshake and making me grin around my straw.

"You've seen me fight?" I ask him, my brow quirking.

"Yeah, the fight with the cop. That was fucking brutal." Pride shines in his eyes as I preen in my seat.

"I rarely fight to kill, just incapacitate, but thanks to our big brother here and our late father, I've taken a liking to it." I run my finger along my throat.

"Come back to work with us," Carm implores. "You can get to know Emmett and also train each other. He's great with knives and guns and you're great with combat."

"I don't know about knife training. After seeing Father's body, I think she's got that down," Emmett states. He doesn't seem too torn up about our father's death.

"Fine, teach her how to throw them and how to hit a target with a bullet," Carm remarks, patting his back.

"I'll think about it," Emmett and I say at the. Same. Fucking. Time.

"Oh, fuck no," I breathe out as Carm gets stuck on a fit of laughter. "You got the bill." I point to him and growl before pushing out of the booth and start walking to the door. "Peace out, assholes."

I walk into the gym and standing at the desk is Shay in all her bitchy glory. She hasn't spotted me yet because she's looking down and scrolling on her phone.

"Ahem," I clear my throat.

"Shit." She looks up, startled, and nearly drops her phone. "Oh, hey, Ember."

"What's up?" I ask. I'm trying to be cordial, but looking at her still pisses me off. I think I just need to uppercut her one time to get it out of my system.

"Nothing really. A lot of people are asking about your classes, though. Are you coming back?" Her mouth stretches into a wide smile as she leans on the counter.

"Probably. I just want to speak to Andrew first. Is he in the office?" She nods, and I let myself in to walk down the hallway toward the office.

After our brief meeting, we came to the agreement that I would resume classes again the first week after school starts. I explained I needed the time off to deal with some family shit and would gladly take the classes up again afterward.

"Are you coming to my party this weekend?" Shay asks as I walk by her, heading to the exit.

"I have to be in New York this weekend," I reply over my shoulder.

"It'll be Friday night. Couldn't you go on Saturday?" The urge to turn on her and tell her to shut the fuck up is strong, but I rein it in.

"I will have to see and get back to you," I tell her in my best customer service voice as I turn to look at her.

She nods and I wave as I leave the building. I don't really want to go to Shay's party, to be completely honest. I still don't trust her and the thought of being in her house just doesn't appeal to me, but keep your enemies close and all that jazz.

Vin has been quiet today and I know why, but I decide to text him so he knows I'm thinking about him.

Me: Hey, babe. I miss you.

It takes a few minutes, but his reply comes through.

Vin: I need to see you. Are you free?

Me: Just leaving the gym. Meet me at my place?

Vin: K.

The Hummer is already in my driveway when I get back to my house. I exit Shelby and cross over to his passenger side, popping up into the vehicle before leaning over to kiss him. He looks handsome in a black dress top with the top two buttons undone and a pair of black slacks. He gives me a quick peck and stares at me.

"What's going on?" I ask. I already know, but this is where my acting skills come in full force.

"Robert killed himself last night." I search his face for a sign of what he's feeling, but there's nothing.

"What?" My eyebrows shoot toward my hairline as I shake my head in disbelief. "That's hard to believe."

"Yeah, it is." He nods and then turns his head to look out the windshield. "We were all summoned to the will reading this afternoon. So I'm sorry I wasn't in touch."

"It's okay. I was busy trying to be normal." I wave him off and fall back into the seat. "How was the will reading?"

"He left me and my mom a good chunk of coin and he put a condo in New York under my name." No sadness, no surprise. Nothing.

"Whoa," I breathe out. "Was he trying to redeem himself?"

"I don't actually care, but it looks like we have somewhere to stay in New York now." He turns to look at me and the green eyes I have come to adore, search mine. Almost like he knows I had a hand in all this.

I nod because inside, I'm elated that everything went to plan, but on the outside, I am stoic and in control. There are no boundaries to what I would do to keep Vin safe. "When's the funeral?"

"Travis and his mom have decided not to have one. I think

they are pretty ashamed of how he went out. He'll be cremated and the rest I didn't care to hear about."

"Okay." I incline my head. "I will call Travis later to see how he's doing."

"He's going to be busy now since he has a business to learn to run and a board to keep happy." He snorts, the sound sarcastic and cold.

"Poor guy. Having control of all that money is just so stressful." I roll my eyes with a snicker.

Vin chuckles and leans over to press a kiss to my cheek. "We're still on for New York this weekend? I'll book the tickets."

"Did you want to go on Saturday morning? I think I want to go to Shay's party and scout out what my senior year is going to look like." I decided on the drive home that if I truly do suspect Shay is up to something, the only way to find out is to be in her house.

"Sure. We can do that." He looks slightly surprised but leaves it at that.

"Okay, I better go in and call Travis. Did you want me to come by tonight?" I ask him, my heart picking up the pace at the thought of riding his face.

He nods and I lean in to kiss him once more. Then he grabs the back of my head and pushes his tongue into my mouth, making me moan as I deepen the kiss. His tongue ring slides along my tongue and I shiver with arousal. When we pull apart, we are both panting and looking at each other hungrily.

"Get in that house now or your ass will be naked in your parents' driveway," he growls, his eyes shining with need.

I snort and open the door, blowing him a kiss. He circles

around the front of my house as I step up onto the porch and then he drives to the end of my driveway, blowing his horn once as he turns onto the street.

"How's he doing?" Dad cuts through the silence behind me as he stands in the open doorway, nearly giving me a heart attack.

Cursing softly at his sudden appearance, I reply, "His deadbeat father killed himself, but he's not too beaten up about it." I turn to go into the house. "But I bet Travis is. I should call him."

"Good idea." Dad steps back and closes the door behind us.

Once I'm in my room with my phone in my hand, I exhale with the images of Robert bleeding out in his bed in my head. I need to pull out the actress Ember here and exude sadness for Travis. He's going to be devastated and I really need him to sense sympathy from me. I lie across my bed and dial his cell phone.

He picks up after a few rings. "Hey, E." The exhaustion in his voice carries through the phone.

"Hey, yourself. How are you holding up?"

"Just trying to get over the disbelief. This is the last thing we ever imagined he'd do," he says, his words filled with skepticism.

"He was really sick though. Maybe he just didn't want to put you guys through any more of that." I try to sound saddened. "He's in a better place." He's burning in Hell where he belongs.

"Yeah, he's where he belongs." His voice hardens for a split second, then he exhales into the speaker.

"You know I love you, right?" I need to make sure he knows he's not alone. Not anymore.

"I love you too, E. I'm going to go check on my mother. She's a fucking wreck right now." The thought of him taking on more responsibilities worries me, but I make myself promise to stay by his side through it all.

"Okay, I'll call you tomorrow," I promise him.

"Good night."

"Night."

Dropping the phone to my bed, I roll over onto my back to stare at the ceiling. I made the right decision about Robert, I just feel bad for Travis.

Vin

This week has been a week from hell. I don't give a fuck that my father died. I couldn't care less. Fuck, a part of me wishes I was there to witness him running that letter opener along his wrists and savoring the way his veins opened. No, that's not why this week has been hell. I have had to put up with Travis more than I ever have before. Am I being a bitch? Sure, but I don't give a fuck. His whining, privileged ass pisses me off. 'Oh, my father would never kill himself. Check every camera.' And then, 'What will we do without him? How will my mother survive alone?' He needs to pull up those big boy pants and be a man.

My mother is all too happy to take the money left to us. She views it as back paid child support, so good for her. I don't want any of it though, and the condo he left me was almost suspicious. It suits Ember's and my needs perfectly. Too perfect. I questioned Travis about it the same day the will was read. I asked him if he told his father to give it to me based on our conversation at the cottage, but he maintains he didn't. So I'm left to believe it was just a crazy coincidence.

Thank God it's Friday and I'm leaving for the weekend with Ember. That was the only thing that kept me from murdering Travis and sending him to be with his precious daddy all week. Ember and I are driving to New York instead of taking a flight because she said there would be too many eyes. I wanted to question her and find out whose eyes she meant, but I let it be since it's convenient, because now I can take my gun without fear.

We have Shay's party to attend tonight before we leave for New York, and I'm suspicious about it. I know that girl and there's no way she's done with Mar. They have been glued at the hip since fucking eighth grade. They have something planned, and I'm thankful Ember can sense it too. She hasn't been as welcoming as Adri, and I admire that about her. She doesn't give too many chances and she sure as hell wouldn't give any to a waste of life like Shay.

I head over to Ember's house to pick up her and Adri. It's the same as it's always been with those two getting ready together. This last week, Ember has done a one-eighty. I don't know what brought her back, but whatever it was, I hope it's here to stay. I park in her driveway before walking into her house, knowing her parents love me and that she's mine.

"Em!" I yell at the bottom of the stairs. "Let's go!"

"Okay!" she yells back from upstairs.

I head into the family room and find Debby and Scott curled together on the couch. I have never witnessed a couple this in love—besides me and Ember—before.

"Hey, Vin," Debby says with a wave as Scott rubs her feet in his lap.

"Hey, guys." I sit in the armchair across from them and turn my eyes to the football game on the TV.

"You're heading straight to New York after this party?" Scott questions. "No drinking, right?"

"Yes, sir." Turning away from the game to look at him, I nod. "Don't worry, I will take care of her."

"I just don't understand why she has to find out about this Tommy person." Debby lifts her head to look at me before shaking it and then dropping back down to the couch with a huff.

"I think we have to let her do what she needs to do." I shrug and lean forward, resting my elbows on my knees. "I'm pretty sure if we try to stop her, she'll just go behind all our backs."

Scott nods and looks at his wife. "He's right, Deb."

"Don't worry, I promise not to let anything happen to her." It's an easy enough promise to make. I would kill for that girl.

"It's the only reason we are letting this happen, son," Scott admits as he continues to rub his wife's feet.

I respect the hell out of them, and it leaves me a little sad that they couldn't have children of their own because they make kick-ass parents. The circumstances of Ember's coming here were tragic, but I'm sure fate had a hand in it.

"We're ready," Ember announces from behind me, her voice sending goose bumps along my skin. Being so engrossed in conversation with Scott, I didn't hear her approach. Not that I'm worried if she heard anything. I turn and take her in. My girl is supermodel material. She has a strappy pair of black-heeled sandals on, and her long, toned and tanned legs are on display. She's wearing leather shorts and her midriff is showing beneath a band shirt tied at her side, ripped at the neck and arms. Her hair is straightened and hanging down to her lower back, and when I reach her face, she's smirking with those plush lips. "Are we going?"

"Yeah," I say as I clear my throat and stand from the chair. "Hey, Adri." Adri waves at me with a little smile on her face. They both look great, and I have no doubt Travis will think the same about Adri.

I grab Ember's bags for the weekend, and Adri and I walk out to the Hummer while Ember says goodbye to her parents. "I'm nervous," Adri whispers as I put the bags into the back.

"About what?" I turn to find her dark eyes wide with a harrowing look.

"I feel like something is going to go down at this party, like what if Marlana shows?" She wrings her hands together as she bites the inside of her cheek.

"Well, Ember won't care unless she tries something, and at that point, she deserves whatever happens, right?" Adri nods and then hops into the back seat as Ember saunters out of the house, her long legs flexing with each step she takes in my direction. My cock twitches in my pants at the sight of her.

"Baby, your boner is showing," she points out, her hand rubbing along the front of my jeans.

"You keep that up and we'll be giving Adri a show. I don't give a fuck," I groan and grab her face. Then I kiss her deep, licking along the inside of her mouth as her tongue flicks my tongue ring, and we both groan. The honk of my horn pulls us apart and we turn to find Adri giving us the middle finger. We both laugh and get into the Hummer before she does something worse like drive away in my baby without us.

We pull up to Shay's house and it looks as though the party is already well underway. Cars are parked all along the street and the sounds of people yelling and laughing can be heard about a block away. That doesn't even include the thumping of the music. She must've warned the neighbors if the cops haven't shut this down yet. We walk up to the house together as a few girls run through the sprinklers on the front lawn, and the guys hang back, watching with beers in their hands.

Ember snorts beside me and I grin, grabbing her hand. She's only ever been to Danny's parties or mine and we don't let shit go down like this. So this is new to her, at least, new to her here in Whitsborough. We enter the house, and we're immediately bombarded by half-naked people making out in the front foyer and girls dancing topless on tables.

"Holy shit," Ember breathes out, her eyes wide as she takes in the room.

"This is a Shay party." The fact that I used to like this type of atmosphere and enjoy these types of girls is weird to me now.

"Let's find the alcohol," Adri says, brushing by us. "I need to dull my sight to this bullshit."

Ember and I laugh as we make our way into the kitchen after Adri. Standing on the counter is Shay herself, pouring vodka into people's open mouths. She's already looking pretty wasted and I can probably bet she'll be out in about an hour.

"Ember!" Shay squeals, throwing her hands up. "You came!"

I look at Ember, needing to witness her reaction. She cocks her eyebrow and points at Shay. "Girl, if you fall, I will piss my shorts laughing at you."

I snort, because she never disappoints.

"Emmberr," Shay whines. "Come up here with me."

"I'd rather shit in my hands and clap," she retorts, clapping her hands together for effect.

I fucking lose it, laughing so hard, and Adri is snorting into a red cup of liquor.

"Ew," Shay replies, her nose crinkling in disgust.

"Exactly." Ember nods, her face filled with mock disgust as her lip curls.

Adri and I laugh again, and Shay looks between the three of us, confused. She eventually shrugs it off and goes back to pouring liquor down people's throats.

"What did I miss?" I turn to find Travis leaning against the wall. Waiting for the familiar rush of annoyance, I'm surprised when it doesn't happen.

"Ember being Ember." I shrug. "Just get here?"

"Yeah, this is a shit-show already," he states as he looks around, his brows creased and his mouth set in a grim line. He looks just as thrilled to be here as I am.

"Seriously."

About an hour later, Travis and I are sitting on a couch watching Adri and Danny laughing with each other. He's agitated about it, I can tell by the bounce of his knee and his clenched fists, but he doesn't do shit.

"Doesn't that shit bother you?" I ask him.

"Yep." He takes a swig of his beer, his eyes completely focused on them.

"Go get her." If that was Ember, I would make sure everyone in the room knew she was mine.

"Nah, let her do what she wants." He gets up from the couch and stalks into the kitchen. Nothing about their situation makes sense, as if there's a piece of the puzzle I'm missing.

I'd have Ember thrown over my shoulder and into a bedroom where I could spank her, then fuck some sense into her. Speaking of, she plops her ass down on my lap and smiles at me. Her eyes are still crystal clear so I'm guessing she's been nursing this one cup all night.

"Not feeling like drinking?" I ask as I run my thumb along her lower lip.

"No, we have a long road trip after this shit." Her tongue dips out to press against the pad, sending sparks of energy up my arm.

I nod. I've been drinking water all night, to most of the drama club's dismay. Not that I care. I never do what everyone else is doing if I just don't fucking feel like it, and Ember is the same. Shay starts yelling and we turn to see her on her phone having what looks to be a heated discussion.

"She hasn't been off that thing all night," Ember grunts. "She's been texting or yelling at someone."

"Hmm." That is a little weird, but fuck, so is Shay.

Shay hangs up and stumbles her way into the room. Then she stops and starts looking around, swaying on the spot.

"She's going to pass out soon," Ember mutters.

"Yeah, looks like it."

Shay spots Ember and her brows crinkle together before she heads our way, and I groan into Ember's hair. "Make her fuck off," I beg.

"Yes, sir." Ember chuckles and stands up.

"Ember," Shay whines, "come hang out with me."

Ember looks at me and smiles. Then she takes Shay's hand and leads her out of the room.

Chapter Nine

"I haaave to taaaalk to youuuu," Shay slurs while almost face-planting into me.

"Alright, girl." I push her back and make sure she's steady on her feet before releasing her. "What about?"

"Nooot here." She grabs my hand and drags me down a hallway, forcing me to keep her straight and praying she doesn't take me down with her if she falls on her face. "Somewhere private."

"I'm not making out with you tonight. I'm not drunk enough," I deadpan as I let her take me through the house.

"Ewww, I'm nooot into girlsss," she sneers over her shoulder, nearly stumbling over her own two feet.

"Gotcha." I steady her once again and she continues forward.

She leads us up an enormous staircase and into the first room on the right. It looks like her bedroom, and it's full of pink things and stuffed animals. I shudder with revulsion at the sight. This immature shit is weird.

"I need to sssssshow you sssssssomething on my phooooone." She's slurring worse now and her eyes are rolling into the back of her head as she tries not to pass out. "But youuuuu caaaaan't get maaaaad at meeeee, oooookay?"

"That depends." I narrow my eyes as my jaw tightens. What the fuck is she talking about?

"Marrrrlanaaaaa isssss bothhhhhering me sssssso muchhhhh and sssshe'sssss thhhhhreatening to tell everyone wwwwwhat I did—" She falls onto her bed, her body bouncing on the mattress as deep snores instantly pour from her mouth. She's passed out.

Fuck's sake. Her phone is poking out of her back pocket, so I roll her a bit and pull it out. It immediately asks for a thumbprint for access. I yank on her hand and push her thumb to the phone, then it lights up with a background of Shay in a bikini. Typical.

I open her messaging app and find a conversation with Marlana, the last message just ten minutes ago. My blood pumps and the telltale tendrils of anger come over me. I open that conversation and scroll up to start at the top. The conversation started about two weeks ago with Marlana messaging her and asking about her party. Shay ignores her, then Marlana messages again and tells Shay that everyone will hear about her and coach fucking in ninth grade if she doesn't answer. *What the fuck?*

I look over at Shay and really scrutinize her. Is that what she's hiding? She fucked a coach at school? I wonder which one. I go back to the messages and see she answers Marlana, asking what she wants. Marlana sends her a link and tells her to show everyone this video on her projection screen at the party. I press the link and my body goes completely stiff, like someone has doused me in ice water.

"I'm getting good at making you squirt, huh?"

"This pussy loves her daddy, huh?"

It's a pretty clear video of what went down between me and Vin in the dressing room at the theater party last year. I'm bent over the stool with my hands on the vanity top, my extremely wet pussy spread open by Vin as he slaps his cock against it. My fluids are running down the insides of my thighs, my legs quivering in the aftermath of my intense orgasm. Vin strokes his cock and the piercing on top glints in the light, then he slams back into me with hard, quick strokes. The sound of my arousal is clear through the video. Finally, he throws his head back and lets out a guttural groan as he comes inside of me.

"Gonna be hard to walk."

Then the video goes black. I'm still holding the phone as I tremble with anger. I knew the door was fucking shut, and I should have realized Marlana would have had something to do with us finding it open afterward.

I shoot Vin a quick text message using Shay's phone and forward the video, telling him to get his ass up to her room. Then I message Travis and Adri with my phone, telling them to come upstairs as well. I erase every damn thing on her phone in the meantime. Text messages, pictures, and videos. When that's done, I pull out the SIM card and flush it down her toilet, then I drop her phone in there for good measure.

"Ember?" Vin yells out as he runs into Shay's room, his eyes wild and his teeth bared.

I come out of the bathroom and stare at him. What he finds on my face causes him to pause and swallow hard. I look empty again because I can feel how much of the darkness is back and the need to kill vibrates along my fingertips.

"What the fuck was that Shay sent me?" he whispers angrily, then looks at her bed and finds her passed out.

"I found it on her phone with a pretty damning conversation between her and Marlana." I come around the bed to stand beside him, both of us looking down at her with disgust.

Travis and Adri run in next, both of them looking back and forth between Vin and me. "What happened?" Adri finally asks, looking at Shay on the bed. "Did you knock her out?"

"She's passed out. She brought me up here to tell me that Marlana was blackmailing her to show everyone a very intimate video of Vin and me tonight at the party." Adri gasps as she shakes her head, her face turning a few shades paler.

"How would Marlana get such a video?" Travis asks me as he kicks at Shay's feet hanging off her bed.

"She found us at the theater party and taped it without us knowing," Vin answers, his voice like stone as his body trembles with suppressed anger.

"Wow," Adri breathes out as she rubs her fingers to her temple. "What are you going to do?"

"I already erased it from Shay's phone, and I destroyed her SIM and cell phone, but I need to get to the source to delete the data there. I'm sure Marlana has that saved into a cloud system," I grit out as I cross my arms over my chest, all of us still peering down at a snoring Shay.

"She would have that file saved on her computer too," Adri states quietly as if in deep thought.

"I know how to wipe a computer system." I wave her off and step back from the bed, readying to leave the room.

"You do?" Travis asks, his head snapping up to look at me as his brows come together.

"Yeah, I need to go now." I brush past them and head downstairs. Vin is close behind me with Adri and Travis trailing behind him. I rush out of the house and onto the front lawn. It's littered with beer cans and teenagers either making out or puking.

"Travis, can you take Adri home?" Vin asks him as I continue toward the Hummer.

"Wait!" Adri yells out. "Where are you guys going?"

"We have to drive to New York," I tell her over my shoulder.

"Oh, right. Okay." She sounds a little lost. "Have a safe trip."

With my mind on the confrontation I'm planning, I don't acknowledge her as I stand in front of the Hummer and Vin stops to talk quietly with Travis. Finally, he heads over, unlocking the vehicle so I can get in. We both sit inside and he takes a slow breath. "So, Marlana's house first?"

"Yes." My answer is immediate as I pull on my seat belt.

He drives for about ten minutes and then pulls up to a smaller home. It's still large compared to the average home, but when you compare it to any of our neighborhood homes, it's smaller.

"Her room is the one on the bottom right. There's no alarm system," he states as he undoes his seat belt to lean over the wheel, looking toward her window.

I try to ignore that brief pang of jealousy that hits my lower belly. Of course he would know where her room is and whether she has an alarm system. They've only been fucking for years.

So much for ignoring.

I jump out of the vehicle and head toward her window. The purple-headed bitch is sitting on her bed texting. I can only imagine it's Shay she's messaging, probably trying to figure out what's going on. Well, she's about to find out.

"Hey," Vin whispers behind me. "Step to the side of the house. I'll get her to open the window and let me in, then you come in after."

I nod and do as he says, watching as he taps on the glass. The thirsty bitch is quick to open her window before breathing out Vin's name.

"Hey, Mar." I hear him shuffle around. "Can I talk to you? Ember just broke up with me tonight and I don't want to be alone."

Motherfucker is smart, I'll give him that, but if he touches her, I'm taking a testicle. A few minutes later, I sneak back around to her window and peer inside. I find him sitting on her bed with his head in his hands, the actor in him making an appearance, as Marlana rubs circles into his back. *This bitch.*

I jump into her room through the window, and she gasps as Vin closes his hand over her mouth and holds her in place. Marlana begins to struggle and stops as soon as her eyes land on my face, making her body go stone-still with fear. "Thank fuck. I was trying not to vomit while she was touching me," he groans as his nose crinkles in disgust.

"Give me your phone." I stick my hand out to her. "Now."

She hands it over with a shaking hand and I give her phone the same treatment as Shay's. Only this time I pocket her SIM card and smash the phone under my shoe.

"Where's your laptop?" I ask as Vin drops his hand from her mouth, the skin pink from how hard he was holding her.

"There." She points to her desk with a whimper.

I walk over to her desk and sit down. She's amazingly quiet, and it's nothing like the Marlana I know. I guess us being here in her room with no one close enough to help her is scary. I open her cloud and enter the virus Carm taught me, then I put it on her laptop as well. Everything she ever had saved or downloaded there is gone. Then when I double-check to make sure it's done, I smash my fist through the screen. I don't register the pain. I stand up abruptly and exit through her window, because if I stay any longer, I might kill the bitch.

I pull out my phone and fire off a quick text to Carm.

Me: Set me up with a fight tomorrow night. The same kind Father used to.

Devil's Offspring: You sure?

Me: Yes. See you soon.

Chapter Ten

It's been a long drive, but thankfully, Vin did most of it. He was nervous about me driving his baby, so he literally slept one hour and then drove the rest of the way. He is currently sleeping in the lush master bedroom of this very impressive condo. It has three bedrooms and four bathrooms. Each bedroom houses a king-sized bed with luxurious down covers and satin sheets. Robert was a master at throwing his money around. The floor-to-ceiling windows all over the penthouse condo are breathtaking, and we have a gorgeous unobstructed view of the Empire State Building. Tonight, the lights on it illuminate in soft blues.

All appliances and electronics in this place are top-of-the-line, and even the windows have some sort of lining on them which can shift to block the sun at the press of a button. I'm still having a hard time adjusting to wealth like this. Being so close to the only other home I've known is reminding me that I didn't come from this sort of lifestyle. Memories of a life filled with struggle and pain flood my mind, contrasting with the lush amenities around me. Hunt's Point is about twenty minutes from here, so I can be there and back within two hours, and I can bet Vin will still be sound asleep. My phone pings with a message. *Finally.*

Devil's Offspring: A car is downstairs.

I don't answer him and grab one of the three sets of house keys on the hook. Then I sneak my way out of the condo without making a sound. Not that Vin would hear me in this massive fucking place. Did I mention there are only two penthouses on this floor? Yeah, Robert sure loved his decadent life.

I'm dressed in my usual fighting attire: black leggings and a black sports bra with a hoodie on top. I've already taped my hands so that I don't need to waste more time when I get there. I've been announced as the showcase fight tonight, and I'll show up just as I'm about to be called to the ring.

A blacked-out sedan idles on the street, and I know that's for me. I slide into the back seat and the driver turns to give me a once-over. "Hey, Blur." He nods with a smile. "We're excited to have you back."

I nod back my acknowledgement as he pulls out onto the street and we're on our way to the warehouse. The warehouse that leads to the underground ring. The place I spent a week in captivity, and the place where I killed my father. I should feel some sort of trepidation now, right? Would it be so terrible if all I had thrumming through my veins was excitement and anticipation? I know, I'm so fucked-up.

The twenty minutes fly by and then I'm being led into the warehouse that will bring me down to the ring. As the elevator doors open, I come face-to-face with Carm and Emmett.

"Lil' sis," Carm purrs, his eyes lighting up with excitement. "We are happy to see you."

"Who am I fighting?" I nod to them both and step inside the elevator car, standing between my brothers.

"He's a child abuser from up in Melrose. Beats on his stepson while the mother gets doped up on crack. The Office of Children and Family Services apparently doesn't deem him a threat, even though the kid has been in the hospital three times already this month." Carm's face hardens as he tells me the circumstances, his hands curling into fists. Emmet grunts on my other side, the crack of his knuckles telling me he'd love to be the one in the ring with him.

"This won't come back on you?" I ask curiously, not actually caring how it affects him.

"Nah. A Head in that area is related to the mother. A cousin, I think. He's the one who came forward when I put the word out about needing a fight. He's a spectator tonight, so don't disappoint." He gives me a wink and then shakes out his fists.

I couldn't disappoint if I tried, because I'm literally vibrating with pent-up anger from the entire Marlana and Shay situation. I can't kill either of them, so I might as well kill someone else who deserves it. The elevator lurches as we descend to the bottom, and the excitement grows in my belly. The spectators enter through an enormous set of doors at the front and head down a steep staircase to get here. They don't use the same entrance as the fighters in case someone tries to pull some shady shit to hedge the bets.

"Why did you call for this fight?" I turn at the sound of Emmett's voice, his eyes shining with concern.

"Because I had two choices. Come here and release this shit inside, or end up in jail for murdering schoolgirls," I retort angrily as Carm chuckles and reaches around me to clap Emmett on the back. Emmett rolls his eyes and looks back at his phone, his disinterest obvious.

We exit into a hallway, and I'm led into the closet-sized room I've used for every one of my fights. Carm shuts me in and tells me to warm up as he and Emmett stand outside the door. Huh, it's weird to have brothers and to have them be somewhat protective.

I run through all my warmups, and a few minutes later, "Bodies" by Drowning Pool starts—my theme song. A knock sounds on the door, and I pull my hoodie over my head as it swings in moments later. Carm is motioning me to move and follow him to the ring as the crowd screams wildly for me. The rush of adrenaline is so intoxicating, and I can't wait to sink my fists into some flesh.

I run up the four steps and enter the cage, throwing my hood back to stare into the eyes of the man across from me. He's about mid to late thirties, Caucasian, with stringy brown hair. He's tall and built, which pisses me off to know he beats on a child. His eyes are dodgy as they skim over me and then out to the crowd. He didn't choose to be here, and I know he was told the rules. Kill or be killed.

He gives me another sweep from head to toe before snickering. "Seriously?!" he screams out to the crowd, his arms wide as he leans forward. "This is what you send in to fight me?"

I don't address him since I'll have him lying flat without a heartbeat in no time, anyway. Why converse with the dead? This isn't a séance. I yank off my hoodie and throw it into the corner. He does another scan over my body, and this time, his eyebrows raise. *That's right, motherfucker, I'm stacked for a girl, huh? And these scars are battle wounds, you cunt.*

"Okay, guys! This is your showcase tonight! We have Blur back in the building." The crowd screams and the MC has to pause. "And she is fighting… Child Beater!"

"What the fuck?" my opponent snarls and looks around with confusion, making me snort with amusement.

"The rules are different for this round. Tonight, these two must… fight to the death!"

I do some jumps on the spot to get my blood pumping and keep my muscles limber. I notice this guy now has a smirk on his face as he leers at me. "Did you hear them, little girl? I'm a child beater."

Again, I ignore the prick, and as soon as the whistle blows, I'm on him. I rush at him as his right fist comes out to hit my face. *Amateur.* I dodge and slam my right fist into his rib cage, then I pivot on my right foot and move behind him before he recovers. He stumbles forward and turns around quickly with a snarl when I hit him twice in the kidney and once in the back of his neck.

My vision goes red, and I give him an answering growl as I rush forward again. He once again tries to hit me with a right hook, and I dodge it like the first, slamming him with an uppercut to his chin. His teeth bite through his lip and his blood sprays forward onto my face. It rages me on further, and I strike him with a left hook, watching as he lands on the mat with a thump. Quickly, I jump on him and pummel his face with both fists. His cartilage crunches and his skin breaks open under my knuckles. It doesn't stop me though, because the warmth of his blood running down my arms just adds fuel to my already blazing inferno.

I grab a hold of his shirt and pull him up while I stand, then I move behind him and drop to one knee, bringing him back down with me. I wrap my arms around his head and lean forward until my mouth is against his ear.

"This is for the kid you've been using as a punching bag. Say hello to the Devil, his name is Raphael, and tell him I can't wait to see him again." Then, with a push and pull motion, I snap his neck and he drops to the mat… dead.

I barely register the crowd as they scream and shout my name. Grabbing my hoodie, I quickly exit the cage behind Carm and Emmett as they lead me down a familiar hallway and back into the room I spent a week in. The room has been fixed up since my last visit. There's new plaster, and paint covers the holes I smashed into the walls.

"I thought you would want to shower before you go back, and there's a change of clothes for you," Carm states as he stands just inside the door, Emmett beside him.

"Yeah, cool," I reply and begin to pull the tape off my hands.

"Ember, you were fucking scary in that cage," Emmett breathes out, pride shining in his wide eyes.

"Once we train, I'll make sure you are too," I tell him, holding my fist out for a bump.

He stares at the blood coating it but doesn't flinch as he bumps my fist with his. He's not afraid to get blood on his hands. Big boy points for him. I head into the shower to wash off the blood and then change. When I'm done, I follow Carm to the elevator, the ride to the top a quiet one because Emmett isn't with us.

"Hey, so tomorrow you will be back? To train with Emmett?" he breaks the silence.

"Yeah, I need the workout too." The tension is already forming in my muscles from the lack of training.

"Okay, cool," he murmurs, his eyes on the side of my face.

"I'll be bringing Vin. It's time he meets you guys." I turn to look at him, to gauge his reaction.

"Okay, that's cool," he repeats with a nod.

The elevator doors open then, and I follow Carm out onto the street, where the same sedan and driver are waiting for me.

"All right, get in," Carm says as he opens the door. "I'll see you tomorrow."

"I got her from here." When I hear his voice, I stop and turn around to look into a furious set of moss-green eyes.

Oh, fuck.

Vin

She's sitting quietly in the Hummer as I drive back toward the condo. She really thought she was being stealthy, but the second she snuck out of the condo, the sound of the door closing woke me up. I've always been a light sleeper. I didn't bother to chase her down and demand she tell me where she was going. Instead, I trailed her. I followed the sedan all the way to a deserted warehousing district, and when I saw the crowds entering, I had a knowing feeling of what I was walking into. After paying the admittance fee, I followed everyone into an underground fighting ring.

A fight was already going on in a concrete arena as I came through the doors and it didn't look to be what anyone was really interested in. People drank their beers and chatted amongst themselves as I stood at the far back wall, trying to catch a glimpse of my fucking girlfriend.

"Blur is here tonight, bro," a guy in front of me said, the name perking my ears up.

"That's why I'm here. I only come when Blur is fighting," his friend replied.

"Were you here for her last fight? The one when she refused to fight her opponent?"

"Yeah, well, it looked like that guy had already been beaten to a pulp. Then he gets shot in the head. I scrambled out of here so fast and was nearly trampled by people." They both nod like that was a good time for them and continue drinking their beers. I may not have known much about Ember's life before she came to Whitsborough, but she's had plenty of time to fill me in.

The song, "Bodies," started playing and the crowd went mad, effectively shutting up the guys in front of me. I watched as they threw some crackhead-looking guy in the ring, and then from the corner of my eye, I saw Ember—or should I say *Blur*—heading for the ring. In front of her were two guys, both similar in stature, but that's all I could see because they had hoodies sitting low on their faces. She also had her face obscured by her hood, but I would know that walk anywhere.

When the MC announced the fight was to the death, I lost my shit. I tried to push through the crowd to get to the front, but it was impossible and I ended up stuck halfway to the cage. This guy, her opponent, showed signs of being a certified crackhead and I know how unpredictable fucking crackheads can be because I've dealt with my fair share of them.

The fight was intense, and even though Ember is capable of holding her own, I found myself praying she made it out unscathed. Which she did within ten minutes, but when she took that man's life, I began to fear for the weight she added onto her soul. She's been battling dark energy since she's been back and I worried I was staring straight at her demons inside that cage.

"What happened to Tommy, Ember?" I ask her, breaking the silence inside the vehicle.

"Carmelo shot him in the head while I was being held in the compound. It was either me or Tommy," she whispers, her head hanging as she wrings her hands together in her lap. I can sense how hard this is for her, telling me, but if we're going to be here together, I need to know everything.

"Carmelo is the half brother?" I press her for the details as I stop at a red light, and I find her nodding when I look over at her, her eyes still on her hands

"He's the one you saw me with tonight." Her voice is strained as I'm sure she's reliving the memories that haunt her dreams.

"Is Ray your father?" The light turns green and I press the gas, weaving my way through other cars to get us back quicker.

"Yes." She takes a deep, audible breath. "He was, but his real name was Raphael, and I killed him." The last few words are spit out between her teeth, the hatred in her tone for her father evident.

I turn into the condo's lot and park the Hummer in the underground garage before turning to look at her. My chest is about to explode as anxiety rips through it. "What happened? What did he do to you?"

"He kidnapped me from school and held me in a room. I was forced to train with Carmelo who helped by preparing me for the people I was forced to fight. In the beginning, I had hopes of escaping, to come back to you, but that changed."

"How so?" I reach over to run my knuckles along her cheek as she turns to look at me, her eyes swimming with tears.

"He was the kingpin for the Eastside Rampage and my mother was the informant that put him in jail for fifteen years. When he got out, he caused the fire that killed her and almost killed me. When he confessed that to me, I knew I was going to kill him." Her eyes harden as the tears slowly fade, and she flicks them between mine, gauging my reaction. Her hands still in her lap for just a second before she runs her palms over her thighs.

I'm stunned into silence and understand why she didn't tell me what happened. She was worried I would see her differently, and she's right, in a way I do. She's a survivor, regardless of what she's doing to make sure she continues living.

"Okay, but why the fight tonight? Why kill someone?" I ask her once the shock wears off.

"That was a child abuser. I was helping a kid who couldn't help himself," she explains, her cheeks turning red with rage.

"Why did you come here to fight, Ember? All this way to kill an abusing asshole? It doesn't make sense." I drop my hand from her cheek as she growls, her irritation soaking the air around us. The need to ensure my fingers stay safely away from her teeth overrides my need to touch her.

"I need a release, okay? Because if I don't, I'm going to end up killing people who do stupid shit toward me or my family!" she yells into her hands as her body vibrates with anger.

She's clearly hit her limit for interrogations tonight, and I don't push her anymore because I know what it feels like to have pent-up aggravation pulsing inside of you. "Let's go upstairs. You must be beat." I rub a hand along her shoulder before opening my door.

"That's it?" She looks at me questioningly. "You still want to be with me?"

"Ember, I told you before. This, you and I, is it for me." I smirk at her, hoping she realizes I mean every word I say. "I will love you forever, no matter what you do."

"This won't be the last one," she whispers, her tortured expression wiping the smile off my face. "I can't stop yet."

"What are you going to be? A savior for people who can't save themselves?" I ask, the question sounding absurd. She looks deep into my eyes as a grin slowly crosses her gorgeous mouth, proving just how manic her moods can be when she's in this state. Fuck, I think I just gave her a way to kill people and be happy about it. "Come on." I hop out of the vehicle and motion for her to do the same. "Let's get some sleep."

Once we're in the elevator, she turns to wrap her arms around my waist as I run my hands up her back, feeling how small she is. Sure, she's muscular, but you would never guess a killer resides inside this skin.

"Will you come meet Carm tomorrow?" She looks up into my face, her eyes looking hopeful. "And Emmett?"

"Emmett?" I repeat.

"It's a long story, but he's my twin brother." Holy fuck, can this get any more convoluted? Just when I think I have the information down and digested, she throws more at me.

She sees the confusion on my face and takes my hand to lead us to the condo. Once we're inside, she grabs us each a beer from a very stocked fridge, and we sit at the large dining table. "I'm just as confused," she admits. "I still don't understand why my mother never said a damn thing. Not about Raphael and not about Emmett. How did she live each day knowing her child was out there somewhere?"

"Are you sure he is who they're saying he is?" I take a swig of beer, letting my skepticism permeate the space between us.

"Yes. It's like looking in a fucking mirror," she says, then takes a sip of her beer.

"Did you ask him or Carm? They must know something." It's a long shot considering Ember was raised by her mother and she didn't say a damn thing.

"They don't. Emmett was raised by Carm because Raphael was in jail, and Carm says he never knew who I was or who Emmett's mother was until the night they captured me." She drops her chin to her hand and stares off at the wall, her mind working through the details. She's probably relieved to finally speak to someone else about it all and I'm glad she chose me to trust with all of it.

"There must've been a reason your mother did what she did." I can't see the woman who raised my girl to be who she is today doing anything nefarious to her children. It doesn't make sense.

"There's no excuse for abandoning your child," she retorts,

downing the rest of her beer in two gulps. "Let's get some sleep."

I nod and let it go for now as I follow her into the ostentatious master bedroom. Robert had no problem spending his money on unnecessary luxury things and it only rubs an already raw wound. At least this is now mine, a small consolation prize, but I'll take it. We both strip down to nothing and climb into the lush bed, sparing no more words as I make love to the girl who was made for me.

We're back at the abandoned warehouse with the massive underground compound. Ember explained that this is where the gang operates from and that her father lived here. This is also the place he held her mother captive. She tries to hide it, but the pain flares in her eyes whenever she brings up her mother.

As soon as we are out of the car, two large men pat us down and then lead us into the depths of Hell. I sound overly dramatic, but fuck, this place reeks of blood and desperation.

We're led into an office and one of the guys with Ember last night is sitting behind it. He's muscular and around my height, but where I'm built, this motherfucker is stacked. His neck looks like a fucking cobra's, and I'm slightly jealous. Looks like I'll need extra gym sessions to run with this crowd.

He stands up from the desk, coming around to the front as he wraps Ember in an awkward one-armed hug. She shoves his arm away with a hiss at the same time he reaches his hand out to me.

"Hey." We shake hands, his firm. "I'm Carmelo."

"Vin." He sizes me up while I do the same to him. I don't

know him, and I don't trust him with Ember, but I'll wait it out because she's been different, happier since they've been in the picture.

A side door inside the office opens and in walks a guy who shocks the shit out of me. I must look deranged because my jaw is fucking unhinged. When Ember told me he was her mirror image, I thought maybe she was exaggerating, but no, if my girl cut off her hair, they would have the same head.

She chuckles and nudges me with her shoulder. "Told ya."

Emmett stays standing across the room and gives me a slight nod. From my first impression, his personality is nothing like Ember's. He seems more subdued and quieter, where she is up-front and in your face.

"I'm going to do some combat and knife training with Emmett today," Ember informs me as she stands in front of me.

"All right. Should I come back to get you later?" I smile down at her, happy to see that spark back in her eyes, regardless of what she had to do to have it.

"Do you like to shoot?" Carm interrupts us, his head tipped to the side. He doesn't look like Ember or Emmett. I honestly wouldn't guess they were even related.

"Yeah." I shrug as Ember's smile grows.

"How about you and I hit the gun range? And if you're any good, I will let you take your pick from our arsenal." *Arsenal?* Who is this guy? The Godfather?

"Okay, cool." I nod as Ember leans up to kiss my cheek. If this keeps her happy, I'll dance the two-step with her cobra-necked brother.

Ember heads back through the side door with her twin, glancing back at me to give me a soft smile. I'm not comfortable being here. Being caught up in any type of gang life isn't safe and Ember is more than caught up. It doesn't matter though, because I would never leave her to deal with it on her own.

"Follow me," Carm says as he guides us out of the room and down another long hallway. The walls are concrete and the air is cool, making the place feel like a true basement.

We enter a room with racks of guns lining each wall. All ranging from handguns to rifles to RPGs. My cock stirs in my jeans, and I grin. The room is any man's fucking wet dream.

"Pick one out and let's get to it," Carm remarks with a matching tilt to his lips, knowing exactly what this room is doing to me. I grab a Glock 17 because I know this gun. I've used this gun before and it's a comfortable fit. "Ah, the Glock. Nice pick," Carm states.

I follow him into the range area and am shocked by the size. Ten aisles line up, side by side, fully equipped with ear protection and goggles. Fifty feet down each aisle is a paper target, the sight almost making me giddy.

"I'm sure you have some questions for me, and I will answer them all, but first I need to tell you exactly what's going on," Carm begins as he lays his gun down on the counter and I do the same. "Ember has someone looking for her. This woman is dangerous. Her name is Jennifer Talia and she is a senator here in New York. Needless to say, a corrupt one. She was doing some business with Raph, and I suspect they were an item of some sort. She's looking for revenge and I need Ember protected at all costs. So, when you leave here today, I will arm you and make sure you can protect her."

"Ember told me about what happened and how her father had captured her. She also told me you were a part of it. How can I trust that you have her best interests in mind?" I lay it all out on the line. I don't trust him, and unlike Ember, I'm not blinded by a newfound family.

"Good question. I have Emmett to think of, and Raphael knew how close I am to that kid. He used him against me every chance he got. When he told me Ember was my sister and Emmett's twin, I felt bad, but Emmett is all I have." He scrubs a hand down his face. "But as I'm sure you know, and I soon found out, Ember doesn't need anyone's help. She single-handedly took out our leader."

I want to question him further about where his loyalties lie now and if Ember is as important as Emmett, but I don't think I'll get the complete truth. "What are you doing to find this Jennifer bitch?"

"I have the other heads of our corporation searching for her weaknesses." He nods, sounding purposely vague. "We'll get her." I take his word on it for now, but I'll need more information sooner rather than later. If this bitch thinks she can harm Ember, then she has another thing coming.

We line up in our own lanes and I spend the next hour popping paper men off. For as rusty as I am, I still hit the bullseye multiple times. When we're through, Carm sticks to his word and lets me pick any gun I want. I stick with the Glock and tuck it into my pants, then he sets me up with some ammo and we head back to wait for Emmett and Ember.

When Ember gets back, she says goodbye to Carm and he slips her a piece of paper. To the untrained eye, it would've easily been missed, but I don't miss a fucking thing. I continue to watch as she nods to them both and slips her hands into her hoodie pocket. Maybe it's another fight to the death, and if that's the case, I will be there with her.

We head to the Hummer, and as soon as the doors close, she turns to me. Her face is filled with hesitation as she bites her bottom lip.

"I have to come back next weekend." She reaches her hand out and places it on my arm. "Will you come back with me?"

Relief hits me right away. She's not hiding from me anymore and it can only mean that she trusts me wholly. "Of course. Why are we coming back? Is it another fight?"

"It's a hit." I'm not sure how I feel about that, but I would never tell her what to do. If this keeps her straight, then I won't interfere, but I won't let her do it alone either.

The rest of the weekend we chill out and go over this hit she has the following weekend. We plan it out, starting with scoping this guy's job and the surrounding people. This isn't some crackhead off the street. He's a district attorney who likes to be paid off to let murderers back out on the street. Ember explained that one of the Head's sons was killed by a guy who was let out on a bribe.

And just like that, I'm a fucking sidekick.

Chapter Eleven

Ron Chambers, District Attorney for the Bronx, and an overall dickhead of epic proportions. The file I've received shows he's let out at least twenty rapists and murderers to line his corrupt pockets. One of the ten Heads has requested this man be 'dealt with.' He lives in a fancy condo building on the penthouse floor. One of two penthouses on that floor. Sound familiar? That's right, this bitch shared a penthouse floor with none other than Robert Greene, and now Vincent Greene. This couldn't be any easier unless he tripped off his balcony while drunk. *Hey… that's actually a good idea.*

Since we've been back, I have had Shay and Adri both blowing up my phone, the former begging for forgiveness and the latter begging me to forgive Shay. All calls were muted and messages deleted. I'm just not there yet. The best thing Shay could've done was tell me straight up as soon as she received that video. I get it. She fucked the coach at school, and blackmail is a bitch, but she literally had pornography on her phone with the purpose of distributing.

Travis says he was shocked when he found out one of his baseball coaches was boning a student at Precious Blood Academy, but in the next breath, when the shock wore off, he said it wasn't hard to believe either. That's as much as he would say and I decided not to push him on it. He's also been calling me and asking me more and more about the virus I put on Marlana's computer, where I got it from and what exactly it does. I'm not stupid, I know why he's asking, and if I wasn't so fucking pissed and seeing red that night, I would've kept my mouth shut, if only for this exact reason. He's seeing similarities to the same virus applied to his security system, but I can't do anything about it now. I just have to ride it out.

Back to this file, it's fucking detailed and I'll have to thank Carm for that. Right down to this man's favorite food—lasagna— and how he likes to spend his Saturday night soaking in his hot tub on the balcony. He also has a pet cat, and he's never been married, although he has a long-term girlfriend and she had an abortion a few years back. This guy just feels all over scummy. He is handsome, I will say that. His always-coiffed blond hair sweeps back over his head and his very fake orange tan makes his baby blues shine brightly. The sneer of his smile might make some panties drop, but after all I've learned about him, I can only see evil.

When we got back from New York, my parents had so many questions and even more when I said I was going back the following weekend. Vin convinced them I needed closure and that he would be with me every second. This mollified them and I instantly felt like a dick. All they ever deserved was a child to love, and instead, I'm making parenthood difficult for them. I wish I could stop everything and live the life I dreamed of when they first brought me to Whitsborough, but I can't.

I decide to put the file away to get ready, having finally given in to Adri's begging and planned a dinner date. She's been after me about it since I've been back from my fight in New York. I've put her off for three days and I can't do it any longer without her causing a scene. After taking a shower, I let my hair air dry into a mess of waves, then I apply a light layer of makeup. Grabbing a pair of black skinny jeans, I quickly slip them on and choose a white flowing blouse to complete the look. I'm actually excited to venture out of this house for a few hours because I've stuffed myself in my room for the past three days.

My parents are sitting in the kitchen and reading the newspaper when I make my way downstairs. "Hey, guys!" I chirp. Then I head to the coffee machine on the counter and pour myself a large cup, groaning when I inhale it.

"Hey, Ember," Ma says, her face still in the paper. "They're having a memorial for Robert tonight, candles and all. Do you want to come with us?"

"Yeah, sure," I say around a sip of coffee.

"You've been holed up in your room after the trip. Is everything okay?" Dad asks, his brow quirked as he looks at me.

"Yeah, I just miss Tommy. I have plans with his foster brother next weekend." A complete bullshit lie. I was never fond of Tommy's foster brother.

"Vincent is going for sure as well, right?" Ma interjects. She's trying not to sound worried but it's thick in her tone.

"Yes, I like having him with me." I take another few sips of coffee and abandon the rest before placing the mug into the sink. They both nod and return to their papers.

The lies are only growing and soon they'll be a mountain beneath me, but there's no way I'm bringing them into the bullshit I find myself in. I can handle it on my own without putting them in danger. "Be ready tonight at eight," Ma calls as I get ready to leave.

"Okay, love you!" I yell back as I open the front door.

"Love you too!" they say in unison, bringing a smile to my face.

I get into Shelby and drive to Adri's house with Rihanna's

"S&M" blaring out of the speakers. After pulling into her driveway, I give a quick two honks on the horn as I jam out. I have yet to meet Adri's parents. She says they aren't home much because they travel a lot and when they are home, it's all work. I feel bad for her because she has no siblings and they've left her to raise herself. My parents say that Adri's parents were always the hippies of the bunch and never easy to track down.

She comes out of her front door, wearing a pretty purple sundress, the color reminding me of Marlana's head. I close my eyes and focus on my breathing at the sudden rush of anger as my fingers curl around the steering wheel tightly, the music long forgotten. This technique is the only one that pulls me back from the brink of a full outrage.

The door opens and she sits in the passenger seat as I turn down the music and give her a smile, pushing away my mood. Adri has been tentative with me lately, and of course, I know why. So I always try my best to reassure her that I don't want to lose our friendship.

"Hey," I say to her.

"Hi. How are you?" she replies quietly as she fastens her seat belt.

"I'm all right." I shake my head with a chuckle. "I have to go to Robert's memorial tonight."

"Yeah, same. Travis asked me to go." She nods and turns to look out the window as I pull out of the driveway.

"How are you two?" She lets out a long sigh as I pull up to a red light, and then shakes her head.

"He's been home a lot with his mom. I try to get him to come out, but he worries about her." I can tell she's worried too and that in turn makes me apprehensive. Robert was a sleaze and I'm hoping his wife was unaware of it.

"What's wrong with her?" It's a loaded question, the answer I'll be using to consider whether or not Mrs. Greene needs to be paid a visit.

"She's depressed and doesn't want to leave the house. Although, for as long as I can remember, she never left it anyway." She shrugs.

"I see," I mutter as I begin to ponder breaking into Travis' house again to set up my own surveillance.

"Ember, about Shay—"

"No," I cut her off quickly. "I will have nothing to do with her again. You do you, but if you continue to push her on me, I won't have anything to do with you either."

"Okay," she concedes with another sigh. It's obvious Shay has been a step in during my absences, but I won't let the boundary I've already set be walked all over.

We head over to the local burger joint and I pull into the parking lot. A bunch of kids from school are loitering around the front, their obnoxious banter filtering in through the windows of my car. I haven't really faced anyone yet except for at Shay's party, but I mostly kept to Vin's side, because they wouldn't dare approach me while he was present. I bet they probably have questions about why I didn't finish the school year.

My parents told the school administration that I had a death in my family in New York—not too far from the truth—and that I needed the time to grieve after having two deaths so close together. I'm sure that story has been twisted into something much more elaborate to satisfy the teenage mind.

We approach the restaurant as a few of the guys standing

around the front elbow each other and the murmuring starts. "Hey, Ember!" one calls out. "Will you be back to school in September?"

"Yeah." I nod, waiting for the next shoe to drop.

"Cool." They nod their heads in return and then grin at each other. Their sneaky smirks aren't settling right with me, so I decide to throw in a bit more information.

"Yeah. House arrest for murdering the neighbor's cat is only like 3 weeks." I shake my head and wave my hand around like it's no big deal. "I told them I needed it for the midnight blood ritual, and it's better than using a newborn baby, ya know?" Both their eyebrows shoot up as Adri stifles a laugh behind her cough, but I continue to look around at all of my peers from school with my face full of innocence. "Next time, I plan on using someone with a big mouth. That way, they can tell the Devil all the shit I've been doing and I can get into Hell with no trouble." My smile is so large that I must look psychotic.

"My mom works in the office," a girl pipes up. "She told me Ember had a death in the family."

"Yeah, that was told so you guys wouldn't freak out when I came back. It was just a cat anyway, not like it was a human… yet." I snap my teeth at her, and she yelps with a jump backward.

Adri and I enter the restaurant laughing our asses off. That will be a new rumor in no time, and to be honest, I'm hoping they fear me and leave me alone for my senior year.

"That was fucking hilarious." Adri chortles.

The Hummer pulls into my driveway as my parents and I wait until Vin and Sharla step out. We all decided we would go to this memorial together. I almost laughed out loud when I thought about Robert rolling in his grave the second I stepped foot inside that building.

"Hi, guys," Sharla says, coming forward to hug each of us.

"Hey, Shar." Dad pats her back. "Are you riding with us? Let the young ones go together?"

"Yeah, that sounds good." She nods and then heads for my parents' Mercedes.

We all pile into our vehicles and head to the local community center in downtown Whitsborough. Robert is probably looking down his nose at this place right now. How dare we hold his memorial in a community center? I don't hold in my snort this time and Vin looks at me with a brow raised.

"Seeing Robert's condo makes me think he'd hate the thought of his memorial being here," I explain.

"That's the only reason I bothered to show." We chuckle together as he pulls into the center's parking lot.

My cell phone pings with a message and I pull it out of my pocket to read the text.

Womb Sharing Demon: We training again this weekend?

"Womb Sharing Demon?" Vin snickers, reading over my shoulder.

"Where's the lie?" I ask him with my brow raised. "You don't even want to know what your name used to be in here."

He laughs and shakes his head.

Me: Yeah. I'll see you Sunday AM before we leave.

The memorial was going well until Travis' mom had a fit in the middle of Travis' speech. She started screaming for Robert to come back and help her because she couldn't live without him. To me, she looked strung out. Her blonde hair was limp and greasy, and her skin flushed with a sheen of sweat. Seeing her made me pity Travis that much more. It looks as though he had two fucked-up parents. I make myself promise to hang out with Travis more because his life doesn't seem to be all rainbows like I once thought.

After all the fake displays of condolences—trust me, they did not love this man—from the community, we all headed home. I spent the rest of the night planning my next weekend in New York, making sure every detail was thought through.

Chapter Twelve

After taking another three fingers and carving 'Ephesians 5:25' into his chest, he finally passes out. Why carve that into his chest, you're wondering? A while ago, Mrs. G, our religion teacher, asked us to read this passage and write about the importance of marriage. I felt it was appropriate for this situation since this fuck was a crummy partner to my mother.

I have blood dripping from my hair down onto my face, and my hands look like I performed surgery without gloves, but I'm not nearly done yet. He hasn't paid for his transgressions, and I can't leave until I'm satisfied with what I've started.

I slap him hard across the face, twice, and smile when he comes to with a groan.

"Please, Ember, no more," he pants, his breathing sounding labored as his life closes in on its end. "Just kill me."

"You're giving up this quickly?" I taunt him with a laugh.

"Yes. I can't handle it anymore." If he thought pulling the sympathy card would work, he must believe his blood doesn't run through my veins.

"I'm sure you didn't think this way about my mother. Was she given a choice?" I snarl in his face.

Then I glide the knife around the edges of his face in a circle and he barely makes a whimper. It doesn't surprise me since his life is almost gone, so I have to make this quick. Have you ever skinned an animal? Probably not, neither have I… until now. His skin curls away from the knife as I slowly peel it back off his cheeks first, and his barely-there whimpers become low whines as I cut around his lips and eye sockets. Then, like ripping a bandage, I have a mask of skin in my hand and blood soaking into my sweater. I throw his skinned face onto the desk and lean back to look him over.

He's so near death, his chest rattling with fluid every time he takes a quick breath. The blood that once ran profusely barely dribbles now and I'm coming down from the adrenaline that brought me here in the first place. I want to go home and be with my family and Vin.

I pick up the gun I left on the desk before pointing it between his eyes, and he looks up at me as he smiles faintly.

"You've made me proud, sweetheart."

I pull the trigger as his head snaps back, blood and brain matter splattering the wall behind him. It's done.

Four bullets…

CHAPTER THIRTEEN

A few days and a long drive later, Vin and I are back in the Upper East Side condo preparing for tomorrow. I'm excited and the need to release the darkness gathering inside of me is strong. The nightmares are becoming more frequent, and each morning I wake up a little more agitated. Vin has been subdued and reserved, making me worry about if I'm forcing him into doing this against his wishes. I've told him, more than once, that he doesn't have to be a part of this, but he won't hear any of it. Even if I want to talk him out of it, I need him.

After printing off a copy of the lasagna recipe I plan to use, I take a shower and get ready for bed. Vin is lying on the bed in his boxers, scrolling through his phone as his jaw tics with tension. My mouth goes dry just looking at him. His skin is glistening from the body lotion he applies after his shower and his hair has the damp curled look I love so much. He's so fucking gorgeous. He catches me looking at him and sends me his signature smirk, his luscious lips making my pussy clench in anticipation. I drop my towel and walk toward him as his eyebrows lift and he sets his phone aside. My heart beats a rhythm only for Vin. He owns it and he owns me. Body and dark soul.

I stand at the edge of the bed and squeal as he quickly jumps toward me, grabbing me by the waist. The next instant, my back bounces off the plush mattress and I moan as Vin's tongue licks across my pebbled nipple. He heads down over my stomach and bites into my hip, the sharp sting of pain making me gasp as I grow wetter.

"Is my pussy loving when her daddy bites?"

Jesus, that mouth.

Vin opens my legs and uses his thumbs to spread open my pussy. Then he does one full swipe with his tongue, from my ass to my clit, his tongue ring digging in deliciously. His breath blows across my exposed clit as I writhe against the bed, pulling a chuckle from his chest. He pushes in one finger, and I whimper because it's not near enough. My hips rise toward his face, my body asking for something my mind hasn't even processed yet, but I'm not complaining. His chest vibrates with a suppressed laugh as he covers his mouth over my clit and sucks, his finger still pumping in and out of me. He doesn't let up and soon enough, my orgasm creeps over me like a rolling tide, flooding my entire body.

Then he gets up onto his knees and drops his boxers, his cock standing straight as the piercing at the tip glints in the light. My stomach tightens at the sight as my arousal hits me all over again. He comes down on top of me, his arms caging me in on either side of my head, his eyes boring into mine. Vin is always searching my soul, making sure I'm still his, and even though it's difficult for me to form the right words, my body speaks well enough. His mouth hits mine and I sigh into him as our tongues battle for dominance. His cock nudges my entrance and I moan as I lift my hips to meet his. It takes one painful thrust before he's seated deep inside me.

"You're so fucking tight, Ember. Squeeze my cock, baby."

My pussy automatically clamps down with his instruction and I lock my legs around his waist, urging him to move. He groans deep in his throat and slides in and out, but I need more, so I dig my heels into his lower back and pick up the pace. Then he chuckles into my ear and slams into me in response. *Finally.* This is how I like it. The sound of my pussy reverberates around the room as his balls slap off my slick skin, then he slides his hands under my ass and tilts my hips just right. When he pumps into me again, his piercing drags along my G-spot, guaranteeing a messy bed when we're done. Not that I mind.

As per usual, he doesn't disappoint. My body erupts with intense pleasure as the evidence of it slides down my ass crack and onto the bed. He pumps right on through it though, the loud, wet sucking noises the only thing echoing off these bedroom walls. Not too long after, Vin groans through his release, filling me with his hot cum as my body still rides the high of my own orgasm.

"Let's clean up and change these sheets or else it'll soak through." He snickers, always so smug when he makes me come like that.

I wake up early the next morning, even though it's a Saturday, and start making the lasagna. I need it to look and smell amazing so it'll entice the asshole to his death. Carm has come through with my request for sleeping pills, so this will help me out with step one of the plan to make the piece of shit sleepy as fuck before he takes his evening dip. I crush those up and mix it into the cheese that I will top on it as it comes out of the oven.

As the lasagna bakes, I head into the bedroom to start dressing in my usual black attire. Vin is lying on the bed watching me, his arms tucked beneath his head and a small smile playing around his mouth. "So, first I go drop this lasagna off to him and say it's a new friendly neighbor thing?" He raises a brow. "Isn't that backwards? He should bring me a case of fucking beer or something. What if he doesn't want it?"

"It'll work, and if it doesn't, shove a piece down his throat." I wave him off as I grab my clothes from my duffel bag.

"What?" He sits up quickly, looking at me with both eyebrows raised this time.

"I'm kidding. I'll always have a backup plan." I really do have one, it's 'think of a backup plan on the fly,' but I won't admit that to him right now.

He drops back down onto his back in relief and continues watching as I dress in black leggings and a black hoodie, hiding my knife inside the large front pocket.

"Can I see that knife?" he asks, holding out his hand. I toss it onto the bed and he picks it up, pulling it out of the sheath. Then he whistles as he holds it up, the sharpened edge shining under the light. "This is sharp."

"Sure is. I've cut off fingers with that," I say nonchalantly as I step into my running shoes.

"What?" He immediately drops the knife to the bed, giving me a confused look.

I don't answer and give him a shrug as I pull the face makeup out of my bag, then head into the bathroom. As I am applying the full white all over, Vin steps in, his eyes growing wide and his mouth turning down.

"I can't have anyone seeing my face," I explain as I color in the skull parts with black eye shadow.

"It's like the skulls on your knife," he remarks as he keeps his eyes on me, the shock slowly bleeding away.

"Yeah, it's called a Sugar Skull, originating in Mexico for Día de los Muertos. I researched it as soon as I had the chance." I look at him through the mirror. "This knife and I have a connection and I wanted to learn everything I could about it."

I continue applying the makeup and he stays close, remaining quiet and perched on the closed toilet seat. The timer on the stove goes off and it signals the start of our plan. We both head out to the kitchen and pull the dish out of the oven. I coat the top with freshly shredded cheddar mixed with the sleeping pills and watch as the powder disappears as it melts into the cheese. Then I set it on the counter to cool for a bit and pace the living room. My energy is flying high as adrenaline courses through me.

"The master bedroom window opens outward, and I've pulled out the screen. It's a bit of a stretch, but you should be able to reach his balcony. Slowly skim the ledge and then you just pull yourself over," Vin says, standing next to me. "What happens when you get over there?"

"This building has no cameras on the balconies, according to the original plans, but there are cameras in the hallways. The cops will see you dropping off that lasagna to him. So we have to be prepared for questioning." I avoid answering his question as I turn to pace another line.

"How are you doing it, Em?" He grabs my arm to stop the pacing.

"Trust me, I have a plan." I don't, but I don't want him worried any further. I work better on the fly and if he figures out I don't actually have a plan, he'll call this entire thing off. Being deceitful to Vin is the last thing I'd ever want to do, but I would if he tried to force me to stop.

He nods and stalks forward to grab the lasagna off the

counter before heading directly out the door. I rush after him and stick my foot in the doorway so it doesn't close and I can eavesdrop on the conversation. Vin's quick knock on the door reaches my ears and I wait, holding my breath.

"Hey, man. I just moved in and thought I'd bring over a neighborly dish of pasta," Vin says, his forced pleasantness nearly making me snort.

"Robert Greene sold his condo?" the man asks, his voice a deep baritone, sounding cold and calculating.

"No, man. I'm his son. Robert passed away… cancer." Vin bleeds some sadness into his voice, and I thank my stars he's a fucking actor.

"No way! Shit, I'm so sorry to hear that. Look, Robert and I were friends. We've helped each other out." *I'm sure you did, dick face.* "If you need anything, I'm just down the hall. And thanks for this, man, you didn't have to."

"I love to cook, so yeah, I hope you like lasagna." Vin sniffs. I can only imagine his eyes are filled with fake tears too. "And thanks for the offer. I don't know anyone here yet."

"Lasagna? No way! That's my favorite." The crinkle of tin foil travels down the corridor. "Wow, this looks great. I'll pop over tomorrow with something for you as well."

"Alright, thanks again. Have a great night."

"I will now." The click of a door tells me part one is done as Vin's footsteps head back toward our condo, and I pull open the door and step back as he enters.

"It's a good thing my father befriended every corrupt individual in New York. Makes this shit easier," he mumbles as he heads off into our bedroom.

"True that." I follow behind him as I nod.

The plan is to wait about twenty minutes, then I'll make my way onto his balcony. We both sit by the open window and listen for when this guy starts his ritual Saturday soak.

"Fuck, your face is creepy. I don't even recognize you," Vin mutters, his eyes roaming over my face.

"That's the point." I smile widely as he cringes.

"Have you used this face before?" He reaches out and runs his finger along my red-painted lips.

"One other time," I admit quietly, hoping he doesn't ask any questions because I won't be able to lie to him.

"I see." He thankfully leaves it at that and turns to look out the window.

The balcony door slides open from our piece of shit neighbor's apartment and we listen as he fires up his hot tub. He's muttering about how fucking good the lasagna is and how he's going to buy Vin a fucking carton full of wine. Then the sounds of old-school R&B hits our ears.

"Ugh, I'm so creeped out by this weirdo." I shudder. "Pony" by Ginuwine filters through to our window and I gag dramatically as Vin chuckles. The distinct splashing of this guy lowering himself down into the hot tub sounds as he finishes with a sigh. He must literally be right beside us.

"I'm so goddamned tired, fuck," the guy mumbles. "Must be those two pieces of lasagna."

Shit, he ate two pieces. That's like four pills equivalent, or a fucking quarter of that dish. He really does like lasagna.

"I should get over there now before he passes out." Vin gives me a nod as I stand in front of the window, taking a deep breath.

Then I pull my body out onto the ledge and look down. It's a good thing I'm not afraid of heights because we are thirty floors high. People are still walking along the sidewalks looking like little ant colonies from up here. I look straight ahead toward the Empire State Building in all its fucking glory as dark clouds move across the skyline, covering the iridescent moon.

Looking to my right, I find Ron's balcony just within reach, but I will have to shuffle over about two steps to get a good grip on it. The balcony is all glass, so I see the hot tub against the edge and him lying in it with his back to me. He still hasn't fallen asleep because now he's singing along to some Ashanti and Ja Rule song, albeit a little sluggish.

Vin is halfway out the window when I shuffle the few steps. I look over at him, blowing him a kiss as his mouth stretches into a wide grin. I'm going to sit on that mouth when I'm done.

I drop my sleeves down over my hands because I can't leave prints anywhere, and even though this gives me less grip, it's a necessary risk. I grab onto the balcony railing and step up onto the ledge. He still can't see me because his back is to my front, but at this angle, everything is visible on the balcony. His hot tub is a four-seater, quaint and cozy, and he has a table on either side made from some fancy-looking stained glass. His balcony floor is covered with that fake grass shit to mimic being in a backyard and he has an old-school CD player on the edge of the tub plugged into an extension cord coming from inside his condo. This is where the outdated tunes are coming from.

Ron lays his head back, his eyes closed and his face looking peaceful. If he opens them, he will have a clear view of me and all my glory standing over him. I reach into my hoodie pocket and finger the knife, hoping I won't have to use it. This can't look like a crime scene.

He keeps his eyes closed and his head sways softly as he murmurs the words to the crappy-ass song he's listening to now. I roll my eyes and slowly shuffle along the edge until I come to a spot that's clear for me to pull myself over. He doesn't even flinch as my feet hit the balcony *grass*. I take in the scene before me and quickly think over my options. Affirmative on the no cameras, the cozy hot tub, and a patio set with a barbeque, and that's it. But an idea forms as I stare at him relaxing in the tub.

"Huh?" He's looking at me as he tries to sit up, the water splashing around his body. His eyes droop heavily as his mouth hangs open. "Who are you? Am I dreaming?"

Without answering, I walk closer to the edge of the tub as drool rolls down his chin. Number one rule: Never get into a hot tub after taking sleeping pills. "Killing me softly" by The Fugees begins to play and I snort at the coincidence.

His head falls back against the edge again as faint snores fill the air. With my hands still covered by the sweater, I lay one on top of the CD player and give it a good shove. It hits the water as sparks fly, the electrical current making his relaxing soak deadly. Ron's body begins convulsing and his eyes snap open, his jaw tensing. The veins on his neck and forehead stand protruding as his skin becomes deathly pale. The whites of his eyes slowly bleed red as blood vessels burst open and his lips pull back across his clenched teeth. As quick as it started, it's done, and he lies floating on his back with his bloody gaze to the sky. The electric arcs still dance along the water's edge, so I am mindful of not touching any part of the hot tub as I pull myself back over the railing and shuffle along the balcony's ledge once more.

As soon as I am back in front of our window, Vin reaches out and grabs me around the waist. Then he pulls me inside as his mouth lands on mine in a punishing kiss. When he finally pulls away, his face is lined with my white and black makeup, giving him a creepy mask.

"Everything go okay?" he asks, his eyes scanning over me quickly.

"Swimmingly." I grin.

Thankfully, with the darkness sated once more, I fall asleep with no haunting images of deadbeat fathers and chopped-off fingers.

Vin

The next morning, we're awoken by a pounding on the front door. I groan and unwrap a sleeping Ember from my body and throw on some sweats. When I get to the door and open it wide, I come face-to-face with two police officers, the sight of them sending my stomach flipping with nerves.

"Sorry to wake you, sir," the one on the right says. "We were wondering if you heard anything on this floor last night?"

"Heard anything?" I repeat with a yawn, my acting skills on point.

"Yes, there was an accident in the condo next door," the left one answers.

"Accident?" I widen my eyes as I look between them, filling my voice with concern. "Like what kind of accident? Is that guy okay?"

"You knew him?" Right narrows his eyes.

"He was my neighbor. I introduced myself last night." I run my hand down my face. "Are we not safe here? What happened?"

"He had an accident in the hot tub last night. Your neighbor is deceased," Left replies as they both scrutinize me for a reaction.

"What kind of accident?" I rear my head back. "I thought this building was safe," I mutter, playing my part.

"Sir, it looks to be just an accident on the victim's part, not anything to do with the building." Right's eyes remain narrow as he explains the situation, but Left is looking a little sympathetic.

"Okay. Is there something I can do?" I ask, sounding every bit the neighborly neighbor.

"No, sir. You've answered all the questions we have." Left nods and takes a step back, Right following suit. "Please try to enjoy the rest of your day."

I keep the grim expression on my face as I step back, watching as they head back down to Ron's apartment. Then I lean against the door after I shut it and let out a breath. When I look up, Em is standing in front of me, wrapped up in a sheet from our bed.

"Clear?" she whispers, her face puffy and her voice sounding hoarse with sleep.

"Yeah, baby."

Her phone pings with a message from the kitchen counter and she walks over to open it up. A grin forms on her face and she looks back at me. "Carm says it's all over the news. Tragic accident. DA dies in a hot tub." She shakes her head slowly with surprise. "And he says for me to come by to pick up my payment." I stand beside her and read the text, not liking the apprehension skating along my spine. This guy better not be using my girl. "Is it weird that I didn't discuss payment?"

"Yeah, baby." I *tsk.* "It's a little weird."

She smirks and skips—yes, she fucking skips—back to the bedroom.

We pull up to the compound, but before we can enter, we're both being patted down by two goons. I have nothing on me, but they find the knife in Ember's hoodie pocket. When one of them tries to remove it, she shoves her palm into his nose, the crack making me wince, then she grabs the guy's hand that was in her pocket and snaps that back too.

I'm worried about my sanity because I'm so fucking hard that the zipper of my jeans is cutting into my dick. She looks at the guy writhing on the ground and then flicks her eyes to the other dude with his hand held to his nose as tears run down his cheeks.

"Problem?" she asks him, her voice even despite quickly taking two guys down.

"No, Miss Torres. He shouldn't have done that." He's smart enough to step out of her reach, respect shining in his eyes.

She nods and then leads us both inside. She no longer corrects anyone when they refer to her as a Torres, as if she's accepted what and who she is. It makes no fucking difference to me. If she calls herself Big Bird suddenly, she would still be mine. I like how tough Ember is and I like that I don't have to watch her back. My girl can fight and she's been doing it for so long that she no longer has to plan her moves. It's like breathing for her. Most guys would feel useless, emasculated even, but I know what I'm capable of and until she needs my help, I'm willing to watch her sexy-ass take control of most situations.

We enter the elevator and Em pounces on me as I chuckle against her mouth, pulling on her hair to expose her throat. Then I lick my way up to her ear and flick it with my tongue ring. Her moan is so loud that it vibrates off the elevator walls. I grab her thigh and pull it up to hook around my waist and grind my hard dick into her heated center.

"This is just gross," a voice full of disdain interrupts us. "That's my fucking twin."

"Turn away," I growl back as I continue to ravish my girl. "I'm about to fuck your *fucking twin*." Ember moans and grinds against me harder. My mouth always gets her worked up.

"Guys! Come on," Emmett groans, but makes no move to walk away.

Ember pulls back with a snicker and rubs her hand over the bulge in my jeans. Then she turns around, grabbing my hand and leading me out. Emmett looks at me with a glare and I toss him a wink. There's nothing anyone could ever do to pull me off of her. If I really wanted to, I'd fuck her here on the floor just to prove my fucking point.

I stay behind and lean against the wall as Ember goes into Carm's office, folding my arms over my chest.

"Hey, do you like motorcycles?" Emmett asks me, his eyes flashing with excitement. It's so weird how identical he is to Ember. I don't think I'll ever get used to it. Both of them are manic in their mood swings and I begin to fear having the two of them in the same room.

"Yeah." I lift my eyebrow in question.

"Come see what I got myself for my birthday, bro." He grins, his excitement bleeding over to me.

I shrug and follow him to a set of steel doors. He leads me inside and toward a candy-red Ducati. I chuckle because it's the same color as Em's car. Maybe they have that twintuition shit.

"Ducati." I whistle as I walk around the bike, taking in all the angles.

"A Ducati Panigale V4," he breathes out, caressing the seat.

"Engine?"

"A 1,103-cc desmodromic 90-degree V4," he replies while nodding, then leans against the bike.

"I don't know what any of that means," Ember says, sidling up beside me. Surprise along with irritation flows through me because I didn't even hear her come in. Again. It should be disconcerting but I think I'm slowly getting used to it. "But that sure is a pretty color."

I chuckle and pull her into my side to kiss her head. "It's the same color as your car," I tell her with a grin.

"Yeah, it is!" she exclaims with a laugh.

"Really?" Emmett's eyes light up.

"Yeah. You should come see it." She nods enthusiastically. Watching these two siblings bond is reminding me of the one I lack with my own brother.

"Yeah, I should. What kind of car?" He straightens from his bike.

"Shelby!"

"It's a 1967 Mustang convertible. GT500KR," I answer for her with a snort.

"Shit, seriously? How the fuck did you get your hands on that?" Emmett's hushed tone relays just how rare that car is.

"Our uncle is so fucking cool." She nods, and I nod as well because Scott is fucking golden.

"I'd like to come see it," he whispers and bites his bottom lip.

"Come next weekend. You and Carm," she says excitedly. "You can meet Adri and Travis too."

"That's not a bad idea. We could rent a hotel suite for the weekend and maybe I can find out who the new Head is for Toronto," Carm suggests, looking at me, then to Ember. "You sure you don't know who it is, Ember?"

"I'm sure." She nods.

"Okay." Emmett grins. "Let's go to Whitsborough next weekend."

175

Chapter Fourteen

I am one-hundred-thousand dollars richer. That's the going rate for an accidental-looking assassination. I tried to give Vin half, but he screwed his face up at me like I was losing my mind, so fuck him. And I did, on top of a pile of one-hundred-dollar bills.

I wanted to tell my parents about Emmett and Carm so they can meet, but then Carm reminded me about my open investigation and the murder of my father. All things Ma and Dad are in the dark about. They would have so many questions that I just couldn't answer for them, and what if they tried to take Emmett from Carm? So I have to keep them a secret, but not from Adri or Travis. I just have to swear them to secrecy. It'll be a relief to off-load everything to them and to have some—not all—secrets out in the open.

Vin is hosting a barbeque at his house while his mother is at mine for their weekly gossip fest, so it's just the four of us. We can talk about Emmett and Carm arriving tomorrow morning with no listening ears.

"I can't believe you have a twin brother," Adri mutters, her brows crinkled in confusion.

"Yes." I nod. "And an older half brother."

"How?" Travis asks.

"I've been remembering what happened in New York. My birth father and my half brother captured me the night of the play, brought me back to New York, and held me in a compound." It's the most condensed version of what truly happened, but neither of them needs the details.

"Held where?" Travis sits forward in his chair, his face filled with curiosity and his interrogation game on point as usual.

"With the Eastside Rampage. It's a gang that I was affiliated with before moving here, and the night they captured me, I learned their leader was my father." I sit up straighter in my chair, preparing for the onslaught of questions burning in both of their eyes.

"Are you sure that's really true?" Adri interjects, shaking her head in disbelief.

"Yeah, it's true. Not only do I resemble my father, but my identical twin brother is proof enough." I try not to let the irritation of bringing my father up simmer inside of me.

"How was a twin kept a secret this entire time? Your mother obviously knew she had two of you, right?" Travis questions, getting right to the heart of it.

"I don't have answers for that. I'm still figuring it out. My mother kept that from me." My heart thuds inside my chest at the mention of her and her apparent betrayal.

"This has to stay between us because it's more complicated than it seems. We can't blow this open right now," Vin stresses to them. "We are trusting you with this because Ember views you as family."

"Some of us here are actual family," Travis mutters as he slumps back in his chair.

I move to where he's sitting on one of the patio chairs and kneel in front of him, placing my hands on his knees. "Travis, you're right. You and Vin are brothers by blood." Sympathy rolls through me as I stare into his pain-filled eyes. "But you are also my brother through love, and Adri is my sister through love. I love you guys so much and I just want you to meet my family," I explain to him gently.

He leans forward and wraps me in a hug, the tension bleeding out of him as I rub his back. I can only imagine how frustrating it can be to have a brother who wants little to do with you. Especially now, just after he loses a father and has an absentee mother, but with time, I am confident Vin will be the brother Travis deserves. He has already come so far.

I move back to my seat beside Vin and try to ease the anxiety inside of me. This is draining, trying to explain situations without actually explaining shit. I can only tell them half-truths in the best of scenarios. "Any more questions?" I ask them as I hold my hands open.

"I have so many," Adri replies, her eyes shining with mischief.

"Okay, I will answer what I can." I clasp my hands back in my lap.

"So, where is your father now?"

"Dead."

"How?" she asks, her eyes widening as the mischief disappears.

"Murdered. That's all I can say."

"Okay... and Tommy? Was he murdered too?"

"Yes." I nod.

"By the same person?" Travis cuts in.

"Might as well have been. That's all I can say about that."

"Are you safe, Ember?" Adri's face is filled with worry as her eyes run over my face.

"As safe as I'll ever be."

"What are their names?" she continues.

"Carmelo is my older brother, and Emmett is my twin."

"Whose blood were you covered in when they found you?" It's Travis' turn.

"I can't answer that yet," I mutter.

"What do you do while you're in New York?" Travis is asking all the right questions at the wrong fucking time.

"Getting to know my family."

"It's a good thing my father left that condo to Vin then." He raises a brow and I swear it's a challenge, but I don't take the bait.

"Yes, it's helpful. Even if he didn't, we would stay in a hotel." He's fishing. I can sense Travis doesn't accept his father's death as a suicide. It's the first time I've felt any sort of apprehension about killing Robert Greene.

"True," he answers, looking me in the eyes.

If he's searching for the truth in my eyes, he won't find shit. I'm an actress, and if I want to disguise anything, I can. Do I regret it? No. Their father was the scum of the Earth, and I did them both a favor.

"Hey, quick question," Vin says while flipping the burgers. "Do any of you know what the fuck happened to our sauna sign?"

Adri chokes on her beer, and while she's hacking out a lung, my head tips to the side as I stare at the sign, acting obtuse.

"Are you talking about the one that says *Use anals at your own risk*'?" I quirk an eyebrow at him. "Because that's sound advice."

"My mother found that last weekend and nearly ripped my head off when I got back." He chuckles and flips a burger. "But it's genius, whoever did it."

Adri is full-out cackling now, and Travis is chuckling along with her.

"I still have a few questions." Travis breaks the moment.

"Alright, shoot," I groan.

We spend the rest of the night having a few beers and hanging out with a couple of fucking investigators.

We're waiting in the parking lot of the same diner I met Carm and Emmett in before, all four of us leaning against Vin's Hummer and enjoying the afternoon heat. The summers here in Ontario are hot, which is a relief because I wouldn't be able to live somewhere that was cold all year round.

The faint rumble of a motorcycle sounds in the distance, and Vin glances at me with a grin. "Carm wouldn't let him drive here on that thing, would he?" Vin asks with a chuckle.

"I doubt Carm has much say in most of Emmett's decisions," I reply.

Sure enough, the candy-red bike roars into the parking lot as my helmeted twin brother pulls up beside us. He revs his engine a few times more and I roll my eyes. *Fucking child.* Then he flips up his visor and throws me a grin as Adri gasps from behind me.

We both turn our faces toward her as she breathes out, "Wow, you really are identical."

"I think I'm slightly better looking." Emmett shrugs while pulling his helmet off his dark brown, disheveled hair.

"And my dick is slightly bigger," I retort, then hit him on the shoulder.

"Then you got a monster between your legs, sister," he throws back with a wink.

"Oh, dear God, it's double the Ember," Adri remarks, shock still lining her voice.

"Where is Carm?" I ask the womb-sharing demon.

"Should be here soon. He drives like an old man," Emmett says with a snicker.

"Emmett, this is Adrianna Hinton and Travis Greene. Guys, this is Emmett, Ember's twin brother," Vin introduces them.

Emmett sizes up Adri and then Travis as well, his eyes flicking between the two. He finally holds out his hand to Travis to shake and then to Adri. "It's amazing to meet you," he tells them politely.

Travis has said little, and he's looking at Emmett like he's trying to figure him out. It's a little unnerving with Travis because I can never predict what his mind is piecing together.

A few minutes later, a blacked-out sedan pulls into the parking lot and then beside Emmett. The driver's side window slides down and Carm's stern face appears. "Hey, little dick, I told you to stick close. What was that shit you were pulling on the highway?"

"See? I do have a bigger dick. Even Carm says so." I snicker and slap Emmett's arm.

"You drive like a geriatric." Emmett rolls his eyes, then turns to me. "Don't make me whip it out."

"Okay, okay. Let's go eat before I lose my appetite," Vin groans with a huff as he walks off toward the restaurant.

Emmett and I laugh as we all make our way inside while Adri continues to keep her eyes on us like we're a sideshow, and I understand why. We are eerily similar. Our hair is the same shade, as is our eyes and the beauty mark below the right one. Not to mention the curve of our lips… identical. We're a carbon copy of each other. His skin seems to be slightly lighter than my darker tan and he stands much taller at around the 6'2" mark. He is broad-shouldered, and at seventeen, he's nearly the same size as Carm.

We all sit in an oversized booth made to resemble the old-style bed of a pickup truck with protruding wheel fenders on the back of each side of the booth. They even have the old-style whitewall tires in them. This diner is so cool and has fast become my favorite place to eat. I order the steak on a bun with a vanilla and chocolate swirl milkshake, then grin when my twin orders the same. He catches my reaction and shrugs his shoulders.

During dinner, as everyone is talking, I monitor all the interactions. I thought at first Emmett might have been checking out Adri, but when he did the same with Travis, I chalked it up to him being curious about who's around me and not him being romantically interested. Which is fine by me because I don't need this situation to become any more complicated than it already is.

A plate of funnel cakes lands in front of me by our server, and I gaze around the booth with confusion. I didn't order dessert. Emmett catches my eye with a wink, his mouth curving into a mischievous smile.

"Twintuition," he says with a shrug as I shovel a forkful into my mouth.

"Cool," I mumble around the doughy goodness.

"Emmett," Travis begins. "How did you feel when you found out you had a twin sister?"

"Like I was drowning. I couldn't get any air into my lungs, and I thought I might pass out," he says nonchalantly. "But then I met her and the empty void I've always lived with was finally filled."

Everyone around the table is smiling, or in Adri's case, almost crying, but I'm fucking shocked. I'm a terrible person because the first time I met him I felt nothing. Now though, he's right. The part of me that has always craved family and something constant is now filled, thanks to him and Carm.

"Ditto," I say around a mouthful of funnel cake.

After eating, the guys are all gathered around Emmett's bike, talking about God knows what, while Adri and I are sitting in the Hummer nursing full bellies.

"Girl, your brothers are so fucking fine," she groans, watching them out of the window.

"Ew, shut up." I slap a hand to her arm.

"Seriously! Carm is hot in that older, hot, bad guy kind of way, but Emmett? Holy shit, he is probably the sexiest thing I have ever seen, like right up there with Travis." Her eyes are drilling holes in the back of my twin brother's head and it's taking everything in me not to throw up in her face.

"I just ate, Adri. Don't make me regurgitate," I snap as irritation floods me. My reaction is a little puzzling because it's not about jealousy, it's my protectiveness rising.

"Is he single?"

"Are you crazy?" I swing my gaze from Emmett to her. "That's just looking for trouble. Don't pin Travis on my brother." That's the real problem. I don't want Emmett to find himself in the center of a years-long feud, being used as a ploy to make Travis jealous because that's who she's truly in love with.

"Ugh, fine." She crosses her arms across her chest, the petulant expression on her face making me gnash my teeth together.

A tapping on my window pulls me from my murderous thoughts, and I turn to find Carm's eyes, the dark brown orbs dancing with amusement. I lower the window and he sticks his head inside with a grin that echoes my own. "Hey. Can you swing by the hotel later? I got something for you."

"Yeah, sure." I shrug, releasing the breath trapped inside my chest. Anger will always be my constant companion. I just need to be able to deal with it better.

"Okay, cool." He nods, then flicks his gaze to Adri, that glimmer of amusement growing. "It was nice meeting you, Adrianna."

"You too," she whispers hoarsely, a blush stealing up and over her cheeks. I roll my eyes as Carm pulls his head out with a chuckle.

"Em! I'll see you later?" Emmett calls out to me, his words

more a question than a statement and his face slightly tight with panic. It's almost like he fears I'll disappear.

"Yeah, Em!" I holler back. He throws his head back and laughs like I said the funniest shit in the world and the fucker has me chuckling along with him.

"Jesus H Christ. Can you explain to my vagina that he's off-limits?" The laugh falls from my lips as I slowly turn back to her, my eyes narrowing and my chest heating with anger once more.

"I am going to cunt kick you," I threaten her, meaning every fucking word. If it doesn't work, she can't use it on my brother. Her mouth pops open with the threat as her eyebrows skate up her forehead.

"Bye, Adrianna! It was real nice meeting you," the fucking Womb Demon coos, as if he just knows how much this is irritating me.

Adri waves and then covers her ripe tomato face with her hands. Both Emmett and Carm are chuckling, Vin has a shit-eating grin on his face, and Travis stands with his arms crossed over his chest, his body stiff like he's about to kill someone.

Perfect.

"Baby, flash me a titty before we have to go talk business," Vin rasps, making my pussy clench at the deep tenor.

I turn around to face him, then pull my breast from my tank top and squeeze it. He growls and reaches for me just as the elevator pings our arrival. "Uh-uh," I *tsk*, turning around to put my tit back in my shirt.

His heat creeps along my back as he closes in on me, his hand traveling up from my waist to settle around my throat. "You're in trouble later," he whispers against my ear, giving it a bite before walking us out of the elevator and down the corridor.

"I certainly hope so."

We arrive at Carm and Emmett's room, and Vin knocks loudly. His impatience to get this done and fast ringing loud and clear. I lean up on my toes and lick up his cheek.

"Gross, is this how I will always be greeted by you guys?" Emmett whines from inside the room.

"Yep!" I reply, popping the P.

Pushing my way by him, I scrutinize the luxurious suite they're staying in. Floor-to-ceiling windows provide a view of the plain skyline of Whitsborough, and lush couches and rich red carpets decorate the space as oak paneling covers the walls. I find Carm sitting on the couch smoking a joint.

"Can you smoke in here?" Surprise coats my words as I wave my hand in front of my face.

"For the amount I paid, I dare them to tell me otherwise." He cocks a brow, then offers me the joint. I pass, but Vin takes it and sits opposite Carm. His sexy lips wrap around the joint as he inhales, then exhales in a slow breath. Fuck, he's so fucking hot.

"Earth to sister." Emmett snaps his fingers in front of my face.

"What did you fuckers want?" I growl. "I need to go home and do something." Irritation comes on fast and hard these days with little warning, especially when my time fucking Vin is being wasted on bullshit.

Vin chuckles and Carm flicks his eyes between the two of us. Then he leans back against the sofa, his legs spreading. "What are you guys, fucking rabbits?"

"No, I'm the motherfucking hunter and right now he is looking like a fat fucking rabbit," I snarl. Vin laughs again and passes the joint to Emmett.

"All right, shit. I have another job for you, if you want it," he begins hesitantly. When I nod for him to continue, he visibly relaxes. "Another Head heard the work you did and was interested."

"Who… and why?" My arms cross over my chest as the dollar signs begin blooming in my mind, thoughts of humping Vin pushed to the back burner temporarily. I can make a real profession out of my joy of killing.

"This guy works at a juvenile detention center, and he likes the young boys that come through," Carm says through his teeth, my body stiffening with shock as I absorb his words.

"You don't mean—" Vin starts, but Carm cuts him off.

"Yeah… he rapes them, frequently." He throws a folder down on the table in front of me and I stare at the orange color, my heart pounding inside my chest. "Doesn't have to seem like an accident either. Actually, according to the Head, make it as messy as you want."

My arms drop as I take an unsteady step forward to grab the folder off the table. It's light but the information inside will be another heavy burden on my shoulders until I end his life. Flipping over the flap, I scan the page inside.

"Henry Thompson," I read out loud, the name sounding so

average. "Age forty-eight, has a wife and two boys at home." Sounds like the perfect family, but that's just it. Beautiful exteriors hide the most rotten cores.

"He messes with his kids too?" Vin growls, his declaration speaking out loud about what I'm thinking.

"Yeah. His boy goes to school with the Head's daughter, told her some shit and she told her dad," Carm confirms, his tone solemn. "He's willing to pay two-hundred-thousand."

"Okay, I will let you know." I release a sigh, because as much as I want to help the children who can't help themselves, getting into assassination contracts is dangerous, despite the money being amazing.

"If it's next weekend, I won't be able to hang with you on Sunday because we have the Head's meeting, but Saturday works," Carm explains as he leans back against the couch once more. The scruff on his chin has grown out a bit and his eyes are cushioned by large bags. Clearly, my brother isn't sleeping. Taking on the evil empire our father was building is taking its toll on him.

"Ember can come and chill with me this weekend," Emmett pipes up, his excitement a drastic contrast to Carm's exhaustion. "Drive your car down and we can hang out, maybe do Coney Island."

"I'll let you know." I smile at him. The thought of having a bit of one-on-one time with him is appealing and a little nerve-wracking. How would I even act with my twin brother? What would we talk about besides blood and knives?

"I can help you with the guy too. You decide." His grin is malicious, and the sight pulls on one of my own, knowing we probably are the most identical in this moment. Emmett would be a great help. He whips knives around like no joke and has a killer aim with the gun too. Before I agree to anything though, I need to talk to Vin, and I'm sure they both understand that.

"We also have another issue," Carm states, sitting forward again, his shoulders tightening. This must mean business. "Ms. Talia has sent a message to me. She wants to meet up the weekend after the Head meeting."

"Sweet," I breathe out with excitement. "I can take her out then." My mind begins spinning with ideas of how I would torture the woman my father was supposedly in a relationship with. I could give them his and hers matching face masks.

"It's not that easy, sis." Carm holds his hand up, halting the fun time I'm having inside my head. "She's government. She'll have guards with her."

"What's the plan then?" The folder in my hand crinkles as I tighten my grip.

"I meet with her and find out what she wants, take note of her surroundings, and then I'll stick a tail on her." He pins me to the spot with his eyes, an alpha sizing up his opponent. Carm is my blood, but I'd be lying if I said I didn't sense the competition growing between us. In a few years, I'll be more capable of running a diabolical organization than he is. Not that I'd want to. "We have to be prepared that she's informed of exactly who you are and where you live, because like I said, the bitch is Government."

"Can I take this?" I lift the file, letting the argument of Jennifer Talia go right now. Carm can have his space to take the bitch down... until he fucks up.

"Yeah, let me know during the week, alright?" The dismissal is heavy in his tone and I'm fucking fine with that. There's nothing more that needs to be said anyway.

"Yeah, cool." With a quick glance at Vin, I jut my chin toward the door. My need for him comes rushing back and I want to go home to fuck his brains out.

CHAPTER FIFTEEN

It's Thursday night and Ember is driving to New York tomorrow to spend the weekend with Emmett and take out some pedophile piece of shit. Having her here in my bed is only prolonging the anxiety I'll have until she's back, but there's no way we'll be apart until she leaves. I hate that she's going without me, but I can't suffocate her, and I have to trust that her mob family will protect her if she needs it.

"What do your parents think you're doing?" I ask her, because they wouldn't let her go to New York without me.

"They think I'm going to some cabin spa retreat up north with Adri." She winces. Ember loves Debra and Scott, so the betrayal is probably bothering her. "I bought the tickets and she's just going to take Travis."

"And this hit?" I run my fingers through her damp hair, tugging slightly at the ends as she wraps herself up more in my blanket. We're fresh out of the shower, having spent most of the evening fucking. "What do you have planned?"

"I read his file. He likes to take overnight shifts at the detention center, so Emmett and I are grabbing him early when he gets off." There's more to it than that, but I let it be. I won't stifle her, and I have all the confidence in what she can do. After hearing Carm say this Talia bitch probably knows where my girl lives, I feel the need to monitor her house for any suspicious activity. That's what I'll be doing this weekend and possibly hanging out with Scott. I love when he has to search for a classic car. That shit is fun to do.

"I'll be okay," she purrs as she sits up and settles herself between my legs, running her tongue along my hip.

"I know." My voice is filled with hunger but my answer is immediate because it's the truth. Ember has proven herself when it comes to staying alive.

This weekend, I plan to spend some time with my mother as well. It's been a while and she's been noting my absences. She loves Ember but she's also worried that I'm getting in too deep as she questions Ember's healing from her kidnapping daily. I can't reassure her about shit because what Ember went through is fucked-up, and she will continue to recover from that for a while. She was fucking kidnapped and forced into killing people all for her deranged biological father. My mother will just have to be content with knowing I found my one person in this world and that I will never be alone again. No matter how crazy Ember is.

When you grow up with a jaded mother who had a terrible experience with love, you soak up her attitude, and eventually, you think it's your own. I had girlfriends and slept around, but girls were never a priority to me. Bagging them when I wanted was easy, but so was dropping them when I was done. Marlana was one of them. I took her virginity in grade eight, and we had been off and on until Ember showed up. I did nothing with any girl in public because I wanted to make sure they and everyone else understood that they weren't a permanent thing. They didn't have the power to fucking break me or ruin my whole life. Like what happened to my mother.

My classmates whispered about me and most of those rumors made me cringe. I guess I was a bit of a fuckboy. Using my looks, I got laid whenever and however I pleased. Then Ember came, just fucking stormed into my life like a tornado, and ripped open the concrete encasing my dark heart. Her personality and determination swirled around me until my jaded heart was torn from me and landed in her hands. She shows me I'm capable of love and of being loved, that I can shower her with affection no matter who's watching, and she'd never use that against me.

"What are you thinking about?" Her turquoise eyes find mine as she rests her chin on her folded arms on my stomach.

"How damaged my mother is, even after all these years. She still holds that pain and deceit in her heart from eighteen years ago. She's never attempted to move on with anyone else." How can I convince my mother that I'm in love when she doesn't believe in it?

"Vin, I think she does that for you," Ember breathes out, her words making me pause.

"What? How?"

"Because she wants to make sure you're her number one. That no matter what, no one else is more important. Your father made your lives hell and I doubt she wanted a repeat. You've been through enough already. That's what I think my mother thought too." She says the last few words in a pained whisper, her face morphing with sorrow. Ember still hasn't completely dealt with her mother's death, and as time moves forward, I worry for the day she crumbles.

"I think it's more like her never wanting to endure that pain again," I counter as I really process it. "Or a mixture of both."

Robert Greene swept my mother up into an intense affair full of empty promises, and then he dropped her when he found greener pastures. Unfortunately, he didn't wrap up his dick and won a hateful son in the lottery of unprotected sex. The more I think about it—

and I have thought about it too many times over the years—the more I understand that he would have never been with my mother. Greener pastures aside, my mother is black and his family was a prominent white one here in Whitsborough, their white skin dating back centuries. While I was in his house, all the portraits were of white families, taken with prestige oozing from their pores. Not a face of color was in sight.

"Why didn't they work?" Ember breaks the silence as her eyebrows come together. "Why did he leave her here and go off to college? Besides the obvious asshole behavior."

"She didn't fit the life he and his family wanted," I grit out as anger begins to rise inside of me.

"How so? Sharla is a fucking gem." Ember just doesn't perceive race. My girl is pure and doesn't hold hatred based on race, only on the actions of a person.

"They would prefer someone… whiter." I shrug with a nonchalance I'm not feeling. Here in Whitsborough, it's predominantly white. A few families of color are sprinkled throughout, but it doesn't escape me how little lives inside our town's borders.

"No!" she breathes out in horror. "That's so disgusting."

"Well, you can't kill all evil, baby," I say with a chuckle as I drag her up my body to kiss her cheek.

"You have no idea." Apprehension skates through me as I gaze into her mischievous eyes. Sometimes I want to dive into her mind and find everything she has planned to do and the things she's already done, just to understand her better. Then I give myself a shake because no matter what I find in that beautiful mind, it won't change who Ember is to me.

"How often are you going to masturbate this weekend?" she asks, and I can't stop the laughter that bubbles out of me. Breaking the tension of our heavy conversation, she tips her head to the side as she releases a long sigh, so impatient for the answer.

"A lot," I admit as a smile climbs over her mouth. "I'm going to miss my pussy."

As her eyes darken, they instantly fill with lust. I love that I can do that to her. She pushes herself up—still naked from our shared shower—and straddles my lap. Her body is riddled with scars and it makes me proud every time they're on display. Em is muscular and cut. Her muscles are defined on her arms and stomach, not an inch of cushion except for her tits and ass. I grab both cheeks in my hands and squeeze, then bring her center down to run her wetness along my hard dick. She moans, throwing her head back and her dark brown hair skims along my thighs. Then she runs her hands up her stomach and grabs her tits, pinching her nipples and gyrating against my dick. No matter how many times we fuck in a day, we can always fuck some more.

Ember falls forward, her mouth latching onto mine as she sucks my bottom lip and gives it a bite. I pull away, then kiss her again with more intensity, my tongue intertwining with hers as she sucks it into her mouth like she's sucking my cock. I groan and lift her ass up to impale her on my cock. She releases my tongue to throw her head back and scream. Thankfully, my mother is at the restaurant tonight. I tilt Ember's pelvis forward and start pumping into her, using my piercing to drag along that spot inside, my favorite spot. She's grabbing her tits again as her moans become fiercer. Then my balls tighten, the urge to come spreading up my shaft. I'm not going to last much longer.

She picks up the speed and grinds down onto me, then she screams as fluid gushes out of her and over my lower belly, sinking down into my ass crack. With just two more pumps, I'm coming so hard inside her as my body jerks with the force.

"Going to miss my cock," she mutters as she falls onto my chest, her eyes growing heavy with exhaustion.

I chuckle and pick us both up, still joined, to wash up in the bathroom. Yeah, I'm going to miss this for the next few days. My hand will never be enough ever again.

199

Ember

I'm sitting in a blacked-out sedan with Emmett as we wait for this piece of shit to finish his shift. Emmett hasn't been as chatty as usual since we left the compound, and I'm not sure what's up his ass.

"That face makeup is the creepiest shit I have ever seen." *Oh… maybe that's it.*

"Don't tell Carm I do this," I say to him as I point to my face.

"Sure, whatever." He leans away, his eyes rounding with fear. *Little pussy.* "This isn't the day of the dead, you know?"

"It sure is," I reply. "For Henry Thompson."

"Oh." He nods as a smile crawls over his mouth. The first sign of his usual demeanor shining through. "That's good."

"Mm-hmm." Turning back to watch the front of the detention center, I let the silence ground me. That is, until Emmett breaks it again.

"Your friends are cool. Well… Adrianna is cool. Travis seems like a prick." He's looking out of the windshield as he runs his fingers through his wavy hair, a contemplative expression on his face.

"Nah, he's just going through shit," I explain. "If anyone is the prick, it's Vin, and you guys get along just fine."

"Vin is a prick," he agrees with a chuckle and a shake of his head, "but I respect him. He takes care of you. Travis just looks like an asshole."

"You'll see. Once he's used to you, he's not."

We both fall silent as Henry Thompson steps outside the detention center. We're parked across the street, and as soon as he gets in his vehicle and turns out of the driveway, I'm on his ass. Carm put a few tails on him this past week and I learned which way he takes home. He drives through a really shabby side of town, and this early in the morning, rarely anyone is out.

Pervy turns down the road highlighted on the map I was given, and I speed up, turning in behind his car and hitting his back bumper hard enough to jolt him. I watch through his rear windshield as he throws his hands up and hits the wheel before pulling over onto the side of the road and turning on his hazards. So far, so good. Next step, we wait for him to get out of his vehicle. Then Emmett—since he's closer to this perv's type—will approach him.

His door finally opens, and I exhale the breath I hadn't realized I was holding.

"Showtime." Emmett grins at me and then exits the car. That son of a bitch just might be as crazy as me, and fuck if I don't like it. He really is a little demon.

"Hey, man!" Emmett yells out. "We're so sorry about this. We're so used to nobody being on this road." My brother's arms spread as he shakes his head, looking every bit contrite.

"What are you kids doing out?" Henry doesn't sound pissed, just curious, and I thank God for Emmett's appealing looks.

"Oh, you know, being kids." Emmett sticks out his hand toward Henry. "Thanks for being so understanding."

The guy nods and looks at Emmett's hand, slowly reaching forward to clasp it. I let out a sigh of relief and lean forward the second he realizes he made a big mistake. Emmett moves fast and puts him in a choke hold with ease. Then I pat myself on the back for how well I taught him.

Showtime.

I step out of the car to lean against the door, and as soon as Henry's gaze flicks toward me, his skin goes pale and he stops struggling. "Henry Thompson?" I call out. He doesn't make a move to answer me, his jaw clenched tight and his eyes the size of saucers. I stalk over to him and lift the laminated identification card hanging around his neck, reading his name beneath his photo. "Good." I smile widely. "Put him in the car."

He begins to struggle again, grunting as his fat belly restricts him from actually fighting back. Emmett is trying to keep his hold, but it's quickly turning into a problem. I walk back up to them as I pull my knife from my pocket, slamming the butt end of the handle into Henry's temple and he drops like a sack of potatoes.

"Let's tie him up and shove him into the trunk," I say to Emmett as he toes the perv's fat stomach.

Tossing him the rope from my sweater pocket, we tie Henry's arms behind him and drag him to the trunk, both of us sweating as we slowly lift him inside. Once he's secured and with a fresh piece of duct tape over his mouth, we head out to our predetermined location. It's secluded inside an abandoned warehouse near the Rampage's compound. Far away from eyes and ears.

We pull up the open garage-style doors and drive right in. I unload our fold-out lawn chair from the back seat as Emmett grabs more rope, then we both head over to the trunk and open it to peer inside. We find our friend wide awake and looking terrified.

"This must be the look the little boys give him," Emmett sneers, mimicking Henry's horrified face.

"Yeah, that's probably pretty darn close," I agree as Henry begins to moan, the sound muffled by the tape.

We haul him out of the trunk and throw his ass into the chair before tying the rope around his waist and the chair to secure him further, leaving his hands tied. Emmett ties his feet together next as Henry attempts to kick out at him, earning a swift punch to his nuts. His eyes roll back as his body trembles with the pain, giving Emmett some time to make sure he's tied in well. The duct tape around his mouth is staying put because of the chance of him being heard. Besides, what I have planned will make him scream for a while anyway.

"Am I doing target practice first?" Emmett asks, his face shining with anticipation as he lifts his sweater to reveal a band tied around his waist, filled with throwing knives.

"Soon. First, I want to explain to our friend here why we're doing this." I look back at Henry, his wide eyes on my face as he whimpers and shakes his head. "Henry, how many boys have you touched or fucked?" He tries to speak as his eyes become glassy with tears, mumbling some bullshit, I'm sure. The duct tape is keeping his bullshit inside his mouth though, working overtime. I *tsk* loudly as I exhale a huff of breath, my eyes rolling with exasperation. "Please tell me you didn't deny those charges. That means you haven't asked for forgiveness. Being an angel of death—"

"More like Devil in that getup—" Emmett mumbles, cutting me off.

"I must make you see the error of your ways," I finish while glaring at Emmett to shut his fucking mouth.

I stalk forward and pull out my trusty knife. As soon as Henry sees it, the motherfucker pisses himself. I don't let it deter me as I reach forward and grab his ear, twisting the cartilage.

"Now, we will try this again. Hold up your fingers. How many little boys have you touched or fucked? Let's say in the last… three weeks." His hands are tied in front of him, but his fingers aren't, not that I expect him to do as I say.

He shakes his head again and is full-on sobbing now, snot running down over the duct tape. I take the knife and slice his right earlobe off, the blade running through it like butter, and whip it to the ground. Henry screams—thank God it's muffled—while Emmett laughs maniacally and I hum my appreciation for my pretty knife.

"That knife is sharp. It went through his ear smoothly." Emmett whistles as I grin at him, holding the knife up as blood runs down the gleaming metal.

"It belonged to our daddy." I look back at Henry as his screams die down and he sniffles, crying like a baby. "I killed him too," I tell him, whispering like it's a dirty little secret as I clean the knife off on Henry's shirt and slip it back into my pocket.

The fucker begins fighting his restraints and trying to break out of the chair. Emmett and I stand back to take in the show, both of our heads cocked to the right and arms folded over our chests. It's almost like watching a deer caught in barbed wire. Finally, the chair tips to the side, and Henry—with all his pissed-pants glory—is face-planted to the floor beside his discarded ear.

"Target practice on the fat ass," I instruct Emmett. "Just one though."

Emmett pulls up his sweater again, yanks out a knife, and tests its weight in the palm of his hand. Then he throws it straight up in the air, catches it, and flicks his wrist. Within a second, that blade is buried deep in Henry's ass cheek, his muffled screams bringing identical grins to our faces.

"Nice shot." We fist bump, then he runs forward to retrieve his knife and sets Henry back up to sitting. Although the asshole is having a hard time now with the stab wound in his ass.

"How many kids, Henry?" I ask again as Emmett cleans his blade off on Henry's shirt.

Henry drops his chin to his chest, letting loose a high-pitched whine as I once again stalk forward to grab him by the hair and lift his head up. His eyes are still the size of saucers and the snot has mixed with the blood along his face. He's just a nasty mess, especially with the stench of piss. I pull out my knife and start carving into his skin. It's fucking hard to do with the bitch thrashing about, but I manage.

"Nice!" Emmett exclaims behind me. "You have lovely penmanship."

"Thank you." Smiling, I look at my handiwork and preen. I love when people truly appreciate my artistic talents. *Perv* is written beautifully into Henry's forehead.

The blood runs from the cuts on his forehead down over his face in thin red rivulets. It looks so pretty, and I'm dying to do more. I wipe my knife with the back of his shirt before pointing it into his face.

"Hold up those fingers, Henry," I snarl. "I want to know how many."

Emmett forces Henry's arms up, but the stubborn fucker keeps his hands fisted. So I slap him hard in the face and growl. When he doesn't budge, I squeeze a pressure point in his hands and his fingers fly out as he whines. Then I pull my knife out and slice through the four fingers on his right hand, leaving just his thumb. The little bitch immediately passes out, making me growl with frustration.

"He'll die of blood loss soon," I muse as I tap a bloody finger to my lip. "Go ahead and throw some of those knives into his belly. Let's see if we can't wake him up."

I sit on the ground and slip my knife into my pocket to watch Emmett toss his blades one by one into Henry's butterball gut. By the eighth one, he finally wakes up with a scream.

"Keep them in. I want him alive for the grand finale," I tell Emmett as I stand, dusting my jeans off with bloody hands.

Bending down in front of Henry's face, I grin as I rip his buttoned-up guard's uniform top open, exposing his nasty hairy chest. Then I pull out my knife again and start carving the words into his chest. He doesn't fight as he grunts through the pain, resigned to his fate, and I seal the deal by sinking my knife into his eye socket, his body immediately tensing and then slumping forward in death.

"'Kiddie Fucker,'" Emmett whispers, his voice a mix of awe and horror.

"Yeah, Kiddie Fucker." I nod and slap him on the back. "Let's string him up outside so someone can find him exactly like that."

Emmett withdraws all his knives from Butterball and we work on hanging this motherfucker up outside the warehouse doors.

Chapter Sixteen

Ember

I spent the rest of Saturday with Emmett at Coney Island. I had only ever been one other time with my mother. It took her weeks to save up for it and we suffered for a month afterward, but it was worth it. This time around was just as much fun without the worry of how it would affect my bank account. Emmett acted like a big kid the entire time, begging me for prizes and to go on the rides together. He even made me eat a fucking nasty corn dog by guilting me into 'sibling experiences.'

We're currently driving back to Hunt's Point in Shelby, both tired out of our fucking minds, having near to no sleep. Despite that, today was important. I bonded with Emmett, my twin brother. We bonded, I mean, first over killing someone together, but after seeing the innocence in each other. First evil, then being assured we're also good, a balance of sorts. We both understand that the scales can always be tipped, and he gets that the killings actually balance me after I tip too far toward evil.

Emmett says he doesn't have any urges for blood or to kill, but if I need him, he would never say no. He doesn't have a darkness and would much prefer not to do it, much to our father's disdain while he was growing up. My twin is like our mother, with only a touch of our father. He doesn't shy away from darkness, but he doesn't let himself thrive in it either. That soothes me and reminds me I also have her inside me… somewhere.

"You sure you want to leave tonight?" Emmett asks as I pull up to the compound to drop him off.

"Yeah, I'll nap first," I lie before he can protest. "I miss Vin." It's the truth, the only honest thing I'm saying right now.

"I miss Vin too." He grins, his eyes filled with amusement. "Make sure you tell him for me."

I laugh and lean over to hug him, and his scent combines with mine, reminding me of our mother. Suddenly, I realize I don't want to leave him, and I think he feels the same with how hard he's hugging me back.

"Come to Whitsborough next weekend," I tell him as my arms tighten around him.

"Okay," he mumbles sadly, his face still on my shoulder.

Finally, we break apart and I don't miss the look of melancholy before he quickly covers his features with his—and my—mischievous grin. He gets out of the car and jogs to the compound, looking back once to give me a quick wave, then disappears inside. It's at this moment I realize I want Emmett to live with me in Whitsborough and I want him to be loved like I am. I'll have to think of a way to tell my parents that doesn't implicate me in the murder of our father.

Being back in the condo without Vin is strange. Lying to

Emmett wasn't easy, but the Head's meeting is very important. I have to prepare myself for what I'm going to walk into tomorrow, which is a bunch of presumably older men who run different districts in New York for drugs, prostitution, and weapons. Except in my case, I am the Head of Toronto.

I will need a good night's sleep to deal with the chaos I'm about to unleash. Chuckling softly to myself, I try to imagine what Carm will look like when he lays eyes on me. I'm not worried in the least about the aftermath, because this is karma working for his involvement in my kidnapping.

The next morning, I wake up early enough to apply my decorative skull makeup because I don't want to go with my face showing. My features make me look young and innocent, and no man in that room would take me seriously. Unless I stab them, and that, unfortunately, is only a last resort.

This time, instead of leggings and an oversized hoodie, I go with black skinny jeans, black leather boots, and a white V-neck with a leather jacket on top. Then I style my hair into a messy bun on top of my head and deem myself Head material.

Pulling up to the compound, the guards at the front recognize my car but are apprehensive about the face makeup. Once I give them a quick nod, they let me in, and I don't spot another guard until I hit the double doors of the conference room. The two guards stationed outside immediately grip their guns and I halt.

"Guys, I wouldn't do that if I were you." I shake my head and *tut*. "Shooting a Torres will have you skinned and in a shallow grave within the hour."

"Is that Ember?" the first one asks, his head tipping forward as he slowly lowers the gun.

"Shit, I can't tell," the other answers, speaking as though I'm not standing in front of them.

"Look, I'm here for the Head's meeting and you're making me later than what I already am." I shoo at them as I approach the doors.

They both nod at each other like my attitude confirms it's me and then move aside. I push the double doors inward and find it hard to contain my laughter when everyone turns to look at me. Some look amused, while others look confused. I can't wait to smack the smiles off their faces when they realize this isn't a joke.

"Hello, fellow Heads." A maniacal grin stretches across my mouth as I spread my arms out wide and Carm nearly chokes as he gulps to take in air. "As you all know, Robert has passed from cancer and signed his Headship over to me."

I pull the paperwork out of my inner breast pocket and throw it on the table as the two men closest to the papers read them over and nod to the rest.

"Ember Craven?" A distinguished man gives me a once-over, his designer suit and coiffed hair hiding the fact that he's a fucking criminal.

"Yes?" My grin spreads across my mouth, showcasing my teeth as a few murmurs circle the table.

"Why would Robert pick you? We were told to expect a son." I open my mouth to say something snarky about men needing to be surrounded by dicks when Carm cuts in.

"That's probably because she's a Torres." He says the words softly as everyone's heads snap around to look at him in tandem.

"A Torres?" an overly obese man wheezes out. "How is that? Raphael had only two sons." My nose crinkles as I watch a drop of sweat drip from his jaw to land on his collar.

"I don't have time to give you the talk about the birds and

the bees, not that it matters." I shrug as I internally shudder at his lingering look. "When was the last time you used it anyway?" I point to his crotch.

A few of the men chuckle while some look irritated. Carm looks like he's about ready to pass out as he runs his hands through his hair obsessively, the stress oozing out of him.

"You wouldn't be able to handle this job, little girl," a tall, dark, and handsome man spits out. I'm stunned for all of ten seconds as I soak in his perfect features, then I snap out of it, finally absorbing what the dick said.

"You don't think so?" I sneer out as Carm opens his mouth to speak. "I got this." I stop him as I raise my hand.

"No, we don't," *Wheezy* throws in his two cents. He's just butt hurt because I called out his inability to piss standing up.

"Who put a hit out on a certain DA a few weeks ago?" I ask as I near the table to place my hands on the wooden top and lean over to look each of them in the eyes. Wheezy's eyes widen, outing himself instantly.

"You," I smugly say, pointing at him. "Thank you for the one-hundred-grand." He coughs as his face takes on an abnormal shade of maroon, reminding me of Adri's hair. I walk around and go to stand behind him, placing my hands on his shoulders. "It was convenient that the CD player was plugged in on the ledge of his hot tub." I squeeze his shoulders. The details of the hit weren't privy to the public, only to Carm and this guy, because the police didn't release them.

"Last night, I had a little more fun with a certain juvenile detention guard." I snicker as I take a seat on Carm's right. Robert's spot. "So much more fun than the last." Tall, dark, and asshole quickly swings his head to glance at me. Ah… fucking kismet, this is.

"Holy fuck," someone mutters, the horror in their voice telling me they saw the photos on the news this morning. That shit was nasty.

"How?" Tall, dark, and dickhead asks.

"You may also know her as Blur," Carm interrupts, his eyes shooting daggers at me as his skin blooms red. I toss him a demure smile and then focus back on the others.

"No way," Tall, dark, and cunty says, leaning forward. "You're my favorite fighter."

"What's your name?" I ask him sweetly, batting my fake caterpillar lashes. "I can't keep trying to come up with synonyms for asshole in my head."

"Wade," he replies with an amused smile.

"I'll be changing a few things for Toronto." My hands land on the table again as I get right down to business. I'm a Head now, whether or not they like it. "I won't be distributing drugs, guns, or whores any longer. Instead, I will offer my services as I have been doing for you already."

A few disrupt and argue until I pull out my father's knife from my jacket pocket, unsheathing it to twirl the sharpened point on my index finger. The sharp pinch is euphoric and the blood drips from my finger onto the table as the tip of the blade digs into my skin. This quiets them down quickly. When I deem them contained, I sheath the knife and lay it on the table in front of me.

"I will offer all of you, and anyone you deem fit, the services I provided for the two of you recently, but… on the condition these targets deserve death. Not some lovers' spat or territory disputes. Real evil inclinations."

"Men and women work in the Toronto territory," someone

else pipes up from the end of the table. Perhaps the man with the obvious toupee and patchy skin. I bet he distributes meth and dips his dick in prostitutes as a pastime.

"Pull them out. I have my own team." I don't care to employ drug peddlers and whores.

"You are more your father than both of his sons," Wheezy breathes out, the collar of his shirt now saturated with his sweat.

"I'm sure you mean that as a compliment." I lift a brow at him and he nods back nervously. "And I probably would take it if I hadn't actually murdered the piece of shit myself." Now everyone has the common sense to regard me as unstable, and most of all, capable of horrendous acts of violence. I grin with amusement as they squirm and mutter shocking words of disbelief. "Do we vote? Like raising our hands? Aye or nay?" I sweetly ask Carm as I raise my hand.

"No need to vote. You're the Head of Toronto. What you say goes. Although the funds will significantly drop if you are providing just a singular service," he advises, sounding bored.

"Perfect!" I say. "Proceed with the meeting."

"We are here to discuss profits from the last quarter. So, I will run through Heads and if you dispute, please wait until the end. Head One: Six point two million…"

I don't pay attention to a sizable chunk of the rest of the profits because my ears are ringing as I choke on air. Did he fucking say millions?

"… Head Nine: Three point five million, and Head Ten: Four point one million. Any disputes?"

Nobody disputes it, because why the fuck would they? That's huge money, and these Head motherfuckers make that every three months? I have to calm myself and realize this is because of drugs, guns, and sometimes forced prostitution.

I raise my hand, making Carm raise his brow. "Sorry, which Head am I?" I ask him.

"Head Ten."

"No disputes." I shake my head quickly, then continue to shake it as I look down at the other end of the table. "No fucking dispute here," I reiterate to the rest. The money is already made and here for the taking.

"Your finances will go down drastically unless you take on a large workload," Carm warns me, a ghost of a smile playing around the edges of his mouth.

"I'm good." And I am, that's a lot of money. I'll be set for life, and so will my kids, then their kids, and their fucking neighbor's kids… Shit. I lost you? Yeah, I lost myself in that one too.

The meeting wraps up as soon as I begin to doze off. These grown-ass men complaining about rival gangs and such are boring as fuck.

"Okay, we will reconvene at the end of October." They all start getting out of their seats when Carm turns his attention to me. "Ten, can you please stick around so we can iron out some details?"

"Yeah, sure." I roll my eyes at him, knowing I'm in for a berating.

"Blur, are you going to be fighting soon?" Wade asks as he walks backward toward the door.

"Not unless you're my opponent," I throw back. He laughs and shakes his head like I told a funny joke, then leaves the room. I wasn't fucking joking though.

"Don't you think this is something you should've told me about?" Carm asks as soon as the door closes behind the last Head, his mouth turned down in a frown.

"Why? Because you're my brother?" He nods. "Forgive me, but I barely know you."

"Right." He scrubs his hand down his face. "This isn't a simple job—"

"Stop." I hold my hand up to cut him off. "I'm not going anywhere, so skip the lecture and get to what you really want to talk about."

"Did you kill Robert?"

"No, he killed himself." I cross my arms over my chest as he exhales a frustrated breath. The doubt is apparent in his eyes, and rightfully so.

"Why would he sign you over the business when he was adamant his son would take over?" He thinks he's got me when I take a minute to answer, his smug smile making it difficult to keep my hand from slapping it off his face.

"Because he found out who I was and he couldn't convince his *mutt* of a son to take it." I give him a smug smile of my own.

"I can't even right now." He throws his hands up and sits back in his chair. "We have a bigger problem."

"What now?" Irritation bleeds through my tone as the smile falls from my face.

"My meeting with Jennifer Talia. It's this evening," he reminds me, his brows coming together in irritation.

"Right!" I snap my fingers. "I should stay and scope her out."

"I can't have you doing that, Ember. It'll be too risky. You need to go home. Now."

"Carm, you *need* to put a tail on her, and we *need* as much information as possible."

"Fine." He shakes his head. "I have a headache. I'll call you this evening."

"Here." I pull the gun he gave me out of my sweater pocket and put it down on the table. "I don't want this. I find I'm better with a knife."

"You sure?" he asks, and I nod at him before pushing up out of my seat and heading for the door. "Fine, I'll call you."

"Make sure that you do, or I will come right the fuck back here and search for her myself." I slam the door behind me. He better not fuck it up.

This was a productive-ass weekend, if I do say so myself.

Vin

I'm laughing my ass off at my mother right now because she is so fucking jealous that Debra won a free all-inclusive getaway weekend for two from their spa. She says Debra should take her, despite it being a romantic trip. I told her that Scott works so much and this would be good for them, but she just rolled her eyes.

"It's just not fair!" She stomps around the kitchen, sending me into another bout of laughter.

"Ma, I'll buy you an all-inclusive getaway, okay?" I promise, wiping the tears from my eyes.

"No! I want to win one!" She pouts as she hits me with the drying towel over her shoulder.

"You're too much. Either accept a gift or knock it off," I say with a chuckle.

"Ugh… fine," she concedes and goes back to the sink to dry the dishes.

My phone pings with a message and I smile, knowing it's my girl.

Em: I'm home. Miss me?

Me: Come here so I can eat you out.

Em: LOL, later! I have to celebrate with my parents. They won some shit.

I chuckle again and then look at my mother.

"What?" she asks. "Who is it?" Her fists land on her hips as her eyes narrow on me.

"Em. She's celebrating with her parents on their winnings."

My mother growls and storms off to her bedroom as I laugh heartily, making her curse before she slams the door.

Me: K. C U later.

I'm curious about Ember's weekend. I'm sure if I looked online for news in New York I would find her guy, but I want her to tell me about it instead. There's something about telling me that sets her off, and I can't pull her off my dick for hours after. Selfish, I know.

I'm also curious to find out how she and Emmett got along. I want Em to have a big family and more people to count on besides me and her aunt and uncle. Emmett seems like a good fit and they're so similar that it's a little freaky to be honest. When he grins like he just fucked some shit up and he's proud—same as Em's. When he chuckles like an evil villain—same as Em's. His whole fucking face is Ember's, but their personalities are slightly different. Emmett is quieter and more reflective, whereas Ember will say and do whatever the fuck she wants. I believe Emmett will balance her and she will also pull him out of his shell a bit.

A yawn rips from my mouth and I stand to head upstairs to my room, deciding to nap for a few hours until Ember comes by.

Her hand skims up my leg and by the time she reaches my dick, it's ready to go.

"You're late," I mumble, still half asleep.

"Sorry, they wouldn't go the fuck to sleep," she whispers harshly. "I considered cutting their throats…"

"Em!" I hiss and sit up, alarmed at her words, my body stiffening and my eyes widening on her laughing face.

"Guess I shouldn't joke about shit I actually do, huh?" She giggles.

"Yeah, no." I shake my head, relief hitting me instantly. She had me worried there for a second.

She plops down on my bed beside me and I cup her face with my hands. I missed her scent and the touch of her skin. I run my nose along her throat and then press my lips to hers. Her mouth is so fucking soft, and the noises she makes, just for me, are fucking sexy. Her tongue works its way into my mouth and she flicks my tongue ring, and it takes all my effort to stop this from going any further.

"Tell me what happened," I prompt her, knowing she needs to release the energy trapped inside of her.

"First tell me yours," she counters, her eyes pleading with me for normalcy.

"Sure." I shrug as I twist a piece of her hair around my finger. "I spent most of it at your house. I helped Scott find a 'Cuda."

"A fish?" Her nose crinkles.

"A car." I pinch her nose and laugh.

"Oh!" she breathes out, her face relaxing. "That's so cool." I nod and then wait for her to fill me in on her weekend.

"I took Emmett with me. It's different having someone else take part in the extermination but normal at the same time because he thinks like me, you know?" Her turquoise eyes bore into mine as they fill with pride. "We waited for him to drive home and I rear-ended him. He got out and we nabbed him." Her voice cracks with emotion and she looks at me, her throat working on a swallow before she admits, "It got pretty intense. I haven't tortured anyone like that since…"

Her voice breaks at that moment and she stops talking. I run my fingers over her cheek as she closes her eyes and breathes deeply.

"Since… your father?" I take a guess.

She nods and buries her face into my neck as her arm wraps around my waist. I knew Ember did some dark shit while she was taken, and most of it she did to her own father. I don't push her for more as I slowly rub circles on her back.

"My mom is so jealous that your parents won the all-inclusive getaway." I chuckle, trying to lighten the mood. She pulls her head from my neck with a soft snort.

"Really?" She smiles, relief rushing through her eyes.

"Yeah." I lean forward and kiss her forehead. "I had to promise to buy her one too. When do they go?"

"Next weekend. I was thinking of inviting Emmett and Carm here while they're away." She bites her bottom lip as her eyebrows fall in thought.

"That's cool."

"I want to figure out a way to tell my parents about Emmett. I just have this yearning for him to stay here in Whitsborough with me," she reveals, her chest swelling as she fights off more emotions.

"Really? How would we do that?" I ask as I tuck her hair behind her ear.

"We?"

"Yeah. We. For always, whenever you need me," I throw her words from the performance night so long ago back at her.

Her eyes instantly become heavy with lust and she sits up to rip off her T-shirt. She has nothing on underneath and I groan as her tits bounce with the motion. Her fucking tits are amazing. She stands up by the side of the bed and rolls down her black yoga pants, her abs flexing as she bends, and when she stands back up, she's completely naked.

"Touch yourself," I demand, my voice husky with need.

She runs her hand down over her breast, lightly pinching her nipple. Then her hand continues its downward path over her flat stomach and over her bare pussy to cup herself.

"Spread her open and show me how wet she is for her daddy."

Ember groans as she lifts her right foot onto the bed and spreads her pussy with her fingers. Her wetness coats her pussy lips, making my mouth water with anticipation.

"Two fingers, fuck yourself," I command her as I sit up to get a closer look.

She sinks two fingers inside her cunt and my dick twitches, wishing I was inside her. The sucking sounds permeate my ears and

I reach inside my boxers to stroke myself as she pulls out her fingers, each one glistening with her wetness.

"Taste yourself." She opens her mouth and seals her lips over her fingers, slowly sucking her juices off them.

Grabbing her around the waist, I throw her on the bed as she squeals, and then I press my body against hers. "I love you," I tell her.

"I love you forever," she breathes out as her hands run down my back, her nails scraping along the skin.

Shucking off my boxers, I settle between her legs, lining myself up and slowly pushing into her. Her wet warmth envelops me and I succumb to instinct as my mind shuts down.

"Vin, harder," she demands, her fingers biting into my ass as she tries to grind against me.

I lean down and suck her nipple into my mouth, flicking it with my tongue and ignoring her demand a little longer. Her pussy contracts around my cock, telling me she's close. I slide my hands under her ass, grabbing handfuls, then tip her pelvis up and pull all the way out, only to slam back in. Balls deep. Ember trembles and groans as I repeat the process a few more times, her body tensing beneath me. Reaching between us, I pinch her clit between my fingers, knowing my girl likes a little pain with her pleasure.

"Vin!" she screams as her pussy squeezes me, the tight grip making it difficult to move.

"That's it, baby, come all over my cock." I remove my hand and thrust inside her, grinding my pelvis against her clit.

She keeps mumbling my name through her orgasm; the sound filled with awe and love, making it hard to hold on any longer. I begin to really pound into her, my balls clenching tight just before

I come so deep inside her. I stay rooted firmly, letting both of our releases mix as they run out of her. My balls are sticky, but I can't move. Being inside her is my favorite fucking place in the world.

Moaning softly, she moves, the mess making her sticky too. I pull out as my cum follows and runs down to her asshole. "Vin, please get me something," she groans, knowing I'm just staring at our cum.

After cleaning us both up, I rouse Ember because Scott would kill me if he found out she was sneaking out of the house to come here. "Babe,"—I kiss her forehead—"you got to get back."

"I know," she whispers sleepily, her eyes still closed as a wrinkle appears between her brows. "Are we still too young to live together?"

"I think so?" I shrug as I pull her into me, her warm body relaxing against mine. "Plus, we need money to survive."

"We have money."

"My mom…" I stop. The thought of my mother ever living alone gives me anxiety.

"Yeah, I know," she says as she opens her eyes and gets up. "Don't think about it. I was being stupid."

"Em, I'll have to think about it sooner rather than later. We can't be married and live with my mom," I confess to her. Being with her forever has been playing heavy on my mind. Ember will be my wife, whether it's tomorrow or ten years from now, but it doesn't erase the worry I have about leaving my mother.

"Married?" Her head snaps around and her eyes search my face, as if looking for any sign of jest.

"Well, yeah. What did you think this was?" I raise a brow at her. Doesn't she think of this? Of us? Is the future something she refuses to think of, given what she does for a living?

"Whenever you said things like that, I didn't take you seriously," she admits, her eyes filling with tears as her throat works to speak.

"Even from the very beginning, baby, when you refused to be claimed, I knew it was just a matter of time. You're it. I want nothing else. Of course I'm marrying you. Of course you're having my babies. And most of all, you will always be my family." I reach out to catch a tear as it slips from her eye.

"I want all that," she breathes out. Family means everything to Ember, and I don't just mean by blood, it's the ones she chooses as family too.

"Soon, baby, when high school is done. When we can legally move like adults, we will do what we're meant to do." My fingers skim along her cheek and into her hair as I bring her mouth to mine.

"Okay," she mumbles against my lips. She kisses me goodbye, then stands to dress as I rake my eyes over her.

"I love you," she says and bends over to kiss me again.

"Forever," I promise into her mouth.

She pulls away and blinds me with her wide smile as she slips out of my room and out the front door.

It's Friday morning and the week has flown by. This is the weekend Ember's parents are going away and Emmett and Carm are coming to spend the weekend with her before leaving Sunday morning. My phone pings with a message and I open it expecting Em but discover it's someone else.

Scott: Hey, son. Do me a favor. Since Ember sneaks to your house every night anyway, can you keep an eye on her this weekend? Might as well sleep here.

Well, Em wasn't as sneaky as she thought.

Me: You got it, OG.

Scott: Bring your own beer.

Me: Damn, ok.

Scott: Check out the garage later, find out what was delivered today.

Me: 'Cuda?

He sends me a thumbs-up and I chuckle. I can't wait to rub it in Em's face that her father knew what she was up to this entire time.

The respect I've always had for Scott is high. He has been more of a father to me than anyone else. I've looked up to him since I was young and he always took me under his wing. He taught me about cars and expanded my interest in them. Now I experience just as much a thrill in finding these oldies as he does. Being in love with his adopted niece is just the cherry on top.

C.A. RENE

Chapter Seventeen

"Ember!" Ma screams from the bottom of the stairs. "Come have lunch with us before we go."

"'Kay!" I holler back as I jump off my bed.

I throw on a hoodie and join them in the kitchen. This weekend, Emmett and I are going to come up with some explanation about his existence so he can finally meet our family. They'll accept him with open arms. It's their nature. Their hearts are just so big.

"Vin is going to stay with you here this weekend, saves you from sneaking out and going to him," Dad says with a knowing grin and a wink.

"Well, that was a lot of work for nothing." I pout as I fall into a chair at the table.

"We have video surveillance that alerts us about movement outside," he replies with a lifted brow.

"I avoided cameras," I explain as I pick up my fork and stab it into the roasted chicken on my plate.

"Not well enough." Ma laughs as she pokes me on the arm.

"Maybe I wanted you guys to know." I shrug—I totally did not.

"Sure." Dad grins again before biting into a piece of chicken.

"What time will you be back on Sunday?" Would it be too much if I surprise them with Emmett on Sunday?

"Not sure. This entire weekend is a mystery. We are supposed to just relax and let everyone plan everything for us. Don't expect it to be too early though." Ma sighs with contentment.

From the moment they picked me up in New York, they've been nonstop on the go. They work too much and are selfless in their love for me. "You guys deserve this break. You work way too much."

"I agree." Dad looks at Ma affectionately. "We need a break, but we're going to miss you."

"You can come along!" Ma says, clearly excited. "We can just pay for Ember. Why didn't I think of that?"

"Guys…" I put my hands up. They've officially hit the limit of the love I'm willing to accept. "I love you and all, but we are not making this a weird third-wheel romantic weekend. Please go. I'll be fine here for a few days."

"You sure? You can have your own room and visit the spa for massages," she continues, excitement flaring in her eyes.

"Trust me, I'm sure. None of that sounds appealing. Do they have punching bags and ring matches?" I ask, knowing that will put a wrench in the plans she's already making.

"No." Ma scrunches her nose.

"I'm good here then."

Dad chuckles and gets up from the table, ruffling Ma's hair, then kissing me on top of my head. "We should hit the road."

"Yeah, at this rate, we will waste the first day of our free weekend." Ma nods as she stands from the table. Then she gives me one more longing look before smoothing my hair back. "You'll call us if you need anything, right?"

"Yes, Ma." I stand and wrap my arms around her waist, breathing in her scent.

I follow them outside and help put their bags into the back of the same Mercedes they picked me up in. Suddenly, a rush of panic comes over me and I'm not sure why. Maybe it's because this is my first real weekend of not having them here with me. Yeah, I leave for New York, but they never leave me here. Calming myself down, I plaster a smile on my face. They really deserve this and I won't let my abandonment issues resurface to stop them.

"We stocked the fridge and left some cash in the top drawer of your dad's desk," Ma says, her eyes skipping from me back to the front door, almost like she's thinking of just staying home.

"We will still monitor the surveillance, but if anything comes up, no matter how small, call the police." Dad wags his finger at me.

"Don't go all Blurry and try to take on anything yourself," Ma adds, making me snort. If only she knew what I was capable of.

"Got it! Don't worry, I'll be fine," I say, exasperated. I grip them both in a group hug, letting their warmth seep into my skin. My eyes tear up as that familiar lump grows in my throat. *They won't be gone forever,* I remind myself.

"I love you guys." I clear my throat to prevent my words from cracking.

"We love you too." Ma kisses my cheek as her hand rubs my back.

"Behave and don't throw wild parties," Dad warns, kissing the other side.

"No parties!" Ma reiterates on her way to the car.

"Don't worry, I don't like people enough for that." I wave at them.

"Ugh, we got so lucky with her. Antisocial and an ass-kicker." Dad sighs and waves back.

They start the car and drive down the ridiculously long driveway, my eyes blurring as they reach the end. When they turn out onto the road, I'm shocked when a teardrop hits my lip. What is up with me? They'll be back. It's just one fucking weekend. I wipe my tears off my cheeks and run my hand down my face.

Pull it together, Ember!

Emmett shows up around an hour later, without Carm. I invited them both and I'm a little disappointed that Carm isn't here. He was supposed to tell me all about his meeting with Talia.

"Where is he?" I ask, my arms crossed over my chest.

Emmett is pulling his bag off the back of his bike before he removes his helmet, his brown hair swaying in the breeze as his turquoise eyes light up with mischief. "I'm not good enough?" he teases as he drags me in for a hug.

"I invited both of you. What was his excuse?" I hug him back, then lead him up to the front door.

"Apparently, you caused a bit of an uproar with the other Heads. He's been stuck in his office doing conference calls and calming everyone down. He has a lot of backlogged work because of it. Why didn't you tell me about that?" He narrows his eyes, the betrayal clear in their depths.

"Less you knew, the better. I didn't want Carm to know ahead of time." He nods, accepting my reason, and grins again.

"You went in full makeup too, huh?" He chuckles.

"Yeah, I did." I grin back.

"Okay, show me this fuckery of a mansion. It'll be nice spending the weekend in an actual house and not an underground Batcave." He rubs his hands together with anticipation.

He needs to live here. The compound is underground and no matter how luxurious it is, it's not a home. He can ditch the tutors and homeschooling and actually come to Precious Blood with me.

"I can't believe Carm let you come alone," I muse as he looks around the front of the house, his eyes landing on the garage. I'll have to show him that later.

"He's not my father." Emmett shrugs, his eyes coming back to mine. They reflect a maturity older than his seventeen years, making me feel sorry for the both of us and what we missed out on.

"He is your guardian though." I elbow him and he grunts, rubbing his ribs.

"No. Dad was, and when he died, his lawyer filled out the paperwork to emancipate me. I have a lot of liquid funds and can take care of myself." Shock hits me in the chest as I stare at him. He and Carm have always seemed so tight, and I mistook that as a parental closeness.

"Oh, that's weird," I admit. "I just thought Carm would want to be your guardian."

"Yeah, he acts like one, but he has no time to raise me, not with how much he's dealing with." What really hurts the most as I take in his nonchalant expression is the fact that he never experienced a parent's love. I was lucky to have it with our mother and now again with our aunt and uncle. It only proves to me that he needs to meet them.

"Yeah, I get that." I lead Emmett into the house and show him around. He looks exactly like I did the first time I took it all in. He picks the guest room just down the hall from me so he can be close to me, and an hour later, we go to hang out by the pool.

"This is nice." He whistles as he checks out the fountain.

"Would you like to come to Precious Blood Academy with me this year?" I wanted to wait and let him settle in, but the thought of him leaving only makes me more anxious.

"Why the fuck did they name a school that?" He looks at me with a mix of disgust and outrage as I lead him to the lounge chairs in front of the pool.

"Catholic," I explain with a shrug. That should be sufficient.

"I haven't been to a proper school." He looks out at the pool, his expression becoming contemplative.

"Always homeschooled?" It breaks my heart because he's always been alone. He should've been with me and our mother.

"Yeah, always."

"Hopefully we can change that for this year, and you can learn to play with other children." He turns back to face me as I give him a toothy smile.

"Or I can avoid playgrounds and not stab anyone," he retorts, his mouth turning down into a mock frown. I snort out a laugh and he joins me. It doesn't matter what he says to me, the gleam in his eyes when I mentioned him coming to school with me was unmistakable. He looked excited, and to be honest, so am I. "What do these people do for work?" he inquires while looking around at the lush surroundings.

"Uncle Scott looks for classic cars and sells them to his customers. That's how I have Shelby. Aunt Debra is an interior designer. She works for a firm that has a TV show." Pride saturates my tone because even though we live in opulence, my parents worked their asses off for all of it.

"Wow." My chest warms when I hear the awe in his voice. He could be here with us, living this life and giving my parents another child they can love.

"They are really great people. When I first met them, I was angry as fuck at seeing all of this and comparing it to what I grew up with, but they've given me more than material things. I am loved." I press my hands to my chest as my heart beats faster.

"How were you living before here?" he asks me, his face a mask of confusion.

"Mom ran away from Whitsborough to be with our father and her rich parents disowned her for it. We were pretty fucking poor, to be honest. We lived in roach-infested apartments, slept on one mattress on the floor, and ate a lot of ramen because it was the only thing we could afford." Recounting those days isn't as hard as I thought it would be. I miss my mother, but I've stopped feeling so guilty. Now, I'm able to look back on our toughest days and remember being loved.

"Fuck, I'm sorry, Ember." He looks at me with sympathy, his hands wringing in his lap.

"I'm stronger because of it," I assure him. "You don't need to apologize. Our father had the biggest hand in it all and he paid for it."

"Yeah, he did. I'll never forget the morning I found his body," he murmurs as he shakes his head. "I stood in the doorway to his office, staring at him, and then a smile came over my face. Finally, the piece of shit was dead." The smile on his face is radiant and filled with relief, probably the same one he wore that day.

"I couldn't apologize for that if I wanted to. Although, I still dream about the things I did to him." I'm telling him things I've only ever trusted Vin with, and even though it's scary, it feels right to share my troubles with my twin.

"You skinned his face." He scrubs a hand down his own face, exhaling heavily. "The damage to his body was crazy. We all thought a rival gang found their way into the compound until Carm told us the truth. A secret daughter killed him in a rage."

"I wanted to kill Carm too, and I would've if he was still in the spot I left him. I went back to find him," I confess. My chest tightens with anxiety as I worry if Emmett will be angry with me.

"Really?" His eyebrows lift with surprise, and thankfully, no anger.

"Yeah, I hated everyone inside that compound after finding out about what happened to Mom," I explain as he reaches over to take my hand. The second we connect, my anxiety flees and a sense of calm comes over me as I squeeze his fingers with mine.

"Understandably. Carm was the one who kept the guards away while you were with Father. Did he ever tell you that?" When I shake my head, he nods and continues, "Yeah. He ordered everyone away. Told them it was family business." He lets go of my hand and runs it through his hair. "The night I watched you fight, Father told me you came for us, that you chose to become family. I swear I didn't know you were taken against your will."

"I believe you," I reassure him, "but I also don't think of the kidnapping as the worst thing to ever happen to me anymore. If I wasn't taken, I wouldn't have been able to kill that fucker and I wouldn't have found you."

"True." He looks at me as a smile grows along his lips. "I wish I had you when we were kids though." My breath lodges in my throat at his words. Did Emmett suffer as I did when I was a kid? Being an outcast and feeling like something was missing. I couldn't form the proper bonds of friendship, so all I ever had was Tommy, and even though he was my closest friend, I still hid so many things from him. "I grew up alone. I was such a fucking lonely kid. Carm was older and angry all the time. My only constant was the guards surrounding me." He slaps a hand to his chest and looks at me, his eyes shining with the loneliness he once felt, and I vow to never let him feel it again. "I was missing something in here."

"Me too," I whisper, the confession shaking me to my core. He and I grew up missing each other, as if our hearts were once one and forcefully ripped in half the moment we were separated.

"Yeah?" His voice trembles as he stares at me. I nod, unable to say anything else, and he gives me a sad smile. "I would've liked to have met our mother."

"We look a little like her. Our eye color came from her and our smiles," I describe as I poke him in the cheek.

He leans back and swats my hand away with a chuckle, his voice evening as he asks, "Do you have any pictures?"

"Yeah, I have a bunch. Did you want to go take a look?" The thought of sitting down with him and sharing our family photos makes me giddy with happiness.

He nods and gives me a smile before we gather our stuff and I bring him inside. We sit in the den as I pull out the box Vin found and Ma's photo albums from a cabinet I stored it in. I spread everything out and sit back as he flips through them.

"This is our aunt?" he asks, pointing at a wedding photo.

"Yeah, and our uncle. I call them Ma and Dad now. They officially adopted me and since they can't have children, I've been trying to be a worthy daughter for them." The lump in my throat is back as I try to breathe through the guilt growing inside my chest. I'm not worthy of them yet, not with my hands saturated in blood, and I don't think I ever will be.

"That sucks." He runs a finger over a picture of our mother in a Precious Blood Academy uniform, his face unreadable, but the slight tremor in his hand is noticeable. "Why did she leave me?" he whispers, those five words carving a path to my heart.

"I don't know, Emmett," I say as I wrap my arms around him, pressing my forehead to his shoulder. "But I'm going to find out."

"I know you can." The heartbreak in his voice shatters my own as I inhale a deep breath before pulling away to look down at the photos of our mother.

"Ember!" Vin calls out as the front door slams shut.

"In here!" I yell from the family room.

Vin walks into the room with his baseball hat tugged low on

his face, a two-day scruff lining his jaw, and an aura of overall not giving a single fuck. He's wearing a pair of faded blue jeans and a black T-shirt that's molded to his arms and chest.

"What are you guys up to?" he asks as he sits in the chair across from us.

"Showing Emmett family photos." His green eyes meet mine, the heat in their depths mimicking the heat in my bikini bottoms.

"'Sup?" Vin nods at Emmett, reminding me we aren't alone.

"Hey, man. Just trying to wrap my head around some of this stuff." Emmett looks back down at the album in his hands, effectively hiding his emotions from Vin.

"I hear that." Vin exhales as his eyes come back to me. "What are we doing for food tonight?"

"You're staying over?" I smile widely as I imagine having Vin in my bed.

"Can you believe your sister is this badass assassin, but she can't even sneak out of the fucking house properly?" Vin says to Emmett, his eyes filled with mischief.

"Seriously?" Emmett looks at me incredulously.

"Shut up," I groan, tipping my head back.

"Yeah, your aunt and uncle caught her weeks ago and just let her be." Vin chuckles. "She thought she was slick."

They laugh and after a bit, I join in too. It is pretty disgraceful that I don't know how to sneak out of my house. In my defense, I never had a parent who cared if I came and went before, so it's all new to me.

"Carm didn't come?" Vin asks, his eyebrow shooting up as he flicks his gaze to mine.

"Nah, he had a ton of work." Emmett shrugs. "Just me."

"That's cool." Vin walks up to the TV and grabs a PlayStation controller. "You game?"

"Yeah, sometimes." Emmett perks up, his eyes flaring with interest.

"Let's play," Vin says as he flips through the games my uncle has.

They settle into the sofa as warmth gathers inside me at the sight of them together. They are both important to me and I'm happy they're getting along. Tonight I'll spend some time with Emmett and Vin, and then tomorrow, I'll invite Travis and Adri over. It's not selfish to want them both to myself for one night.

Chapter Eighteen

Adri: Hot brother is here? Count me in.

This bitch. Now I regret asking her if she wanted to come hang out with us today. Travis still hasn't answered my text and I'm getting the feeling he is not liking the idea of Emmett being here.

Me: I take it back, keep your slut-ass home.

Adri: C U in 10!

I smile and shake my head. She is my bestie, slut or not. Vin and Emmett are tossing a football around in the backyard and watching them only makes me want this to work more. I want Emmett to live here because I'm sick of that empty place in my heart that only grows when we're apart.

Travis: I guess. Need beer?

Finally, he replies. He doesn't sound too enthused though, but I can work with that. As long as I keep bringing them together and they hang out a bit more, they will like each other. I just know it. I lie back on my lounger by the pool and try to catch some sun, waiting for the others to get here.

"You have Father's skin tone." Opening my eyes, I find Emmett sitting in the chair beside mine.

"I noticed that." Smiling, I nod. "You have more of Mom's skin tone. Be careful, she would freckle in the sun."

"I freckle on my nose and cheeks in the summer." He smiles as he squints, then shields his eyes with his hand.

"Do you have any girlfriends back in New York?" I ask teasingly.

"Nah, not for a while. No one has caught my eye recently." He shrugs, sounding a little like he's avoiding telling me too much.

"What type of girls are you into?" I sit up on the chair and reach for my bottle of water.

"I don't really have a type…" he says, trailing off.

Vin comes over and pulls me up so I can lie on him as he settles in behind me. I love the heat from his skin, and I instantly relax. The scent of his coconut lotion and Dolce cologne is an intoxicating mix and wholly Vin.

"I want to do something different today," I tell them as I wiggle my toes. "I'm tired of drinking beer and chilling by some body of water." Vin chuckles behind me.

"We should get tattoos," Emmett pipes up, his face filled with exuberance.

"Yes!" I sit up as excitement courses through me. "That's a great idea! Do you want something that matches?"

"Yeah, I'd like that." Emmett nods as the excitement grows between us.

"Do you have any tattoos?" I lean toward him as he smirks.

"Yeah, my back is done." He pulls off his T-shirt and turns his back to me. It's completely covered in a large tattoo depicting a scene with a young boy and what looks to be the Grim Reaper holding hands. Trees surround them and the moon is shining down on them. Both have their backs turned, but a side profile of the boy is visible as he looks up at the Grim Reaper with awe. It's fucking dark but filled with sorrow. It somehow twists my insides.

"Why this?" I whisper, the scene growing more desolate the longer I stare at it.

"It depicts the death of my innocence," he mutters as he shrugs his shirt back on.

"What happened?" The words fly out of my mouth with little thought, then guilt crashes through me when his face falls.

"Can we save that for another time?" he asks me, his expression filled with pleading, and I'm glad because I don't think I can handle hearing what happened to his innocence just yet.

"Yeah, we can," Vin answers as his arms tighten around me. "We don't pry."

Relief is palpable as my brother's shoulders relax and his eyes fill with gratitude. "Thanks, man."

"Okay, I want a yin and yang tattoo with Emmett," I say, changing the subject.

"Yin and yang?" Emmett asks as relief shines through his eyes.

"Yeah, opposites that belong together. Me and you. Twins. Get it?"

"I like it." He swallows thickly while averting his glossy eyes.

"I want mine on my shoulder blade. Where are you going to put yours?" I ask him, forcing him to look at me again.

His throat works a bit as he thinks, his teeth chewing into his cheek. "My chest. Over my heart."

"Vin will design it, right, baby?" I look over my shoulder at my man as he gives me a surprised look.

"Me?" His eyes flick between me and Emmett, wondering if this is all a joke.

"Yes, please. Something just for us." I turn back to look at Emmett as my chest swells with emotion. I feared my capability to love as I did before the kidnapping was gone completely, but it's clear I just needed a little blood and a twin brother. "Vin is an artist."

"I can do that." Vin's face lands in the crook of my neck as I grin at Emmett. I can't wait to see what he designs for us.

The doorbell rings and I stand to answer it while Vin and Emmett are in a deep discussion regarding the tattoo. When I approach the door, both Travis and Adri are outside, and by the sounds of it, they're already bickering.

"You want him," Travis says with a sneer.

"Doesn't matter what I want. Ember will kill me," Adri replies, her voice low.

"That's the only reason, huh?"

I pull the door open at that exact moment and stand in front of them with my arms crossed. "What the fuck is the actual problem here?" I snap. Both have the common sense to look chastised for their childish behavior, but it does nothing to soothe the anger coursing through me.

"He's being a jealous freak," Adri points out, her eyes unable to meet mine as she keeps them downcast, her arms over her chest.

"And you're being a bitch," Travis retorts as he pushes by me into the house.

"Hold up," I start as I grab his arm. "I will not have this shit in my house today. Understand? Emmett has no intention of dealing with Adri, and I want him to have fun while he's here."

"Yeah, I hear you," he says and pulls his arm out of my hand.

"And, you,"—I turn to Adri—"stop pitting them against each other. I already told you once to lay off." Her cheeks are red as she shuffles from foot to foot, her eyes meeting mine.

"Ember…"

"No, I'm fucking serious. Whatever game you are trying to play, go back to using Danny instead and leave my fucking brother out of it," I cut her off. Her head snaps back as if I've spat in her face, the look of hurt clouding her eyes.

"I wouldn't do that," she swears with her brows crinkled.

Turning around, I head back to the backyard without entertaining the immaturity further. All three guys are huddled around the table and going over the sketch Vin is drawing as I head to my chair, Adri's shuffling feet sounding behind me. Travis has lost the hostile energy and actually joined in on their conversation, and I smile as I sit down on my lounge chair and Adri sits in the one beside mine.

"I'm sorry," she whispers, the anguish clear in her tone.

"It's okay," I assure her as I turn in my chair to face her. She's wringing her hands in her lap, her cheeks still a bright red. "But you need to stop commenting about Emmett. He doesn't deserve Travis' wrath."

"You think I want that?" She looks shocked, her eyes flicking to the boys at the table. "I don't want to cause any problems."

"Then don't." I look her in the eyes, making sure she sees the warning in mine, and she gives me a quick nod before lying back in her chair. I'm not having a good friend of mine going after my brother because my bestie has hormonal issues. It's just not happening. I'll squash that right here and now.

A few hours later, we exit the tattoo parlor with our new tattoos. Vin designed us a simple yin and yang feather and we changed our minds and placed it on our wrists. That way, when we touch our arms side to side, the yin and yang become whole. It's a perfect depiction for our situation because now that he's here, we're whole.

We all head back to my house, have a barbeque, and hang out poolside. I'm kind of panicking because I still need to come up with a believable scenario to explain to my parents about finding Emmett.

"Listen, you could say Juan found me and we looked so much alike he dug around and learned I was adopted and recently my adoptive parents died," Emmett says, sitting beside me. He knew exactly what I was thinking about, taking our twintuition to the next level.

"That's not half bad." I tap my chin, trying to think of all the holes they can punch in that story.

"Yeah, we can iron it out over this week, and maybe you take a trip to New York to visit me next weekend." Driving back and forth to New York is tedious, especially when I've been doing it on a weekly basis, but this is my brother. *My brother.* I never imagined I'd ever say that.

"Okay, that sounds like a deal." I punch his arm lightly and he turns to look at me, his eyes filled with longing.

"Being apart is hard, Ember," he admits as he looks down at his shoes. "I've never had an actual family. Sure, I had Carm, but he was absent a lot. I can have a real family with you." When he looks back up at me, the look of fear in his eyes tugs on my heartstrings. I'll promise him anything right now if it means he'll be happy.

"We'll figure it all out, I promise."

The next morning, I am awoken by Vin's annoying ringtone. We both groan, and I flip the blankets over my head.

"It's my mom," he rasps, his voice deep with sleep. "What's up, Ma?" He picks up, sounding bothered. "Wait... slow down..." I immediately sit up in bed because the panic in his voice sounds like something terrible is happening. "Oh, my god..." he mumbles, his eyes finding mine, horror growing in his green depths. "When?"

"What is it?" I whisper to him, my heart crashing into my rib cage as my lungs cease.

"I need to talk to Em, Ma," he says, his voice cracking with emotion. "Okay, I will call you back." He hangs up the phone and looks at me.

"Vincent, what is it?" I ask sternly, my mouth drying out as I struggle to swallow the lump in my throat.

"We need to go to the hospital right now." He jumps out of bed and grabs his sweater off my chair. "There's been an accident." His words are rushed as his face drains of color.

"Wait... what?" I shake my head as confusion keeps me rooted to the spot in my bed. Accident?

"Your parents, Em!" he yells, the sudden rise of his voice startling me. "Let's go. They are at the hospital."

"Hospital...?" My body grows heavy and cold all at once. I can't go through this again.

"Ember,"—Vin grabs my face—"we need to leave."

"Vin, I can't move. I'm so scared," I confess as the sight of him blurs with the tears gathering in my eyes.

"Baby, I will be with you through everything, but we have to leave, now." He lifts me out of bed and brings me into my closet. I don't pay attention to what he's dressing me in, and when he leaves me to brush my teeth, I nearly fall to the floor in a panic.

After he's done telling Emmett, Adri, and Travis what's going on, he comes back to sit me on the counter and brush my teeth for me. Then he brushes my hair and puts it up in a ponytail.

"I love you, Em." He kisses my cheek before lifting me down from the counter to lead me out of the room.

We head downstairs to find Emmett sitting at the bottom. "Should I stay?" He looks up at me with sympathetic eyes. "Will you need me?"

I say nothing and sit on the step behind him to wrap my arms around his neck and push my face into his hair. If I had any other choice, I would stay right here, breathing in the scent of my twin and trying not to lose it completely.

"Stay," Vin says. "I'm not sure when we'll be back, but it would be nice to have you here when we do." He's trying to sound strong, but he can't hide the slight tremor in his voice. Not from me.

"Okay." Emmett nods, his hair brushing along my cheek. Then he turns around and hugs me back. "I'll be here waiting for you."

I nod and stand up as Vin moves to my side in an instant, picking me up to cradle me against his chest. Sinking into his warmth, I send up a silent plea to the man upstairs. *I promise to stop everything if it means they're okay.* I don't bother to think of the depths I'll sink to if they're not.

Vin

The hospital they are in is about an hour away and near the spa. My mother is already on her way to meet us, making me worry about her state of mind while driving. Ember has had her head back against the headrest and her eyes closed this entire time. She isn't sleeping but I don't bother her, knowing she needs this time to prepare herself, despite the slight hitches in her breathing now and then breaking my fucking heart.

The spa called my mother because she's usually the one to spend a weekend with Debra, but they didn't provide her with much information. Only that it was a boating accident. It's easy to jump to conclusions with that, and I refuse to let my mind wander to the worst-case scenarios. I have to be strong for Ember, but I can't help this nagging feeling I'm getting in the pit of my stomach. What the fuck actually happened? Scott is good on a boat, actually, he's better than good. He has taken our speedboat out at the cottage many times.

"We're here," I tell her softly as we pull into the emergency parking spot of the hospital. As soon as I park, Ember flies through the door and is across the parking lot, and I run to catch up to her as she reaches the entrance.

"Ember! Vin!" my mother shouts from the front desk. "Over here."

We run to join my mother, who is looking very irate with the woman behind the counter. Ember leans over and looks the woman in the eyes with her very intimidating self. "Where are my parents?" she grits out.

"They won't give me any information," my mother says to

me, her cheeks saturated in tears as her body trembles. I pull her in close, pressing her face into my chest. "I'm not an immediate family member."

"Like hell you're not." I nod to Ember. "She'll sort it out."

"The doctor is on his way out. He will speak to you shortly. Can you please follow me to the waiting area for family?" the nurse says to Ember, the pitying look in her eyes not sitting well with me.

"They come too." She points at us, and it looks like the nurse wants to argue, but as soon as she gazes into Ember's face, she agrees. Smart lady.

This is bad. You don't wait in a family room for minor injuries. Both are strong swimmers, so what type of accident was this? We enter the waiting room, and I sit beside my mother while Ember paces back and forth. She's getting the rush of energy adrenaline brings her, and this is her only option of draining it right now.

"If he is not here in five minutes, I am going to drag that nurse back in here," she grinds out, her body stiff and her fists tight at her sides.

"Geez," my mother breathes out, "she's a force."

"You have no idea."

About four minutes later, a doctor enters the room and I breathe a sigh of relief for the nurse escaping Ember's wrath. He looks at each of us before sitting down in a chair.

"There has been a serious accident involving both Scott and Debra very early this morning," he begins, his tone professional and even. "They took a speedboat out onto the water and collided with the side of a cliff, causing the motor to explode on impact."

"Collided with a cliff?" Ember looks confused as she stands

in the center of the room, her chest heaving as if she ran a marathon. "How?"

"I don't have details as the police are investigating, but we did a toxicology test. It'll be back soon." His words are fading, almost like I'm slowly sinking under water, the waves crashing into my ears. My mother falls against my side as she cries, her body shaking with the force.

"I need to see them," Ember says, her chin trembling as she tries her best to contain her emotions.

"There's more." He scrubs his hand down his face, then looks at each of us. "Scott died on impact, but Debra survived the crash. Another passing boat pulled her out of the water."

Ember sinks to the ground, her body crumbling as she buries her face in her hands. Rushing forward, I crouch down beside her and wrap my arms around her. Her body is limp as she falls against me, my mother's wails filling the room.

"I'm sorry, but there's more." The doctor crouches down in front of Ember and places his hand on her head, the connection making her look up into his face. "They brought Debra here and we performed all lifesaving measures, but she succumbed to her injuries soon after."

Oh, fuck.

Both...

They both passed away.

Ember is now orphaned for the second time in less than a year. The doctor's hand drops away, and she hasn't made a single noise since he broke the news, nor has she moved, save for the trembling throughout her body. My mother's wails intensify when she realizes her lifelong best friend is gone forever.

"I will give you a few minutes." The doctor rises, and with a backward sympathetic glance, leaves the room.

"Em?" I whisper in her ear.

"Yeah?" she answers with a small voice, her eyes on the floor and her body curled inward.

"What do you need right now?" I would do any-fucking-thing right now. Anything she asks of me. Anything to take her pain away.

"I need to find out how this happened." Fuck, her voice sounds so broken. My mother's cries continue around us, the sound only heightening the grief threatening to suffocate us all.

"Ma, please calm down." I look at my sobbing mother with pleading eyes. She lost her lifelong friends, but Ember has lost her parents for the second time in her life. My mother holds her hand over her face and whimpers but nods at me.

At that moment, the door opens again, and in walks two detectives, one female and one male. Both have faces filled with sympathy as their gazes meet Ember still kneeling on the floor. The woman has a makeup-free stern face, her hair pulled back into a tight bun, and stands at around Ember's height of 5'8". The guy is a little on the pudgy side, around the same height as the female, and with a balding head.

"Sorry, Miss," the male starts. "You're the niece?"

"I'm the daughter," Ember answers shortly, her body stiffening as she glares at them.

"Oh, right. Yes, sorry." The man shakes his head. "I was hoping you would answer a few questions?" He has enough sense to look chastised.

"Like what? I wasn't there." I rub circles against her back, hoping the touch reminds her she's not alone, but there's no indication that she even feels me.

"We understand that." The woman moves to take the seat the doctor vacated. "We were hoping you can give us an insight into your parents' life."

"Okay…" Ember looks up at her with a frown, confusion wrapped around that single word.

"These are routine questions," the male states. "Just answer as best you can."

"Did your parents partake in alcohol regularly?" the woman asks as she flips open a notebook and clicks open a pen.

"Regular basis?" Ember repeats as she shakes her head. I don't like where these routine questions are headed. "Maybe a glass of wine with dinner, not much more than that. On weekends, my dad would have a beer while he had sports on the TV."

"How about any prescription drugs?" The male cop leans forward, hanging on every one of Ember's words.

"I don't know i–if they h–had any prescriptions." Ember shakes her head, her confusion making her skip her words.

"No," my mother chimes in, "they were not on any prescribed medication."

"And you are?" the male asks my mother, his tone soft as he takes in my mother's distraught state.

"Sharla Germaine. I was very close to Scott and Debra." Her voice cracks as she sucks in a breath, stopping a sob in its tracks. I'm proud of her and how strong she's staying; she must be dying inside.

"Thank you for that." The female nods. "That's all we need

for right now. I need an identity confirmation on the bodies." She cringes as her gaze swings around the room before landing on Ember. I open my mouth to berate her for even thinking my girl should do that when my mother steps in.

"I will do it." She stands up from her seat, clutching her purse to her chest as tears run in never-ending rivulets down her cheeks.

"Okay, great." The male gives her a small smile and motions her to follow him out of the room. "We'll follow up with you, Ember, regarding any new information we find."

The three of them exit the room, and Ember begins to tremble again, her body nearly vibrating with suppressed grief. Pulling her into my chest, I try to figure out what we are going to do.

"I need to leave and go home," Ember says, her voice shaking.

"Let's go." Standing up, I haul her up with me, keeping my arm around her waist. I'll fucking carry her out of here if that's what she needs. "I'll text my mom and tell her we're leaving."

A nurse is sitting at the front desk as I lead Ember out of the room, and I don't miss the look of pity she sends us. Thank god Ember has her head pressed to my chest because I'm not sure how she'd react to seeing that right now. My girl never wants to be pitied. I'm actually not sure what's happening to Ember right now. I really don't know how she grieves and if this is it. Her emotions are rippling under the surface, that much I know, but they haven't broken through yet and I don't have a fucking clue if they even will.

We get in the Hummer, and I sit back in the driver's seat, my head hitting the headrest. I've been so focused on Em that I've given no thought to myself. These people helped raise me when my father ditched us. Scott was the only father figure I had, and Debra made sure I had a full three meals when my mother worked all day and night. This is the first time I've truly lost someone close to me. My circle is small, and no deaths have entered its circumference before today. In just a few hours, I've lost two.

"Vin?" Ember breathes out beside me.

"Yeah?" I look at her, and she lifts her hand to wipe the tear from my right cheek. I didn't even realize I was crying.

"Oh god." She covers her mouth with both hands as a sob breaks through, the motion jarring her entire body.

"Come here." I grab her and pull her over the console between us. Her knees fall to either side of my waist as her body quakes, and she sobs uncontrollably in my arms. "I will always be here."

"What's going to happen now?" she hiccups into my neck.

"Doesn't matter." I shake my head as tears drip off my jaw. "We'll deal with it together."

She buries her face farther into my neck and continues to sob for her aunt and uncle. For the two strangers who took her in without a second thought and then adopted her, wanting to be her parents. After a while, Ember pulls away and wipes her face. She's red and puffy but still so fucking beautiful.

"Emmett." Her chin trembles again. "He'll never meet his mother's family." Her face falls as the tears run anew, the sight pulverizing my heart in a second.

"Yes, he will. He has you. You'll be the best source to tell him about your mother and her family." Her face falls again before she turns to look out of the window, her jaw clenching with the effort to hold herself together.

"I have to call him." She grabs her phone out of her hoodie pocket as I open the vehicle door and move her to sit in the driver's seat while I walk outside, giving her privacy to talk to her brother.

"Vincent!" Ma calls out as she's exiting the hospital, and I wave her over to me. "It's them." Her voice cracks and the sound is hoarse, and her face looks ashen as her bloodshot eyes begin to water.

"Yeah." I didn't once doubt it.

"Ember can come stay with us. Maybe I can hold off Social Services." My heart drops. I didn't even fucking think of that. Ember is still seventeen, not yet an adult in the eyes of the law. She may be put into foster care until she comes of age. "She is going to be coming into a lot of money as well. Not just Scott and Debra's but also her grandparents' money. We will have to speak to Deb and Scott's lawyer."

"*She* will have to, Ma, not us. All of this is Ember's say," I remind her, placing a hand on her shoulder. I love how she wants to guide Ember and be there for her, but in the end, these are Ember's choices.

"Yes, of course." Ma nods as she strains to hold in her emotions. Then she looks into the Hummer to find Ember hunched over in the driver's seat with her phone to her ear as she rocks back and forth. "Poor girl."

"I'm going to drive her home, and we'll talk to you later."

"Okay." She pats my cheek as she sucks in a breath before walking over to her car, her sobs meeting my ears as she climbs inside.

As we're driving home, Ember finally passes out from exhaustion. I watch her slim shoulders move with each breath and my heart jerks inside my chest. I need to remember, as strong as she is, she's still human, and right now, her heart is completely broken.

CHAPTER NINETEEN

I'm lying on a bed in a darkened room, my eyes slowly focusing as I recognize the room Emmett took when he came to visit. My heart is racing as I sit up in bed. Where are Vin and Emmett?

"Ember, chill," Emmett's sleepy voice rasps from beside me on the king-sized bed.

"Why am I here?" My voice is hoarse with the effort to speak, as if I've been crying for hours. Having Emmett beside me soothes a bit of the agony, but my chest is still ripping with the pain of losing my parents.

"Vin put you here when you got back so you wouldn't wake up alone. You were crying in your sleep and asking for me," he says softly. "So I laid down with you."

"Where's Vin?" I rub the sleep from my swollen eyes and swallow down the sob working its way up from my chest.

"At his house, talking to his mother. I believe he is trying to figure out a way for you to stay with them since you're still a minor." He sits up beside me. "I think you need to contact your aunt and uncle's lawyer and ask about emancipation," he advises as he brushes his tousled hair out of his face.

"Emancipated?" I wince at the thought of no longer being the legal daughter of Debra and Scott Williams.

"Yes, Ember. Child Services can put you into the system for a year until you are of age. Deal with it now. Push the grief down and contact the lawyer. When all is done and secure, grieve. I'll be with you when you need me." He sounds firm but his tone is soft, like he's afraid I'll break, but he's right, I should contact the lawyer. This house, the cars in the garage, and businesses need to be taken care of.

I'm the only legal family left here, and it's my responsibility to maintain our assets. With an excuse to bury the grief, I jump out of bed and head downstairs to my dad's office, Emmett close behind me. Dad has to have the family lawyer information in here somewhere. I sit at his large oak desk and start going through the Rolodex, a few pages yellowing with age. Emmett sits in a chair across from me and scrolls through his phone.

"I tried texting Carm. He hasn't answered me yet," he informs me, his mouth turned down with disappointment. I'm a little disappointed too, considering Carm didn't even bother trying to reach out to me after what happened to my parents.

"He's expecting you home today, right?" I keep my eyes on him as his jaw works with irritation, his thumbs furiously flying over the face of his phone.

"Yeah. Usually he's on my ass when I'm riding the bike, but he hasn't messaged me once." That's a little concerning, and I tap my fingers along the top of the Rolodex.

"Huh." *Tap, tap, tap.* "That is weird. Call one of his minions and find out what the fuck is up." Maybe Carm found himself on the wrong end of a gun. Wouldn't be the first time. There should be some emotion in my words, anything to show my twin that I care about the well-being of our brother, but I can't seem to muster it up.

He nods and rises from the chair to take the call outside. I proceed scrolling through the Rolodex until I come across a Dean, Cole, and Associates. It's the first lawyer's contact information that I've found, so I swipe open my phone. As I'm punching the numbers into my cell phone, a call comes through from an unknown number.

"Hello?" I pick up, my voice a little hesitant. Unknown numbers freak me out.

"Emberlise Craven?" a man with a terrible nasally voice asks.

"This is her." A tremor works its way from the tips of my fingers and up my arms. Is this Child Services?

"My name is Anderson. I am a lawyer with Dean, Cole, and Associates." The relief is immediate as I slump in the desk chair with a loud exhale.

"Wow," I breathe out and shake my head at the coincidence.

"Excuse me?" he says as papers shuffle on his end of the line.

"Sorry, I was just about to call you," I reveal.

"Oh! We received a call regarding Debra and Scott today. I am so sorry for your loss." The emotionless sympathy doesn't bother me in the least. This is business to him and I appreciate him not being fake about it.

"Thank you," I say, and as I'm about to open my mouth to ask about emancipation, he continues.

"I have their last will and testament here in front of me. As you're probably aware, they've left everything to you." More papers are shuffling as he clears his throat.

"How would I be aware?" I ask, my tone petulant as I straighten in my seat, my fingers rubbing into my temple. "We never discussed that."

"Of course not." He pauses, then shuffling filters through again. "You are currently seventeen. Do you have any other family?"

"No. That's the reason I was reaching out to you," I explain. "For emancipation papers. Is that possible?"

"Yes, of course. I'm your family lawyer, therefore, I am your lawyer as well. I'll start working on those papers, and I'm sending over my assistant with the will document." Appreciation flows through me at his no-nonsense way of doing business, and I imagine Dad did as well. The thought has my throat sealing as my sight becomes blurry.

I take a deep breath and push all the emotions back down. "Great. Thank you, Anderson. I'll be in touch."

I end the call and exit the office, bumping into Emmett at the bottom of the stairs. He's sitting with his head in his hands and muttering profanities. "What's going on?" I ask him.

"I got a hold of Trent. He's Carm's right-hand man." He looks up at me, anger flaring in his eyes. "Carm is on his way here and he's bringing information regarding our aunt and uncle's death."

"Information?" My spine straightens as my head begins to throb.

"That's all I got out of him. Fuck, I would guess it was a hit." My heart beats into my rib cage as I grab onto the railing for support. That can't be right.

"A hit?" I sound stupid, my words repetitious, but nothing is making sense right now.

"Ember, he'll be here in a few hours. Go rest until then." Emmett stands and puts his hand on my shoulder, worry reflecting in his features.

"No, I need to call Vin." I fist my hands to stop them from shaking as I bite into my cheek until blood coats my tongue. Pain flares and with it, a sense of relief. I haven't become numb like I was after killing my father. Not yet anyway.

I go back into my dad's office and shut myself in. A hit… Who would want to put a hit out on my family? Was it a Head? But why? Maybe having a young girl in their midst is intimidating?

Once the questions subside, the anger rolls in, red and hot.

Someone put a hit on my family… Someone played with what's mine. Someone is sending me a message, and I have received it loud and clear. The familiar fire of lava pools in my belly, slowly spreading under my skin and heating me from the inside out. The edges of my vision pulse with each heartbeat, telling me what's coming next. I try to breathe through it, I really try to calm myself down, but I'm helpless as my vision bleeds into red, and nothing short of blood will make it stop.

"She's been inside for a while. The door is locked." Emmett's voice enters my red haze, breaking through the rage. "I called you because I'm worried."

"Good choice." Hearing Vin's voice instantly sends a cooling effect over my heated skin. "Em? What's going on, baby?" he calls through the door as he tries to turn the knob. The red is still clouding my thoughts and vision as I stand from the desk and try to make my way to the door. My heart rate picks up again and the lava bubbles. "Ember?" he repeats, his tone a bit frantic. Again, his voice is like a balm, immediately soothing the bubbling rage. I press my face to the wooden slab and take a deep breath.

"I can't open the door yet. I don't feel right." The sound of my voice is muffled as though I'm under water, the sound of my anger rushing through my ears like a tsunami. My confession leaves me breathless as I let the cool surface spread over my face.

"Like what, Em? What are you feeling?" He's right on the other side, the wood the only thing separating us.

"Angry," I growl, my nails scraping over the surface of the door.

"Okay," he rasps. "I'll sit here and wait with you."

The shuffling on the other side of the door sounds as though his back is pressing into it and sliding down to the floor, and his shadow grows in the crack at the bottom as I do the same. My skin is hot and flushed, my chest hurts like I've run a marathon, and my vision is still clouded in red hues.

"Tell me what you're thinking," he whispers from the other side.

"Like I want to kill. To have someone's blood coat my hands as I break open flesh," I answer truthfully with a voice sounding heavy with lust as my chest heaves with my panting. His quick intake of breath sounds through the wood as I continue. "I want bones crushing under my fists as life slowly drains from someone's eyes. Scared, lost, then vacant."

"Fuck." He sighs from the other side. "That's dark, Em."

"I'm dark, Vin," I retort. His closeness and his voice have

lessened the red clouds from my vision and I can finally breathe, filling my lungs with air. The panting has gone and all that remains is anger. I firmly tuck my rage back, waiting for the opportune moment for it to be released.

Slowly, I stand, feeling slightly lightheaded, and reach for the door handle. I unlock it as Vin scrambles to his feet on the other side. Then he pulls me into his arms as soon as he can grab me.

"Are you okay?" he mumbles into my hair as my arms hang limply at my sides.

"No," I answer honestly. "I'm not okay. Is Carm here yet?"

"He texted me and said he was another hour out," Emmett answers, standing over by the stairs with his arms crossed in front of his chest.

"My mother and I think it's best if you stay with us for the rest of this year. Social Services can be a bitch," Vin says, looking down into my eyes.

"Emancipation. I spoke to the family lawyer already." My shoulders slump forward as my adrenaline begins to fade. "I am not leaving my parents' house and all their valuables unattended."

"Okay…" He sounds unsure. "That's another option."

"It's the only option." I pull away from him.

My hands tremble with the aftereffect of my rage and I try to shake them out as I take a deep breath. Emmett is watching me closely with narrowed eyes, and I can't reassure him that this doesn't happen often. I can't console him or his worried expression. So I remain quiet and make my way to the kitchen. Carm needs to hurry.

The doorbell rings and Emmett flies out of his seat at the kitchen table and toward the front door. It's Carm. I watched his familiar sedan enter the driveway from the cameras connected to my phone. Sitting still in my seat at the table, I keep an eye on their interaction at the front door.

"Anything suspicious?" Vin asks from the other side of the table, his hands twitching on the wood.

"Not yet," I answer, my eyes never straying from my brothers as they whisper together.

Then they both walk down the hallway and enter the kitchen. Carm looks tired and unkept, his hair limp with bags under his eyes that almost look like bruising. I sit quietly as he pulls up a chair and sits across from me beside Vin.

"Ember, I am so very sorry for your loss," he starts, sounding tired as he scrubs at his face. "As soon as I received the information, I came straight here."

"You should have called me right away," I grit out, my anger flaring to the surface of my cool facade. "Not make me wait."

"I can never do that. Your phone lines may all be bugged and you don't know who's listening."

"What is it?" Vin waves him on, also done waiting.

"I received a message late last night." His chin drops to his chest as he curls his fingers into fists on the table. "We found one of my men killed and a message carved into his chest."

"Carved into his chest?" Emmett asks Carm but looks at me

with his eyebrows raised. I nod because it's exactly what he and I did to the detention center perv.

"Yes, it said, 'We are even -Talia.'" Carm runs his hand through his messy hair and exhales a heavy breath. "I've been trying to figure it all out."

"'We are even'?" I question as my brows come together in thought.

"Yes, and a separate message carved into his back. 'You took my family, so I took yours.'" Carm sounds defeated as he shakes his head. "I have been trying to locate her, but she is just too fucking slippery."

"I took her family? Hold on… Does she mean our piece of shit father?" I exclaim, surprise making my mouth fall open.

"I assume so. Unless you've been hunting her and her family recently." He slumps back in his chair as my surprise gives way to rage. His brows raise when he looks me in the eyes. "Stand down, Ember. Let me take care of this."

"No way!" I shout as my palms slap against the table, making Emmett wince.

"Yes, way." Carm holds his hands up. "We need to do this smart, Ember. We can't just go in guns blazing, okay?"

"Do you have a location where we can go with our guns blazing? Do you have any information for me? I have received nothing about the supposed meeting you had with her." I lean over the table as Vin's jaw tics with agitation. Something feels off and I'd hate for my brother to meet the pointy end of my blade because it might make Emmett mad at me.

"A man was sent in her place. They asked me to hand you over. I believe this was her retaliation when I didn't comply. There's very little information, I admit, but after today, we are going in full force. I'll have more information for you by the end of the week," he promises, but I'm beginning to realize his promises are all empty.

"You should've told me about that! My *family* would still be alive." His wince has my heart squeezing in my chest. Carm has taken a lot on recently, and if I'm being honest, I haven't really checked in with him. Honestly, I don't think I ever have, but he was my one-time kidnapper and didn't really deserve it. Lately, all I've been doing is asking for his help, but this is important and he's dropped the ball too many times when it came to giving me information I've asked for. "Just get me the information this week." I smile wide and he visibly swallows at my forced pleasantry. "Go on upstairs and get some rest. You look like shit. Emmett, show him the spare rooms."

Emmett nods and leads our brother out of the kitchen and up the stairs. So, this was all Jennifer Talia's doing, and Carm has not given me one thing to work with in the last few weeks. Is she really this evasive or has she just not been made a priority? Thanks to Robert, I have a pretty thick file on Ms. Talia, but I can't work on it with Vin here. As much as I want to clue him in, I can't explain how I got that file and I never want to lie to him.

"I'm going into Dad's office to see if I can find any information on accounts and properties. Would you be able to chill with Emmett?" I give him puppy dog eyes while my stomach sours with my deception. It's necessary and that's what I tell myself when it rolls off my tongue. "I don't mean to make you a babysitter."

"Yeah, it's cool. I should actually go take inventory of the cars in the garage. You'll need help with that business." He swallows thickly as he looks down at his hands, his despair hitting me like a tidal wave. Vin is grieving too. Despite everything I'm feeling right now, I have to remember that.

"You're right." I try to blink past my tears. "He would've really appreciated you doing that."

Vin stands, then saunters over to me and cages me in on the chair with his arms on either side of me. His bright green eyes look deep into mine as he pulls his bottom lip into his mouth, biting down with his pearly white teeth. He's providing me with the distraction I need to push down the grief. Holy fuck, how is he this hot? It's not fair to other men to be compared to this perfection. He notices my close inspection of his mouth and grins, running his pierced tongue along his bottom lip. I moan as I envision where I want his tongue right now. Then he leans in close, his lips glistening as his tongue flicks out and licks along my lips.

"Fuck," I groan against his mouth. "Take your pants off." He's giving me a distraction and it's working too well, not that I mind.

"You want to do this on top of the dining table?" He pulls back and barks out a laugh.

"Yes." I nod emphatically. "Do it." I'm not even bluffing, and it's disturbing that I don't care that my brothers could walk in at any moment. Not that it would deter me at all, because when we're like this, Vin is all I see.

"Can't, baby. I need to babysit," he throws back at me, his smirk cocky as hell.

"Leave now, or I'm taking my pants off," I threaten as his grin widens and his love for me shines bright from his eyes.

"Okay." He leans in and presses his mouth to mine in a very chaste kiss. "I love you."

"Mmhm." I cross my arms over my chest like a petulant child.

He chuckles as he backs up and walks out of the kitchen in search of my twin brother while I shake off the lust and try to calm my clenching vagina. *Sorry, girl. We got work to do.* I head to my dad's office, closing and locking the door behind me, then proceed to my hiding spot. Knowing I had sensitive information, I hid it in the most secure place I could think of. I stuck it into an old binder that I knew my dad wouldn't look in. Finding the file, I take it to the desk before sitting in Dad's over-plush leather chair. Then I take a deep breath and bury my emotions because I need to be analytical with this information.

Opening the file, the first thing I see is her picture with her career and schooling information. She is indeed a New York senator, which these days means shit. If you have the money for a campaign and can lie through your teeth—you're a shoo-in. Studying her picture, I deduce she's in her late forties and slightly overweight. Nothing of actual use to me except to spot her in a crowd, so I commit her face to memory and turn the page.

It shows her three unique properties in New York. This would be easy information to find and not at all hidden. My guess is she either fluctuates between these or doesn't stay in any of them. Again useless, but good to have as a backup. One address catches my eye because it's a penthouse unit in a building next to the one Robert gave to Vin. Do all criminal pieces of shit gravitate to this upscale area?

The next page shows a picture of two young boys. Now we're getting somewhere. I read their birth dates and calculate that they're five years apart. This is an old picture because their birth dates put the oldest at twenty-one and the youngest at sixteen. The oldest named Carlos, last name Vergara—different from his mother's—is currently attending Columbia University's law program. He's in his third year and his grades look pretty fucking immaculate. The younger boy, Anthony Vergara, is attending a private school for boys. It looks prestigious and fucking pretentious. According to his grades, Mommy will have to rely on the oldest to follow in her footsteps while this one lives off a trust fund.

The next page gives me some medical information. Ms. Talia has had two cesarean sections and nearly died while having the second one. Not too useful except to assume that maybe the oldest is the easier golden boy and the youngest may be a pain in her ass, but again, that's just an assumption. The oldest also has asthma and has been seeing a psychiatrist because of depression. According to the psych's notes, he has been under a lot of pressure lately and has been prescribed Prozac.

No noted medical conditions for the youngest except a few ER visits for a broken arm and collarbone because of a dirt bike accident. The youngest seems to have mommy issues and is looking for attention. It's time to plan a trip back to New York. I've always wanted to attend university in the Big Apple, and Columbia is looking more and more appealing.

Vin

Debra and Scott's ashes arrived today and Ember has her emotions locked up tight. Since that day at the hospital, I have barely seen her tear up. This is her hit-planning mode and it makes me fucking nervous. She seals herself up in Scott's office for hours on end and if I don't bang the door down to remind her to eat, she won't. She's planning something and I am readying myself for a bomb.

The toxicology report also came in this morning and we learned that both Scott and Debra's blood alcohol level was almost double the legal limit. No traces of drugs were found, but they were extremely intoxicated. Now that it's confirmed this was a hit on them though, it makes more sense because Scott would never do anything to put Debra in danger. Unfortunately, my mother can never know the truth and she must live with the thought that they put themselves in that situation because they were too drunk.

Carm left to go back to New York yesterday. He tried to convince Emmett to go back with him, but he refused. He's staying here with Ember and enrolling himself into Precious Blood Academy for his senior year of high school. I had thought that Carm was his guardian, but according to Ember, Emmett emancipated himself after his father died, and that's where Em got the idea. Now, we have to figure out how to tell my mother—and the whole town of Whitsborough—where the fuck Emmett came from.

Ember has also come into more money and three properties. Two here in Whitsborough and one in Belize. The second one here belonged to her grandparents and has been rented out for years. She also found a storage unit rented under Debra's name that she's going to check out, which is probably filled with her grandparents' stuff when Debra and Scott cleared out the house to rent. Her family lawyer has also filed her emancipation papers and expedited them. She has a court date this coming Friday.

Planning the funerals rests on my mother's shoulders since Ember has no fucking clue what to do. Ember purchased them a family-sized mausoleum in Whitsborough Cemetery, and she says there will be a spot for all of us, including my mother. Of course, this sent my mother into a sobbing mess when she found out we would bury her with her lifelong friends and Ember's mother. Tomorrow, we have a small service for Debra and Scott at our local church, followed by a small gathering at the mausoleum. Ember wanted nothing too flashy, and we all agreed that her parents wouldn't want it either.

After her hearing on Friday, Em plans to head to New York and check out Columbia University. She says she's interested in maybe attending and that has me baffled. I always thought she wanted to do dramatic arts, but Columbia University doesn't have a program for that, which makes me suspicious of her intentions because Ember is going to Columbia for other reasons and those other reasons must have something to do with locking herself up in Scott's office and this Talia woman. If she doesn't let me in on this soon, I'll fuck the information out of her. A pleasurable experience for both parties.

"Em!" I yell through the door. "Dinner is ready."

"Okay!" her voice sounds from behind the wooden barrier.

I walk back into the kitchen and Emmett is at the stove, helping to prepare the meal, which has been the case all week. "She coming?" he asks, turning to look at me over his shoulder.

"Yeah, I guess so." It's honestly a toss-up whether she'll join us or not. She's been buried in Scott's office for hours at a time since their death and I've tried to stay out of her way, only forcing her to eat when it's been too long.

"Back to New York this weekend." He raises a brow at me as he continues to get the pasta started. "And Columbia?" Emmett is suspicious of his sister's motives as well, and it only solidifies my concerns. They have twintuition after all.

"Mm-hmm." I stand beside him at the stove as he stirs the sauce, our eyes clashing with mirrored worry.

"So, what's the real reason? Does Jennifer Talia teach 'How to Kill 101' on the weekends in lecture hall B? Can I bring my knives?" He drops the spoon to the tray on the counter and pretends to throw blades across the kitchen.

"She hasn't told me yet," I reply as I chuckle at his antics. "But I plan on finding out."

"Fucking right you will." He nods as his hands drop to curl around the back of a chair. His belief in my Ember-whispering skills is heartwarming.

"Find out what?" Em asks as she walks into the kitchen. Her hair is in a messy knot on her head and she's wearing a pair of leggings with an off-the-shoulder T-shirt, which looks exactly like what she was wearing yesterday.

"The reason we're going to Columbia this weekend," I answer her honestly, our eyes meeting briefly before she averts them.

"I told you," she says while studying her nails.

"You lied, but I'm waiting for you to rectify that." Her head snaps up and she gives me a guilty look before groaning.

"Fuck," she grits out, "fine."

Emmett smiles his psychotic-looking grin and brings the pasta he's been cooking to the table. Then we sit down and wait for Em to talk. "I found out that Jennifer Talia has two sons. One of them is an aspiring senator following in his mother's footsteps while attending Columbia Law."

"We're doing a hit this weekend?" Emmett asks, looking awfully giddy.

"No. Reconnaissance only this weekend," she states firmly as she reaches for the spoon to scoop herself a heaping portion. Reconnaissance, hits, blood, fighting, I'll condone all of it if it gives her back her appetite.

"Sounds good," I reply as I take the spoon once she's done and help myself. "You could've just told us all this. We would've helped you."

"I needed to keep myself occupied. Sorry I lied." She looks me in the eyes, shame reflected in their depths.

"Don't do it again," Emmett chastises and wags his finger at her before taking the spoon from me. We all laugh and everything seems normal once again. Well, our normal anyway.

I'm sitting in my Hummer waiting for Em to come out of the courthouse. Her brother is in the passenger seat, bobbing his head to some awful-sounding music filtering out from his earphones. Yesterday, we had a small service for Debra and Scott and the turnout was more than I'd expected. Debra had renovated many homes and Scott provided a special service, and those people were all very sad to learn about their passing. The charities they were involved in for the community showed up as well, and Ember promised to continue their work. Travis and Adri came, him on his own and Adri with her parents. I've been meaning to ask Ember about Travis and his mother, but I keep getting sidetracked. He's been trapped looking after her and has spent very little time with us since our father offed himself. I'd ask him myself but it's still awkward between us and I'm not completely sure he'd even be honest with me.

We decided Emmett shouldn't go to the funeral because we need a foolproof plan to bring him into the fold. Especially before we tell my mother because she's tenacious. Our stories have to add up, and I need to protect Em above all else. My mother is positive that this Ray character is Ember's father, and she remembers he was bad news. So, we are going to work off that. Carm has asked us not to bring him into it, as he has a whole fucking gang to hide. Fair enough.

The Eastside Rampage has commissioned Ember for a fight. It's not a hit, but it's teaching a certain gang member to stick to his lane. The plan this weekend is to do some lookout for Talia's son on Saturday and then a fight starring my girl the same night. Her fighting, killing, and just all-around scaring the shit out of me is wearing thin on my nerves. She puts herself in these dangerous positions for the rush and also for the reprieve it gives her, but fuck, it also adds unnecessary risks to her life. She'll slip through my fingers if I tell her, but I'm afraid that she'll crack soon. Something needs to breach those walls she's constructed and let the dam free so she can fucking heal. She needs to fucking grieve.

The doors to the courthouse open and my sexy-as-fuck woman walks out. Ember's wearing a nude pantsuit today with a lacy, black shirt underneath and some sexy-ass red-bottom shoes. She pulled her hair back into a low bun and wore next to no makeup, yet she still looks immaculate.

"My sister looks happy," Emmett drawls, reminding me he's in the vehicle. "She must've received the news she wanted."

Yeah, she looks smug, which is a fucking colossal relief. Not only does this make life easier without the added stress of her maybe having to live in a foster home, but she also said something about paying the judge a late-night visit if it didn't go her way. "Did you want to go back and grab your bike?" I ask him as I tear my gaze from Ember's approach. "Or are you coming back with us?"

"I should take the bike. I need to spend some time with Carm before I move here." He's being torn in two different directions, but I know his heart is here with Em.

"True," I agree. The door to the Hummer opens and Ember climbs into the back seat. Her perfume wafts to the front and I instantly grow hard. I look at her through my rearview mirror and match her smirk.

"Boys, you are looking at a grown-ass adult." She puts her hands in the air. Despite the humor, she's holding back the sadness consuming her eyes. She would rather be a daughter to Debra and Scott instead of a *grown-ass adult.*

"Congrats, womb-sharing demon." Emmett grins and Em rolls her eyes.

"Emmett is going to ride back on his bike, so we have to head back to the house first." I pull out of the parking lot and head back toward her house, the silence that follows becoming stifling.

"Okay," she finally responds, looking at him wide-eyed. "You are coming back though?"

"Yeah, I am." He nods and turns in his seat to face her. "You'll have to help me enroll for school."

"Okay." Relief eases her tense shoulders as she falls back against the seat, her forehead meeting the cool window.

"We should probably grab a hotel tonight, considering Emmett can't ride his bike for long distances," I suggest as I pull into the driveway.

"That's such a waste of time," Em whines. "Emmett, take my parents' Mercedes and leave the bike at the house."

Both Emmett and I turn in our seats to look at her. Since they returned her parents' car, she's barely even looked at it.

"You sure?" Emmett asks hesitantly, his eyes skipping from me to her.

"Yes." She nods as she opens the door and hops out of the Hummer.

We both turn to the front and side-eye each other, his brow raising as I give him a slight nod. Whatever Ember wants at this point is what will happen.

After switching vehicles and changing clothes, we are finally on our way. Ember is debriefing me on what will go down with the recon mission. This guy—Carlos—lives on campus and rarely leaves on the weekends. He's also a tutor, and on Saturdays, spends his time at the campus library. Our plan is to have Ember dolled up and visit the library, where she will engage with Carlos and try to tempt him to go out with her the following weekend. It pisses me off, but I just have to keep telling myself it's all a ploy. I can't bring myself to be fully on board with this because children should never pay the price of their parents' behavior, but I'm afraid to voice my opinion because I don't want to be left out and have something bad happen to her.

We should find out where Talia is and take the pound of flesh from her. I would absolutely take part in that. Her kids though, may not be evil like her. Take, for instance, Travis and I. He looks emo, sure, and he's looking like a kicked dog these days, but he is nothing like his father, and he would never do the shit Robert did. Me? Sure, I have this dark thread that runs through me and I enjoy certain aspects of life that a majority of people don't. I like to fight, and I enjoy watching my girl commit some heinous acts in the name of justice, but I'm not Robert's level of evil. Point being, Talia's offspring is probably nothing like her. The oldest rarely goes home. That must mean something.

"You're quiet," Em says in the darkened vehicle, pulling me from my thoughts.

"Just thinking." I quickly glance at her, finding her eyes on me, then flick mine back to the road.

"About?"

"This Talia woman and what we have to do this weekend."

She nods and rests her head back against the headrest. She's looking exhausted and I try to remember the last time she actually slept. I've been in her bed every night, but I don't stay all night so I haven't seen her sleep, and that fucking worries me. I make a mental note to ask Emmett to check in on her when I'm not there and make sure she's sleeping. Dire mistakes can happen when you're too exhausted to be ten steps ahead.

Watching the New York skyline and the lights of the Empire State Building at three in the morning is mesmerizing. We finally arrived here about thirty minutes ago, and Ember made a beeline for the cushy shower with the five hundred jets while I just needed to seek stillness and try to calm my thoughts. I never want to doubt Ember, but on this, I believe her logic is tormented with grief. If someone took my mother from me, I would want to retaliate too, but not like this. Not on the children, no matter how many sins of the parents they bear. I have to convince her to stick to the proper target, but I have to admit, it'd be better for her to meet him and maybe learn more about him. That way, she puts a human face and personality to her hit.

Through the reflection of the glass, a flicker of movement

catches my eye behind me. Ember approaches with no clothing on and her hair dripping water down her breasts and over her flat stomach. My eyes flick back up to her smirking face and find her eyes almost glowing in the dark, the bright green-blue stealing my breath. She walks in farther and her toned legs flex, causing drops of water to splash on the floor. She really is the most beautiful thing I have ever seen, and I will always thank god for bringing her to me.

I turn around, rip my shirt off over my head, and throw it to the ground. This week, while Ember was busy, I added some more ink of my own. Something for her—a statement—to say our relationship is forever. Over my heart, I got the infinity symbol. One side has her initials, E.C., and the other side has mine, V.G. Her eyes widen as she takes it in.

"When?" she breathes out, coming closer.

"A few days ago. It's still a little scabby, but it'll heal up in a week."

"Vin, it's amazing. I want one to match." Her eyes focus on the tattoo as I soak in her surprise.

"Okay, baby." I smile as I trail my fingers over her wet hair.

She runs her fingers over the design and her mouth spreads into a wide smile. It makes my heart take off and all I want to do is stuff my cock between those luscious lips. She brings her fingertips to my pierced nipple and gives it a tug, causing a growl to work its way out of my throat. Then she chuckles as her fingers trail south over my abs, slowly torturing me, and I tighten my hold on her hair. My dick agrees and jerks inside my pants. Finally, she gets to the waistband of my sweats and reaches inside.

"I love watching your big dick swing in these sweats and knowing I can have it whenever I want," she groans as she wraps her hand around me.

It's hard to respond when her thumb drags across my tip, making me moan and pump myself into her hand. In record time, she pulls my sweats and boxers down and my dick springs free, nearly smacking her on the forehead. She wraps her hand around me once more before licking from the base all the way to the piercing at the tip, then moans, making me almost shoot my load all over her pretty face.

She sucks my tip into her mouth and her moist warmth makes me fall back against the window, my head hitting the pane with a dull *thud*. The cold glass makes me aware we're both naked in front of a large window. Anyone can look up at us, but instead of that making me self-conscious, I become more heated and overly aroused. I slip my fingers into her hair and tighten my grip, forcing myself deeper inside her mouth. She gags around my length and I pull back a bit to let her breathe. She flicks her tongue against my piercing and the sensation carries all the way to my balls. I jerk inside her mouth and force myself back into her throat, deeper than I was before. She gags again as tears spill out and run down her face. Fucking beautiful.

I force her to release my dick and stand up in front of me. I don't have much longer to go, so I pick her up by the back of her thighs and turn to press her against the window. She gasps when her back hits the cold pane, but I don't care. Everyone should see what's mine. I line myself up with her center, knowing I should prep her more considering how big I am, but there's just something so fucking hot about my cock causing her pain as I force my way in, making her spread and clamp around me like a fucking vise.

I push in and make it halfway before her pussy refuses to take me any farther. Ember's head hits the window as she whimpers, and the sound spurs me on. So I pull back out to the tip before slamming all the way in, balls deep. Her eyes roll back into her head as she swears on a scream. I repeat the movement a few more times as her juices spread all over my cock. The sounds her pussy makes as I slam into her have me gritting my teeth against the release my balls are begging for. Not until she comes first. I tip her pelvis out a bit and force her to lean her shoulders against the window, working the angle that always makes her come quickly. I pound into her until her legs tremble, a sure sign of her impending orgasm.

"That's it. Come all over this dick," I growl between clenched teeth as I continue my assault.

"Fuck, Vin. Fuck!" she screams as her pussy clamps down with her orgasm and thrusting into her almost becomes impossible.

When she finally comes down, I pick up my pace and let myself come, the warm, tingling sensation running through my balls and up my shaft. As I grind my cock into her, she comes again from the motion, her body shaking in my arms.

Then I pull out of her, still keeping her spread wide and propped against the window. Massaging her ass in my hands, I watch as our combined juices drip out of her and onto the floor. My dick twitches and I harden again as I pull her into my arms and carry her toward the bedroom.

"Round two, baby girl."

Chapter Twenty

Vin drops me off about a block away from the Columbia campus library and I walk at a steady pace toward it. Vin demands that he be present inside the library as well so he can see what our target looks like. I'm not stupid. I can tell he has some sort of morality problem with this specific hit, and I can't help that. It's happening whether or not he helps. I lost my family to this guy's monster mother, and I refuse to let that go.

I couldn't live with myself if I let it go.

I'm dressed like a college student with a pair of leggings and a tight crew neck shirt as a sweater hangs around my shoulders. Vin bought me a hot pink Columbia sweater and I cringed the moment he handed it to me, the loud color assaulting my eyes. I piled my hair on top of my head in a messy bun and left my face free of any makeup, save for a sparkling lip gloss. I needed to look a little sleep-deprived and slightly disoriented, like I spent the entire night studying.

Entering the library, I head to the far back right corner because this is where he does his tutor lessons. I spot Vin almost immediately, sitting at a table with a few large textbooks in front of him. I stumble a bit at the sight of him sitting wide-legged with a tight black T-shirt and his baggy jeans tucked into a pair of tan Timberland boots. He has his curly hair gelled on top and a black bandana wrapped around his head. Sure, I was with him in the Hummer on the way here, but I was too preoccupied with my mission to take in his appearance. Well, fuck, I am totally noticing him now and it's making it hard to remember why the fuck I'm here. He sees my reaction to him from the corner of his eye and the smirk that lines his mouth makes his dimple pop. *Sexy asshole.*

I shake him off and continue to the table next to where Carlos is sitting and talking to two girls. They're clearly taking his tutoring lessons, only to giggle and flirt and bat their eyelashes at him. I can understand why. I may love Vin, but I can admit when a guy is hot, and Carlos is hot. He has jet-black hair that's a mess of tangles on top of his head, like he's been running his hands through it all day. His eyes are a honey hazel, and his skin is a couple of shades darker than my own. Even sitting, I can see he's built, and his forearms flex every time he turns a page or points at a particular section.

I take a seat at the table and pull out my laptop, notebook, and pencil. He glances over at me as I bend to place my backpack on the floor. When I sit back up, I go to open my laptop and deliberately flick my pencil off the table. It flies right for his foot and I curse colorfully as I pretend to be annoyed at my clumsiness. He quickly bends down to pick it up before I can attempt to and stands to hand it back, flashing me a stunning smile as I work to clear my throat.

"This yours?" he asks, his voice deep and velvety.

"Yes, thank you." I shake my head, placing my hand on my forehead. "It's been a long night." Taking the pencil from his hand, I give him a bashful smile.

"You're taking summer courses?" he inquires, his hand running through his hair.

I freeze and decide to play coy. I didn't really prepare a schedule for myself to tell him, but I should've realized he'd ask.

"My mother told me to never talk to strangers." I wink at him flirtatiously as his smile grows.

"True enough." He chuckles as his eyes roam over me from head to toe.

"Carlos," one twat whines. "We only have another thirty minutes."

"Right." He nods at her, then looks back at me with a wink of his own. "Try not to impale me with anything else, hmm?"

"I'll try to contain my murderous ways for the next fifteen minutes." Smiling demurely, I flutter my lashes, and Vin's faint snort from a few tables over has me fighting to hold my own in.

Carlos heads back over to his table and I go back to my laptop for the next fifteen minutes, searching through porn sites using the library Wi-Fi—in closed caption, of course. This has been the easiest baiting I have ever done and I am happy about it.

A half an hour later, I've bitten through my pencil in what must look like an intense studying session, but really, I'm working out how a female can take double penetration. I can't wait to speak to Adri about this. We need to discuss what size dildo I should buy so Vin can fuck both of my holes at once.

Carlos' table begins to clear their textbooks away and I quickly switch off my web page to bring up an old essay I worked on this year for English Lit. Luckily too, because he ends up right over my shoulder in the next few seconds, making me turn in my seat and use my shoulder to hide my screen.

"I swear, I have kept all pointed objects securely at my side." I smile up at him innocently.

"Unfortunately, you did. So I had to come over here with no excuses." He *tuts*.

"What can I do for you?" I flutter my eyelashes at him. Fuck, flirting is hard.

"What are you doing tonight?"

Oh, you know, beating the shit out of someone. "Studying." I frown, trying to look put out by how studious I am.

"Would you like to grab a drink?" he asks, a slight flush forming on his cheeks.

"I can't." Making myself look disappointed, I let my shoulders fall forward and pout my sticky lips. "I really need to catch up on work. Next weekend I'm open though?"

"Sure!" he agrees eagerly. "I'll give you my number."

He fires off his number and I program it into my phone. He also goes as far as to make me text him so he has my number too. Thankfully, I purchased a burner phone, so there was no way they would link me to him.

"Your name?" I ask.

"Right." He laughs, the sound rumbly and deep as he shifts on his feet. "Carlos, you?"

"Whitney." I grin. *Thank you, big titty porn star, for the suggestion.*

"Okay, Whitney, I'll text you." He nods, and with one final top-to-bottom look, he saunters out of the library.

Finally. Now I'm all hot and bothered by the porn I indulged in. I look over my shoulder to see if Vin stuck around, but his table is empty. So I pack up all my things into my bag and head out of the library. The sun is setting and the sky is awash with bright oranges and reds. I walk toward the drop-off point and back to the Hummer. I really hope Vin isn't too fucking pissed about my having to flirt with Talia's son because that was the hardest shit I've done in a while. Yes, Carlos is an attractive guy and he seems like he has an outstanding personality—even if it's a bit cookie-cutter—but Vin *sees* through me to the soul inside, and everything about him was made specifically for me.

The Hummer is up ahead, and my heart is racing. I feel like I betrayed him and I never would do such a thing. I hope he didn't leave because he's pissed at me for my superb acting skills.

Opening the passenger side door, I peer in at him. He added his New York baseball hat on top of the bandana and pulled it down low. His jaw is clenched, causing it to sharpen further, and the muscle tics beneath the skin furiously. Don't even ask me why I'm so turned on right now. I'm a glutton for punishment.

"Get in, Em," he grinds out.

Swinging my backpack into the back seat, I pull myself into the Hummer, closing the door behind me. When I turn to grab my seat belt, his fingers slide into the bun on top of my head and grip it tight. I don't move as both trepidation and arousal war inside of me. I'm not sure what Vin is feeling right now and I don't want to make it worse. He tugs my hair sharply, bringing my head into his chest before forcing me to look up into his moss-green eyes.

"I saw what you were doing in there," he rasps, his anger boiling just beneath the surface of his controlled facade.

"Vin..." I try to shake my head and fail because his hand is grasped so tightly in my hair. "I was just following the plan, you remember? The one we decided on together?" My words are breathless and husky.

"We didn't plan shit like that. What you were doing was nothing like we had planned." His lips draw back over his teeth as he takes a deep breath, the motion moving my head in his hand.

"Yes, we did. I told you I would have to flirt to get him to take me out." I narrow my eyes as my anger rises. My hands land on his thigh as my fingers bite into the fabric of his jeans.

"That's true,"—he leans down, bringing our mouths just an inch apart—"but why the fuck were you watching porn?"

"Oh." My breath catches in my throat. Fuck, he saw that?

"Yeah." His mouth twitches as he fights to hold back his smile. "The laptop was facing me, Em. Actually, I'm sure quite a few people got a bit of a show whenever you squirmed in your seat."

"Uh…" Shit. Fuck, shit! I didn't even think about it. I thought I had the screen covered, but clearly, I didn't.

"Threesomes?" His brow raises. "You want two dicks in you, Em?"

"I was…" I clear my throat as his grip loosens and my hands travel up his thigh. "Um… thinking we could try with a dildo, not another person."

"What?" His eyes darken with lust. He's already convinced.

"The whole double penetration thing looks hot, but I don't want anyone else." My hand finds his pulsing cock pressed to his zipper as I give it a squeeze.

"Shit." His mouth crashes into mine and I moan, realizing how worked up I am after watching those fucking videos. "Let's go back right now."

He practically throws me back into my seat and I barely have time to strap on my seat belt before he's peeling out onto the street.

The place is humming with dark energy tonight. It's seeping through my skin as I force myself not to let it consume me. The crowd is different, not so boisterous, and not just here for a good time. They want to witness depravity and I'm the only one who can give it to them.

I'm inside my fucking closet of a room waiting for my name to be announced when Carm strolls in. "Tonight, I have you fighting one of our enforcers. He's a big guy and he's fucking pissed." He begins to pace in the small space, making it more claustrophobic. "I don't want him dead, but I want him regretting what he did."

"What did he do?" I ask as I finish taping my hands. "Give me something here."

"He dipped into the package I needed him to distribute." *Ahh, drugs. Of course.*

"You want me to rough him up a bit? Or rearrange his face and knock him out?" My blood isn't singing with the same adrenaline as it usually does and it should be worrisome, not that I care for my lack of sympathy. Murder has become like Christmas morning for me.

"Knock him the fuck out," he grits through his teeth, looking every bit like our dead father.

"Got it." I nod, averting my eyes from his face. I don't want to detest him for the features he didn't ask for. "Can we get this the fuck over with? I have a sweet thing waiting for me back at my place."

"Yeah." He laughs and leaves the room.

After about ten minutes of stretching and warming up my muscles, I hear "Bodies" on the speaker system and my name being called to the ring. The usual roar of the crowd has dimmed considerably, and a weird foreboding comes over me. This shit isn't right. The door opens and I follow two guards out through the hallway. When we reach the ring, I can immediately tell what the difference is. The stands aren't filled with spectators, they are all gangbangers or men in business suits, and a few Heads sprinkled throughout. I really am here to teach someone a lesson and it's a lesson for everyone else as well.

Gazing into the ring, I find a large man shirtless with only a loose pair of sweats on. That's his first mistake. Always have on as much clothing as you can while still being able to move. Anything loose will be used against you. He has some ink on his chest and arms and he's sweating profusely. I would guess he's coming down from whatever he was distributing recently. His eyes are doing the typical tweaking motion and his jaw looks like it can crack concrete. Definitely strung out, so I need to be careful because this is when a person is the most unpredictable. His arms are bulging with muscles, but his calves look like he has skipped a few leg days at the gym. Based on that, I would assume he's more of a puncher and not a kicker.

I climb the few steps into the caged ring and remove my hoodie. I have my hair braided back into two Dutch braids and I'm wearing black leggings with a tight tank top. My black-taped hands flex as I take in the guy across from me. He doesn't sneer and he's not taunting me about my size. He must know who I am and what I can do.

"Blur." He nods his head in respect, but I don't reply. "I was the man that disposed of your father."

That's when a bit of fear clouds his eyes, and finally, that warm sensation in my gut swirls. I'm a predator and as soon as someone shows me fear or runs, I'm ready to hunt. The warmth grows hotter as it spreads out along my limbs and seeps deep into my chest. If he was banking on working me over with this scared, nice guy routine, then he fucked up because that shit doesn't affect me.

I rotate my neck as his eyes slowly narrow on me. *That's it, get mad.*

"You think you can actually fight me?" he sneers, his last resort to getting a rise out of me. "I'm twice the size of your father. I will snap you in half."

Looking him in the eyes, I grin as the red saturates my vision. The familiar lust for blood courses through me and I lick my lips in anticipation. The MC announces the rules, sounding under water as the excitement encases every muscle in my body, but I don't care because I rarely follow them.

I bend my knees and bring my taped hands up in front of my face. The bell rings, and the guy charges me, his feet sounding like claps of thunder each time they hit the mat. His right fist swings out, a standard fighting technique for anyone who has no fighting technique. I play a little game of cat and mouse to provide a little entertainment, turning away from his fist and bending down quickly to swing my leg out and trip him. He lands face down on the mat with a resounding *thud*, but he jumps back up. I do rapid boxing jumps, moving backward into the center of the ring as his face grows red with embarrassment. Based on that, I can assume his moves will become more erratic as he lets his emotions dictate his retaliation.

He doesn't let me down as he comes back swinging with his right fist—which I dodge—and then coming in strong with a left uppercut. I pull the same twist-out-of-the-way move and drop to swing my leg out, causing him to faceplant... again. His embarrassment should come to a boiling point soon and then we can really start having some fun. The arena is silent save for this guy's panting and my fancy, tapping footwork. He pops back up and growls at me, his teeth looking a little decayed and yellow. *Don't do crack, kids.*

"I'm going to break your little fucking neck," he pants, sweat running down his face. This is looking like the boiling point and I grin.

He runs at me, and as soon as his arm is in hitting range, I drop my back to the mat with my legs tucked up under me. He stumbles as he tries to dodge and figure out my movements. I flip around onto all fours and jump up behind him, swinging hard and hitting his right kidney and then the left. His hands automatically come to lie against those areas, and I grab his wrists, yanking hard until the sweet pop of his left shoulder dislocating sounds in the cage. I drop his arms and he hollers with pain, turning around and looking at me with a bit of a surprise as his arm hangs uselessly at his side.

His right arm is the most dominant but I'm okay with taking this slow because it's turning out to be a good game of cat and mouse. He comes at me again, this time slower and more wary. That's good because it means he can learn, and that's what I'm supposed to be doing, teaching him a lesson.

My body tenses as the red hue thrums with my heartbeat. He lifts his right arm to swing a punch, but as I sidestep, he fakes me out and grabs me by my braid instead. The stinging pain in my scalp has me gasping, and instantly, my blood boils like lava. He whips me down onto my back on the mat and prepares to stomp on me, but as he raises his right knee, I kick his left, a snap sounding like a crack of thunder as the place hushes to an eerie silence. He rolls onto the mat, gripping his twisted kneecap with a yell as I get up and stroll over to him, whistling the theme song for the Dwarfs from *Snow White.* I kick him swiftly, twice in the ribs and once in the side of his head. His brow splits and blood runs down onto the mat.

Then I kneel beside him to punch him twice in the temple,

instantly knocking him out. Standing up, I brush my hands off in an arrogant move and grin, which turns into a genuine smile when I find Emmett sitting in the front row. He winks at me before sprinting up to the cage door to let me out.

I snatch up my hoodie and haul it back down over my head. "That was petty as fuck," Emmett says with a chuckle. "Nice game you were playing."

"I gave him a fighting chance." I shrug as the adrenaline begins to fade and a tremble works its way through my muscles.

"All the Heads are here too." His excitement is like a jolt of electricity as I follow him toward the back.

"That was great sportsmanship," a man in a suit gushes as he looks at me with curiosity.

"She's up for hire." Emmett stops to talk to him as I continue onward. "Talk to your Head if you need her services."

He catches up to follow me to my little closet when Carm steps in line behind us, patting my shoulder awkwardly. "Thanks for that," he says. "Come to my office after for payment."

"Will do."

Emmett follows our brother in the opposite direction as I go inside the room to pull off the tape and to towel off my sweat. I don't want to stay here any longer than necessary, so I bypass the shower, deciding to have one when I get back to the apartment.

Entering the office, I stumble into what looks to be a heated conversation between Carm and Emmett. I push down the feeling I'm interrupting and sit in a chair across from them. We are family, after all.

"Problem?" I look between them. Emmett is red in the face

with his arms crossed over his chest, anger still blazing in his eyes, and Carm falls into his chair with an exhausted sigh as he drags his fingers through his hair.

"Emmett has filled me in recently on him moving to Whitsborough," he says, his brows crinkled as he gives me a pointed look.

"Yeah, and?" I lean back in the chair as he shakes his head.

"I can't protect him if he's that far." He exhales and his shoulders dip forward.

"Carm,"—I lean forward—"Emmett can protect himself."

He looks up at me as a brief flash of anger darkens his eyes before he schools his features. Interesting. Looks like maybe Carm is holding some resentment toward me. That's something I'll tuck away to discuss when we're alone.

"Here's your money." He sounds distant and irritated as he throws an envelope on the desk. "I'll be in touch tomorrow with the intel I gather on Jennifer." I'm being dismissed. If I wasn't so exhausted, I'd be stubborn and stick around just to spite him.

"Cool." I grab the envelope and stand up, stepping forward to hug Emmett goodbye. His frustration is still clear on his face even though the redness has waned.

"I'll walk you out," he says, and I let my arms drop.

We silently walk back down the hallway, not wanting to talk out loud because of the listening ears everywhere, and when we step out into the cool night, I spot Vin's Hummer idling nearby.

"He'll get over it," Emmett mumbles, shuffling his foot along the gravel.

"Maybe,"—I shrug—"but your life is your own. Make your own decisions." He nods and I lean in to give him a hug. He looks so much younger when his face is clouded with indecision.

"Call me." I nod to him and make my way to the Hummer, turning around to watch Emmett head back inside. My stomach twists and I'm suddenly wanting to run back and drag him out, but I stop myself because I have to stand by my previous statement to Carm.

Emmett can protect himself.

Vin

Sharla Germaine is a force to be reckoned with. Since I was a child, she's always been my number one, and I have kept her in that spot until recently. She's told me many times I would replace her one day with the woman I marry, but I never understood what she meant until I fell in love with Ember. Obviously, my mother is important and I love her, but Ember has wormed her way into that number one slot, and my mother knows it.

I catch her sometimes looking at Ember, trying to figure it out, doubting the intensity of our feelings based on our age. She's never really questioned me about Ember and the feelings I have for her. It's like she's written it off as some sort of puppy love. I've been adamant that I don't need to explain myself or my feelings for years, but I may have to make an exception now because I don't particularly like the slight attitude I'm detecting from her toward Ember.

We're having dinner with her tonight at her restaurant because she's been complaining about not seeing me. When I told her about going to New York again with Ember, she lost her temper and told me I needed to give my relationship some space. Not happening. I promised her dinner and told her I was bringing Ember.

And so, here we are.

"Why do you go to New York so often?" Ma questions Em, her brow raised as she drums her fingers on the tabletop.

"I want to check out some universities in New York City. After all, I was born there and I'm entitled to their education," Ember fires back, her brow raising to mock my mother's.

"Really?" My mother finally perks up, seeing an expiration

date on our relationship, no doubt. "That's great."

"What's your exact problem with me?" Em asks, dropping her fork to her plate, getting straight to the point.

Fuck, here we go. I look at my mother with a nod as if to say, *Well?*

"I don't have a problem with you at all." Ma exhales and puts down her fork. "I have a problem with how absorbed my teenage son is with his first relationship."

Ember snorts and shakes her head. "Teenage son? Is that your way of saying he can't have a serious relationship at his age?"

"Of course not, but you're both too young to be making life decisions. Trust me, your mother would be happy I said that to you." Ma's smug expression only has me suppressing a groan. She shouldn't have brought up Em's mother.

"Don't talk about my mother," Em snaps, her face reddening. I understand her irritation, and even though she's stepping into disrespectful territory, my mother should know her boundaries. "And were you not pregnant at our age? I think Vin's life is already an improvement from yours, no?"

I swallow the food in my mouth as my mother sputters and flushes red. Em can be a bit too honest sometimes, but what she's saying is true, albeit a little harsh. Someone is threatening our relationship bubble and she's protecting it like a mama bear. I hold my hand up as they both slowly turn to look at me. I can't have her disrespecting my mother and vice versa. They are both important to me and I don't want to choose.

"You both need to work it out. Don't make me have to choose." I wipe my mouth with my napkin and then push my chair back from the table. "I'm heading out. Em has her car here and she will take you home, Ma." I stand up and pull my keys from my pocket.

"Vincent!" my mother seethes. "Sit down. We need to have this conversation."

I lay my hands flat on the table and lean in toward her, making sure to keep eye contact as I harden my tone. "Ember isn't going anywhere. One day she will be my wife and I need you two to work out your issues. I don't have any with either of you, so I don't see why I have to stay."

"I'll make sure she gets home." Em nods at me with a slight smile on her face. She knows how important my mother is and she'll do everything she can to work it out for me.

"Thank you." I lean over and kiss my mother's cheek, then I give Em a quick kiss on her mouth.

Sitting in my Hummer, I mull over where to go. My house is empty, Ember's is too. There's always Danny's house, and before Ember arrived, it was my go-to. His parents are rarely home and they have little to no time for their teenage son, who is flushing his future down the drain. Danny and I have been best friends since eighth grade, and for as long as I can remember, he's been a privileged piece of shit whose daddy would pay his way out of any trouble.

I decide to go pay him a visit since I've barely spoken to him this summer.

Last summer, Danny had a party practically every other day, and I was so fucked-up most days that I can barely remember those few months. I used the fuck out of Marlana because last summer was when she really fell for me. When I finally sobered up a few weeks before school, I realized my mistake when she began to expect more from me. The hopeful look in her eyes followed me everywhere, and I didn't bother to correct her until Em showed up. Not my finest moment, but I'd like to think that all things happen the way they do for a reason.

I drive up to Danny's street and the heavy thump of bass hits me before I even reach his house. I wonder how much he pays his neighbors to turn the other cheek. His money and wealth were things I resented him for. Sure, my house is pleasant, and it's big enough for Ma and me, but the houses here on this street? They are a ridiculous show of wealth.

Stopping on the street outside his house, I immediately spot Shay and Marlana on the front porch smoking a joint. The yard is littered with a few Precious Blood students and beer cans. None of it is appealing, so instead of parking, I continue by and turn down Travis' street.

He and Danny live just a street apart, and the houses over here are even more ostentatious. Huge, looming, three-level structures with wraparound balconies, immaculate lawns, and majestic statues that sit at the front gates. Travis' house has two exact replicas of the Sphinx at the beginning of the driveway and it makes me snort as I imagine Robert probably thought himself a Pharaoh at one time. Arrogant fucker.

I surprise myself as I turn into his driveway and drive through the open gates. I tell myself it's just to tell him they're open and then leave after. Even though I despise this place and the man who once lived in it, I want nothing bad to happen to Travis or his mother. As I pull in farther, I stop in time to avoid an enormous pile of what looks to be expensive tailored suits and fucking croc-skinned shoes. I throw the Hummer into park and hop out to inspect it further. These suits are Armani and Dolce, fucking silk robes with initials stitched on the front. R.G.

"Christina having a rough day," someone calls out from the front door, startling me. Christina is Travis' mother. I look up to find a woman in a maid's outfit and she looks to be about my mother's age. She's beautiful with a very European look about her. White-blonde hair and bright blue eyes set on porcelain white skin. "Once she tired, I will put back."

"This happens often?" I ask her.

"Once a week. You his other son?" She leans against the brick beside the front door, her head tipping curiously.

"Yeah," I mumble as a wave of discomfort rolls over me. Why the fuck am I here? I look back at my vehicle and contemplate just leaving.

"He'd like a visit," she states, a little quieter this time, making me face her again.

"Is he okay?" I don't know why I ask that instead of just fucking leaving.

"Not really. He doesn't talk to anyone." She looks behind her into the house, then back out to me. "I raise him because his parents not like to be home. He used to talk to me, but… he'd like a visit," she repeats in slightly broken English before walking into the house.

I stand on the spot, unmoving, and try to will my body to turn around and get the fuck away from this circus show. I don't need the extra stress of Travis or his mother. They aren't my fucking responsibility. I look once more at the Hummer and then look down at my feet. *Move, motherfuckers!*

"You should go," a voice sounds from above me. I step back and raise my head, spotting Travis leaning on the railing of the balcony smoking a cigarette. Since when did he smoke? "You're trying to convince yourself to go. Why are you here?" He exhales his drag.

"I went for a drive and noticed your gates were open. Thought I'd come let you know." Lame. I sound so fucking lame.

"Cool, thanks. You can go." He sounds vacant, emotionless, as he flicks his butt down onto the pile of clothing and heads back inside. The ember from the cigarette burns quickly through the silk of a robe, the material practically melting in that spot. Again, I look back at the Hummer and then curse under my breath. It's clear I'm not fucking leaving and I have no idea what's come over me.

The front foyer of the house is intimidating, and I quickly trudge through it. I don't bother removing my shoes as I climb the grand staircase to the second level. Once at the top, I try to figure out which room the balcony belongs to when heart-wrenching sobbing filters through from the door to my left. I stop and listen as a woman keeps repeating *Robert* between her cries.

"They couldn't stand each other when he was alive, but she can't seem to fucking live without him now." I turn to my right to find Travis leaning against his doorframe. "Why are you here?"

"Fuck, man." Shrugging, I scrub my hand down my face. "I don't fucking know. I was driving and just ended up here." Taking in his appearance, I see he has on a wrinkled, black T-shirt with stained sweatpants and no socks. His hair is disheveled on top of his head and he has dark bags under his very exhausted-looking eyes. "You look like shit."

He chuckles drily and pushes himself off the doorframe. "Why the fuck do you care?"

That's what I keep asking myself, yet I still don't have a fucking answer. I look up at him and shrug once more. "I don't know, but I do. Change your clothes and let's go for a drive."

"I can't leave her—" he starts, but I cut him off.

"She's an adult, Travis. Yes, you can. I'll be waiting outside." Before I change my mind, I turn around and run back down the stairs. Then I walk outside and find the pile of clothes smoking as a small flame grows from the now-burned silk robe. Not my fucking problem. I ignore the clothes mound and jump back into the Hummer.

Travis comes out the front door and stops in front of the little burning pit of fire he's created. Then he fucking undoes his belt and jeans, whips out his dick, and pisses on the pile, effectively dousing the flame.

"Jesus Christ," I mutter and avert my gaze. I don't need to see my brother's fucking dick. "Was that necessary?" I ask him as he gets into the passenger seat.

"Yeah?" He lifts a brow. "It could've set my fucking house on fire."

"You couldn't find water?"

"Dude, do you see water anywhere? My piss was the next best thing,"—he puts on his seat belt and stretches his legs out wide—"and fucking satisfying."

I snort and chuckle in response, and soon enough, he looks at me with a grin and joins in. I don't have a destination in mind as I pull out of his driveway, but Travis doesn't seem to mind.

"Your housekeeper is pretty nice." I don't have a fucking clue what to talk about.

"Sonja?" he asks, his eyes showing the first bit of warmth since I got to his house. Then they harden with anger. "She was my nanny. Now my mother forces her to wear that uniform in the house," he grinds out. *Okay, bad choice of topic.*

"I have no idea where the fuck I'm going," I admit. "Do you want to hit up Small's and grab a twelve-pack?" Small's is the one liquor/beer store in our town that will sell to us because Johnny Small likes money more than obeying the law.

"I don't know if I should…" he trails off, sounding torn. He pushes his hand inside the beanie he's wearing—in the middle of fucking summer—and then scrubs it down over his face. I start toward the store anyway because his indecision means a part of him wants to and he's in desperate need of a distraction.

I pull into the parking lot at Small's and run inside to grab the beer. Johnny is standing at the register, his porky belly touching the counter in his sweaty-ass wifebeater.

"Vincent Greene!" he bellows. Thankfully, no one else is in here. "What shit are you up to today? Where's that hot piece of tail that's usually following you?" I grab a case of beer out of the cooler and stride to the front.

"Watch your mouth about Ember, Small, or I will have to teach you a lesson in respect." I slap a twenty on the counter and head out. Small is a dirtbag through and through, but until I'm nineteen and legal, he's our only option to buy alcohol from.

I hop back into the Hummer and look at Travis. He has his phone in his hand and is scrolling through IG. He finally senses my gaze on him and looks up. "What did Small say about E's ass?" He grins.

"Fuck off." I snicker. Small usually talks about every girl's ass under the age of eighteen. "At least we got beer."

"It's a start." He nods and looks back down at his phone.

I take us to the local park—the same one I took Em to when I showed her the box of photos last year—and we both sit on a grassy hill. No kids are here because the sun has already set, so we don't have to worry about them witnessing us drinking.

I'm not sure how I got here with him or what possessed me to chill with the enemy, but I'm just going to go with it. Travis is looking lost without a single friend. He has Em, and sometimes Adri, but they're fucking girls and it's not the same. He has his jock baseball fuckwits, but it's been a while since I've seen him hang out with them. Maybe the death of his father fucked him up, and he has no one who gives a fuck enough to help him.

"Since the f–fuck…"—I clear my throat—"your f–father passed, how are things going?" I sound like a stuttering idiot.

"*Our* father's death doesn't bother me as much as having to be the only one dealing with my mother's downfall," he confesses as I hand him a beer.

"I hated him." I chug back half a bottle of beer. "But I shouldn't have hated you." My brows come together in confusion as I look at him from the side of my eye. *What the fuck am I saying?*

"Yeah," he mutters, tipping his head back to swallow the beer.

"Look, all I'm saying is that I'm here. I'm an option if you need someone." I face him and scrub my hand over the side of my face, sounding like an idiot. Fuck my life.

He nods and stares down at his beer bottle, his finger drawing circles into the condensation. The silence wears on me, but I'm afraid to open my mouth right now in case I spew motivational quotes or something.

"He was a shit dad," he breaks the silence, thankfully. "He was a shit husband. You probably hated me because of how I was living, but I always envied you for having a parent who cared."

"I resented the shit you had while Mom and I struggled. I just had to grow up and see it for what it actually was." Tipping my head back on a swallow, I finish my first beer. "We're brothers, even if I do have tainted blood." I grab the next beer and open it up.

"The only tainted blood you have is the one we share." He finishes his first and I hand him a second. "And thanks… for the brother shit. I needed to hear that." Our eyes meet and I see the sincerity shining in his.

Shame fills me as I try to put myself in his shoes. Travis has never fought against me, and as soon as he broke through to me, he always made it a point to say we were brothers.

"You need to get out of that fucking house," I tell him, his situation finally becoming crystal clear. "This weekend Ember has shit to do with her family, but next weekend you should come chill with us in New York."

"I wouldn't mind hitting up New York and checking out the sights," he says to me with a grin.

"Hell yeah." I hold out my fist as he bumps his to it. "I mean, I'll be a wingman as long as it doesn't cause me to have my balls speared."

Travis snorts on a mouthful of beer and we both end up laughing. "Yeah, E is fucking ruthless, huh? Honestly though… how much does she fucking scare you?" His eyes are wide as he pins me with a look, the mischief swirling in the green irises.

"Honestly? A lot," I admit as he falls back to the hill with a loud cackle. "But she's so fucking hot."

"She is," he agrees as he sits back up, and I look at him with my brow raised. "Chill. She's not my type. I couldn't handle a girl like E. When I first met her, I thought she was sweet and quiet, but we know that's not the case." He shakes his head.

"What's happening with Adri?"

"No fucking clue." He drops his second empty bottle back into the box. "That girl has been confusing me since the ninth grade. She runs so hot and then shuts down and becomes the fucking ice queen. I can't keep up."

"Drama." I shake my head as I hand him another beer. Two is my limit while I'm driving, but he can indulge tonight. He takes it and slings back half the bottle in one gulp.

"I'm done with it. I can't handle more shit right now," he says while peeling the label off the beer bottle. "Adri is too much sometimes. Plus, I think she's into Ember's twin."

"Emmett? No way." I shove at his shoulder and wince when he nearly topples over. "Even if she were, Em would fucking lose it on her. He's off-limits."

"I don't even care." He struggles to sit back up and I have to haul on his sweater to help him. Lightweight.

"All right, I'll talk to Em, but let's do a trip to New York next weekend. No Adri. Just the three of us, but you'll most likely see Emmett. Are you good with that?"

"For real?" His eyes light up as he sways on the spot. "I don't have a problem with him. I'm just happy to have something to look forward to."

My chest swarms with guilt again. I should've done this a long time ago. "Yeah, bro. We'll make a weekend out of it."

After he polished off four beers and nearly fell asleep in the grass, I dropped him off at his house. As I wait for him to unlock his door, I check my phone and find a few messages from Em. My phone stayed in my pocket the entire time I was with Travis, giving him my sole attention.

Em: Your mother is home safe and I didn't get stabby once.

Em: I'll make her love me yet.

Em: Everything okay?

Em: Call me when you're home.

Fuck calling her. I'm going to head over to her house now and sink my cock deep into that warm, tight pussy.

Chapter Twenty-One

Carm: Jennifer Talia has a side hustle. Selling babies under the pretense of adoption.

What the actual fuck did he just send me? What the fuck am I supposed to do with that?

Me: Okay…

Me: Who did she sell babies to? Do we have proof? Where is this bitch right now? Can I snipe her?

Carm: Working on proof. I have a guy with an in.

Are you kidding me? Why am I being fed just enough to be acceptable but not enough to do fuck all with?

Leaving him on read, I let him think I'm still relying on him to help me with taking this bitch down. I can't afford to be on Carm's suspicious side, not while Emmett is still inside of that compound. I have a plan in place to take Talia down, but if I didn't, these morsels he's feeding me would be irritating, especially because this 'intel' was supposed to be given to me two days ago.

It's Tuesday and I have exactly three days to put my plan into motion, starting with texting this Carlos guy on my burner phone. He's playing the cool dude and doesn't want to look desperate by texting me too soon, but I'm not stupid. He's extremely interested. I pull out the phone and fire off the first text.

Me: Hey! How's your week going so far?

Faking a bubbly personality is going to be difficult to maintain. I'll have to cut out his throat sooner rather than later. He lets the text sit for fifteen minutes before he texts back. *Fuckboy.*

Carlos: Hey, yourself! Week is almost done. We still good for Saturday?

Me: It's Tuesday, though! LOL :D Saturday is good.

Carlos: Great! Sorry, just in the middle of tutoring. I'll text you later.

Carlos is not tutoring right now because I know this asshole's schedule as if it were my own. He's done with his classes for the day and should be in his dorm right now. He's probably jacking off his little dick to courtroom terminology.

Vin is spending the day with his mother, trying to calm her down on the whole 'Don't let Ember steal my son' agenda. It probably has something to do with her being a single mother and the fear of being completely alone. Once my life finally becomes normalish, I'm going to find her a dick—I mean, a man.

I was happy when he told me about spending Sunday evening with Travis. He did it on his own and without me yelling at him to do it. He thinks Travis is under a lot of stress and I instantly felt like shit for not checking in on him. It's no excuse, but I have a lot going on right now too.

Vin invited him to come to New York with us next weekend. Thank god he didn't suggest this weekend. I'm not ready for Travis to learn that I'm a homicidal maniac. I let that run through my brain, homicidal maniac… I like it. Has a certain ring to it, like a serial killer or assassin. Actually, I'm all of these things, and not one of them I can put on a résumé, regardless of the awesome skills it comes with.

Sitting at the kitchen table, I open my laptop on the table in front of me, then begin to type out all the skills I've acquired in this profession.

*Punctuality with each kill.

*Leadership skills in planning hits.

*Overachiever in exacting death.

*Passionate about learning new skills for spilling blood.

*Weapons Specialist.

Fuck, that's a near-perfect résumé if I ever saw one.

Vin asked me not to invite Adri on the same weekend we're

taking Travis to New York and I'm already seeing the fallout from it. If Adri ever learns that I kept her out of this, she'll see it as I've joined team Travis. Honestly, I'm fucking Switzerland with them and their fucked-up relationship. I refuse to choose and it's not my place to psychoanalyze them. As long as she keeps her claws out of my brother, I really don't care who's fucking whom.

"Em!" My body jerks at the sudden sound of his bellow. *Jesus, does he not know any other way to announce himself in this house?*

"In here," I grumble as his footsteps thud on the tiles toward the kitchen.

Vin steps into the room in a pair of basketball shorts, no fucking shirt on, and a black bandana on his head. His body is dripping sweat and I'm trying really hard not to salivate on my laptop.

"I went for a jog," he states as he opens my fridge and pilfers a Gatorade.

"Naked?" I ask him, slightly irritated to learn he's running the streets looking like this.

He chuckles and bends down to kiss my pouted mouth. "You're so cute. I'm not naked."

"Whatever." I turn back to my laptop while clicking my tongue.

He leans on the back of my chair to read what I'm typing and nearly chokes on his mouthful of Gatorade. "Are you writing your résumé?"

"Obviously." I roll my eyes and go back to typing out my charitable works in ridding the world of assholes.

"'Looking for a position as a Homicidal Maniac'?! 'An overachiever in exacting death'?!" he reads as he gasps a bit from breathing liquid.

"I have a pretty impressive skill set and I feel underappreciated." I shrug as I type my future goals of owning an empire as my children carry on in my work.

"Underappreciated?" His fingers gripping my chin forces my head to turn and look into his pretty eyes.

"Mmhm." I try to nod but the hold he has on my chin is unmoving.

"That's it." He bends down and throws me over his shoulder, then stalks toward the stairs.

"Vin!" I squeal as I kick my legs against his chest, having no intention of actually pushing him away. "No! I'm not done with my résumé!"

We're both interrupted by the ring of the doorbell, and he groans before smacking my ass and lowering me back to my feet. "You are so lucky right now," he grunts.

"No, you are!" I snap back with a taunting smile and point my finger toward the kitchen. "Did you not read my skills on that résumé?" I run my finger along my throat, then head to the front door. Everything on that paper is fact.

"You watch who's homicidal later when I slay that pussy," he retorts, making me snort.

"Har, har, har," I mock him as I open the door.

"Am I interrupting something?" Adri asks, smiling as she waves at us from my doorstep. I stuff down the slight irritation at her showing up unannounced and open the door wider to let her in.

"Did your phone blow up?" I ask, letting a bit of the irk seep out, and Vin chuckles behind me.

"No. Can I not pop in on my best friend?" She tips her head to the side as she looks back and forth between Vin and me, her face a mask of uncertainty. This is the tough part, juggling my double lives.

"Sure, but don't be mad if next time you catch me in all my naked glory."

"I came by to find out what we're doing this weekend." She hangs her jacket up and begins to take off her shoes. Well, I guess she's staying a while, so I close the front door.

"I have to be in New York this weekend," I state as I lead her to the family room. Every time I come in here, I imagine my dad and ma lying on the couch watching some stupid reality show. I swallow down the lump and repeat my mantra. *Work now, grieve later.*

"Cool, I can come with! We'll make it a girl's weekend!" she squeals as she falls onto the couch, grabbing the throw blanket to cover her legs. The same blanket Ma and Dad used to wrap up in together. I clench my teeth to stop myself from ripping it out of her hands.

"Can't this weekend. I have to help Emmett pack up." I force myself to sit down beside her, my finger running over the edge of the blanket.

"Pack up?" she repeats as I look up at her, her brows crinkled with confusion.

"Yeah, he's moving here," I reveal and brace myself for her reaction.

"Oh!" She tries but fails to cover her excitement. "That's nice. Will he be attending Precious Blood?"

Linking my hands together in my lap, I force a smile and nod. "Mm-hm."

"Sweet!" She claps as her smile grows wide. "Anyway," she wisely changes the subject. "What about next weekend?" Adri looks at me with her big brown eyes, loneliness reflected in the orbs.

"Can't then either. I have to help Emmett settle in, but the following weekend will be all yours." When her face falls, my stomach sours.

Adrianna was my first real friend here in Whitsborough, my first real girlfriend ever, and I've been distant and aloof with her. She's lonely, and even though I'm busy with a life I don't want her to know about, she deserves better.

"I barely hang out with you anymore," she mumbles as her mouth turns down. "You've been so busy."

"I can't help it right now," I supply as I reach across and grip her hand in mine. "After what happened to my parents and trying to figure out all the assets, I've barely had time to breathe. What about Shay? Couldn't you hang with her?"

I hate suggesting it but I also hate Adri being alone during the summer. Shay has done some questionable things but she's the lesser evil here in Whitsborough.

"Yeah, we talk sometimes." She exhales her breath with a shrug and looks around the room, her gaze anywhere but on me.

"Be careful with her," Vin chimes in. "I drove by Danny's the other day and saw her smoking a joint with Marlana on the front porch."

"Yeah, they're talking again." Adri bites her bottom lip as her shoulders fall forward. "That's why I haven't really been hanging out with her."

"Can't say I didn't see that coming." I roll my eyes. "How about Travis? Why don't you check in on him?" I'm not meaning to pawn her off on others, but I have plans I just can't get out of, and she and Travis have a lot of issues they need to work out.

"He doesn't want to see me." She releases my hand to wring hers together in her lap, the nervous energy pouring off her in waves.

"Says who?" Vin asks as he leans against the wall.

After he showed up unannounced at Travis' house, he's had a different attitude about his brother, and it warms my heart the way he's standing up for him now. They've come a long way. Maybe I really was the bridge they needed.

"I tried to call a few times and he ignores my texts." Adri glances at me and then at Vin, her eyes filled with questions.

"Go over to his house," Vin tells her. "I promise he'll be happy you did."

"Okay, I will do that this weekend." She looks back at me with puppy dog eyes. "I really miss my best friend."

"That's my cue to leave." Vin walks to the front door. "I'll call you later."

"Bye!" I call out. Then I turn to Adri and a grin starts along my mouth. "Let's have wine and talk about boys."

Fuck Adri and her peer pressure.

After two bottles of wine and half a bottle of tequila, we

attempted to do TikTok videos and then passed out in the family room. Now I'm waking up to the sun glaring in through the windows while I'm on the brink of death. It's only fermenting the alcohol further in my belly and making me want to hurl.

A tortured moan sounds beside me and I turn my spinning head to find Adri trying to sit up. Her hair is tangled and matted to the side of her face with something that looks suspiciously like drool and her skin is sallow, tinged with green. Fucking serves her right. Raising my hand, I touch the rat's nest at the nape of my neck and cringe. I probably smell like something crawled inside of it and died.

"Fuck," she groans and scrubs a hand down her face. "I hate when we do this."

"Then why do we keep doing it?" I whine, then wince as the pitch of my voice reverberates throughout my skull.

Adri rolls over onto all fours and moans a bit more, the sound making me worried about Ma's carpet.

"I'm going to head home to hurl, shower, and die," she says as she gingerly stands, stumbling a few steps before righting herself. "In that order."

"Call me when you resurrect," I croak out.

The front door shutting has me slowly sitting up, then rising to my feet. I shuffle out of the family room and slowly take one step at a time toward my room. I have so much to do today that was supposed to be done yesterday, but since I pissed that away—literally—I have double the amount today. While I'm hungover, no less. Moving my ass into the shower, I scrub Jose Cuervo off of me and somehow grab clothing to make myself decent.

Today I'm going to work out of my room because I need my marshmallow mattress under my ass. I text Emmett to make sure he can buy the drug I need to incapacitate my victim, and then I look through the pubs and bars in that area. If Carlos has a plan where he wants to take me, too bad because I'll decide on the place and meet him there. I picked the perfect bar that looks small and secluded, and even better, it's only a couple of minutes' walk to Central Park.

I could've played Jennifer's game and make her son's death gruesome, then send her an ominous message, but I'll make it look like a suicide instead. Taking into consideration his hectic lifestyle and the obscene amount of pressure his mother puts on him to succeed and follow in her footsteps, it's not only plausible but downright believable. She'll know I did it though, and then I'll have to prepare for an all-out war. Luckily, I'm now a Head and I have the Rampage on my side, even though my overprotective older brother is making sure I stay out of things.

It takes a few hours, but I finally have my plan down to perfection and I've accounted for any missteps that may happen along the way. I text Carlos and tell him where I've been wanting to go and if he can meet me. He—thinking with his dick—agrees with everything I say, making this the easiest target yet. Exhaustion seeps through my alcohol-soaked brain and I end up passing out with thoughts of blood and revenge.

It's Friday night and Vin, Emmett, and I are sitting around the enormous table inside Vin's condo. Emmett has a raw steak pressed to his bruised eye as he whines about not being quick enough to kill the douche that jumped him.

"He came out of nowhere. I was just about to hop on my bike," he grits out as he shifts in his chair.

My insides are at a fever pitch as I try to hold back the rage.

Nothing about this feels authentic and it's only fueling my anger more. Emmett was being taught a lesson and I have a feeling I know who the teacher is.

"Did you get a look at him?" I ask, my teeth clenched and my fists curled.

"No." He shakes his head and winces. "It happened so fast. He punched me and then he was off running."

"Weirdest jumping ever," Vin mutters, his eyes flicking from me to my twin with confusion. "Why didn't he take anything?"

"Or... it was orchestrated by someone who wants to prove you can't protect yourself," I muse as I stand from the table and begin to pace.

Carm has the most to gain by forcing his brother to stay here in New York. This ruse he's pulling isn't fooling me. Maybe he has Emmett somehow blinded to his ways, but I know how ruthless he can be. He killed my best friend, after all.

"You think Carm would do this?" Emmett asks, a little shocked as he drops the steak from his bruising eye.

"Yeah, if it means it'll convince you to stay here."

The pacing drains a bit of the anger and I can start thinking clearly once again. Carm is about to sign himself up for a lesson of his own, and he's not going to like the teacher much. That I can guarantee.

"I didn't think of that," he groans and presses the steak back to his face. "I don't want to believe it, but if I ask him, it'll cause a problem." It'll cause a problem with me is what he's not saying.

"You sort of failed though," I point out as I come to stand in front of him, flicking the steak.

"Yeah, I did." Emmett nods with a huff.

Emmett came through with the drug I needed. It's a common roofie drug I'll put in this guy's drink, then get him to Central Park before he's completely out of it. Tomorrow evening, I'll make a pit stop at Central Park and stash away the rope and a few other things to get the job done. Vin and Emmett will wait at the park for me and Carlos to arrive, then I will wrap that noose around his neck and swing him from the thickest tree branch.

"We all good with the plan?" I ask them. Emmett and Vin pass a look between them, and I cock a brow. What the fuck was that?

Vin sees my expression and exhales a heavy breath. "We don't like the thought of the son paying the price for his mother's actions."

"Oh?" I tip my head to the side. "What about my parents paying for the price of me killing a psychopath?"

"That's on Jennifer, Em," Vin implores, his hands resting on the tabletop as his eyes plead with me to understand. "*She* made that error. You don't have to do the same."

"It's too late. Even if I wanted to change my plan—which I don't—we wouldn't have time to think up another one. I need to retaliate now." I fist my hands at my sides as my heart thunders inside my chest.

My family was used as a chess piece in Talia's sick game, so why can't I do the same? Why are they expecting me to be the one who rises above? Have I ever given them the impression that I'm capable of that?

"Okay." Emmett nods. "We're with you either way. Always." He can sense that I'm teetering on the edge of control, my grip on sanity slowly slipping away.

"Yeah," Vin agrees, his eyes slipping over me from head to toe. "Always. I just want you to sleep at night."

"Don't worry," I grind out as I let out the breath I've been holding in my chest. "I will sleep like a fucking baby after this."

"Speaking of sleep,"—Emmett stands—"I need to get back to the compound." He drops the steak into the garbage, wasting a perfectly good cut of meat.

"You stay here tonight," I tell him, my tone brokering no arguments. "I don't want you going back alone."

"Fine, I'm too tired to argue. I'm going to shower." He walks down the hallway toward the spare bedroom, his feet shuffling.

"Do you think Carm would do that?" Vin asks once Emmett is out of sight.

"I don't know." I shake my head. "But if he did, I won't mind taking him into the ring to teach him a lesson."

Chapter Twenty-Two

Ember

I settle on waving my hair and leaving it loose around my shoulders. My makeup is light and a little too pink for my liking, but I need to look like a sorority college girl. I'm wearing a pair of light-wash jeans with rips in the knees, a tight, black lace tank top with a pink cardigan tied over my shoulders, paired with light pink Jimmy Choo heels.

This look is screaming virginal and ready for the taking all at once. I finish it with a black clutch and inside is a small bag of crushed pills. I have an idea to order us a shot and distract him so I can pour some of it inside. Then I will ask him to take me on a romantic walk through Central Park. If that doesn't work, I'll tell him I want to lose my virginity in public like a naughty girl. I'm banking on that one to achieve the desired outcome I'm looking for.

My burner phone buzzes beside me with a text and I open the screen to see it's from Carlos. *Obviously.*

Carlos: Heading out in 10. What time should I expect you?

Me: I'll leave in 10 too.

Carlos: KK!

Ugh, he's probably thinking he's getting laid tonight and it's my job to make him believe it, right up to the point he's swinging from that branch.

I walk out of the bathroom and into the living room where both Emmett and Vin are playing some shooting video game. Neither one is aware of me as they scream and swear at each other.

"Ahem," I clear my throat.

Vin looks up first, and his reaction is hilarious. His mouth turns down and his brows knit together, his back stiffening as the controller drops to his lap. "What are you wearing? Is your face sparkling?"

"You don't like it?" I mock pout as my hands hit my waist and I pop my hip.

"Not really." He shakes his head, his eyes roving over my outfit. "You look like Martha Stewart's daughter or something."

"I like it!" Emmett says, sincerity pouring from his turquoise eyes. "You look like a smart schoolgirl."

"Perfect." I snap my fingers. "That's the look I was going for." I bend down in front of Vin and place a hand on his cheek. "I'm happy you like me for me." I give him a quick peck on the lips and laugh when he wipes off my shiny pink gloss with the back of his hand, a look of disgust coming over his face.

"Yeah,"—he looks me up and down—"don't get used to this look and burn that lip shit when you're done."

Earlier in the day, we found the perfect tree in the most secluded spot of the park. My duffel bag is hiding beside it, behind a large bush with an added perk of a bench situated nearby. I plan on guiding Carlos to that spot, giving him the impression I want to fuck him on it. With guys, if you dangle a pussy in their face, they will turn off every other instinct except the one to procreate. Thank god Jennifer had sons and not daughters, otherwise, I'd have to hope they were a little bi-curious.

We all leave the apartment, and when we get outside, we part ways. Vin and Emmett are going to go chill near the spot in Central Park and I'm taking an Uber to the bar. I can't be seen being dropped off by Vin or Emmett in case this guy is waiting for me outside. The same goes with driving Shelby. I can't have any witnesses and she is a car people would remember.

The Uber pulls up outside the bar, and as I predicted, Carlos is standing out front with a smug look on his face. He gives me a once-over as his eyes darken with the telltale sign of lust. This one is going to be so easy, like stealing fucking candy from a baby. I walk up to him, putting a little more swing in my step, and his eyes follow the bounce of my tits until I'm right up in front of him. Then he quickly leans down and plants a sloppy kiss on my lips.

Fuck, that's gross. Can you catch mouth chlamydia from slobber? I school my features and suppress the urge to vomit, then I give him what I hope is the most rapey look ever.

"Do you want to grab a booth in the back or sit at the bar?" he asks as his fingers brush the hair off my shoulders, his hand lingering a little too long near my throat.

"Booth, definitely." I grin and look up at him through my lashes.

"Done." I follow him into the dimly lit, hole-in-the-wall bar and he guides us to one of five booths lined across the back wall. I slide into the booth and I'm pleasantly surprised when he slides in beside me instead of sitting opposite. This will make drugging him all that much easier.

"What can I get you to drink?" A waitress appears, her tits nearly spilling from her low-cut top.

"I will take a beer in a glass," Carlos says. "A clean one."

Ugh, what a pretentious prick. "I'll have a rum and coke in a glass that I'm sure is clean." I nod, unable to hold in the sarcasm. The waitress grins at me and wanders off to place our orders.

"Was I being a dick?" he asks, his eyes lacking empathy.

"No, no." I shake my head. "I was just poking fun at you. Sorry." *I'd rather say you're a cunt the size of the Grand Canyon, a place I'd love to toss your mother over.*

"It's all good." He smiles wide, showcasing his overly bleached teeth.

I plaster on a fake smile and inwardly cringe when my cheeks hurt. His gaze keeps dropping to the very little cleavage I'm showing and it's taking all my strength not to give him one quick jab in the throat.

"So, what classes are you taking?" he asks me, the question perfunctory and lacking any actual curiosity. I could say the urinary trait of felines and he'd probably nod like it's interesting. Still, I need to avoid school details because I don't go to Columbia and I don't want him catching on to that.

"Actually, I want to play a drinking game." I smile as the waitress drops off our drinks. "We take turns naming public places in New York and the other has to drink if they've had sex there.

Kind of like a Never Have I Ever."

His eyes light up and he sucks his bottom lip into his mouth. *Yeah, asshole, you really are a simpleminded guy.* "Okay." He grins. "An elevator."

I don't drink and give him what I hope is a blushing, coy look. His smile widens and he drinks.

"Hmm…" I tap my chin in thought. "In a car."

He takes a gulp of his drink and laughs when I still don't drink. Of fucking course, I've fucked Vin almost everywhere, but I'm the virginal college girl tonight.

"In a movie theater," he says. I shake my head and cover my face with my hands, peeking at him through my fingers. I'm hoping this is how virginal girls look when they're embarrassed. He laughs again and drinks. Ew, he's a real dirtbag.

"Central Park," I whisper. His eyes widen and I'm praying on everything that he doesn't drink. When neither of us takes a drink, I laugh, and it's genuine because this is a sign from god. "I think we should take a walk later." Suggestion is heavy in my tone as he scoots a little closer.

"Yeah, we should." He nods and sucks back his beer. He's suddenly in a rush to finish our drinks, but I need him nice and drugged before we leave.

"Let's have a shot of tequila and get out of here," I breathe into his ear.

"Really?" The excitement shines through his eyes and a familiar tug appears at the base of my belly. No, not arousal, but bloodlust. I'm coming close to enacting justice for my parents' murders, and it feels so fucking good. I let the familiar warmth travel throughout my body like a comforting blanket.

"Yes, really. I just need more liquid courage." When he turns his head to call the waitress over, I slip my hand inside the clutch and pull out the baggy. With his head still turned, I slip my clutch on the floor and kick it to his feet. The waitress comes over and Carlos orders two tequila shots before asking for them to be rushed. The desperation is such a fucking turn off.

The shots are placed on the table with some salt and two lemon slices. Pretty boy here licks his wrist like a girl and pours the salt. "Do you want some?" He holds out the salt.

"No, I'll shoot the tequila straight." Not very innocent girl-like, but it's becoming exhausting. Then I begin to act nervous as I look around the booth. "Do you see my purse anywhere?"

"It's okay, it's got to be here." He looks around and underneath him.

"Is it on the floor?" I let my eyes water as my voice bleeds with anxiety, and when he bends down to check, I pour the powder into his shot, watching as it quickly disappears.

"Got it!" he exclaims as he comes back up with my clutch in his hand.

"Thank you." I exhale with relief and give him an appreciative smile.

His brows crinkle in thought, but he quickly brushes it off and licks the salt. Then we both down the shots and I fold my lips into my mouth to stop my laughter as he fans his face while sucking the shit out of the lemon slice.

"I hate tequila." His face screws up as his throat works on a gag.

"I can tell." I nod as I take in his watering eyes.

He pays our bill at the bar and practically drags me across the floor to the door. Once we step on the sidewalk, we make a left, and at a steady pace, amble our way toward Central Park.

"Do you have any brothers or sisters?" I ask, making small talk and hopefully getting some information along the way.

"No." He side-eyes me. "I'm an only child." Huh, why would he lie about that? "How about you?"

"Yes, I have an older brother." I decide to lie a little too. "He's not around much and he thinks I'm a pest." Not really a lie. Carlos stays quiet and nods a little as he listens. "Your parents must be so proud of you. Columbia Law is prestigious."

"They are," he mutters, not really revealing much at first, but then lets it all out in the next breath. "My mother wants me here, but she's never content, and my father just hates us." He looks at me, his face lined with surprise, like he actually didn't mean to blurt all that out. "Sorry, fuck. I didn't mean to say all that. I don't actually get along with my parents and just stay away."

"I get it." I pat his arm awkwardly, like he has leprosy. "Your secrets are safe with me." My stomach swirls with uncertainty for the first time and I try to tamp it down.

I need to do this for my parents because what better way to get back at Jennifer for fucking with my blood than to fuck with hers? But… what if her blood hates her too and I'm sentencing him to death based on her crimes? Someone could've done the same to me or Emmett for Raphael's crimes. Fuck, someone could've done that to Vin based on what Robert has done and Vin couldn't be any more different from his father.

We approach Central Park and I lead Carlos down the path we scoped out earlier. His steps falter and his pace slows as I look into his face masked in confusion. His eyes are becoming droopy and his mouth curls down into a frown.

"I feel weird," he says as he stops walking.

"Maybe you drank those drinks too fast?" I open my eyes wide and give him an innocent look.

"Yeah, maybe." He grabs my hand and we continue walking forward. "Where are you leading us? Somewhere private? I thought you had done nothing here before?" His voice is filled with accusation.

"This is where I come to read." Fluttering my lashes, I smile up at him. "I don't enjoy being around people." I shrug, and he blinks at me slowly as a goofy smile creeps across his mouth.

"You want us to defile your little reading nook in the park, huh?" He leans in closer and stumbles into me, making me bite back a hiss of irritation. "You want to come here afterward and be reminded that I fucked you so hard on that bench?"

"Exactly," I breathe out in my most seductive voice. "I want to sit here tomorrow and still feel you inside me."

He groans and we proceed deeper down the path. A few minutes later, the bench comes into view and Carlos is now dragging his feet and walking like something off *The Walking Dead*. He spots the bench and makes a beeline for it, sitting down before leaning his head against the back with a long exhale.

"I just need to take a breather," he mumbles. If he opens his eyes right now and looks a bit to the right, he'll find the noose Vin and Emmett hung while we were at the bar. Speaking of them, both are just sitting on the grass on the other side of the tree, watching us. "My mother tells me not to leave campus because they could kidnap me. She treats me like a fucking child when I can look after myself. I can't fucking stand her." He's practically passed out and his ramblings sound like he's talking in his sleep.

Uncertainty swirls again, and this time I listen to it. Maybe Vin was right. Carlos shouldn't be punished for the choices his mother made. If I do this, then I would be no better than her, and I have always made sure my killings were based on that person's actions. With a grunt, I plop my ass beside him as he snores softly.

"He's out?" Emmett asks as he and Vin walk over to us.

"Yeah," I huff as I pick at the sweater around my neck.

"Okay, how did you want to do this?" Vin runs his hand over my hair and his touch cements my decision. *We are not our parents.*

"I won't kill him." I look up into Vin's eyes and then over at Emmett. "We are not our parents."

"You don't have to kill him to send a message," Emmett pipes up. "We'll make this look like a botched suicide. The pills I gave you weren't your typical roofie. These are strong sleeping aids and they leave the system fairly quickly." He walks over to the noose and pulls it down from the branch. "We can wrap the noose around his neck and lay him by the tree, then take some pictures with your burner phone." He comes with the noose in his hands and drops it down over Carlos' head before tightening it around his neck. "In a few hours, you can send those photos anonymously to the police department. It can't be traced."

That's actually not a bad idea. Jennifer will for sure receive those photos, even if the police block it from the media due to who she is. It'll be obvious who set this up, especially when she questions her son about who he was out with the night before. She'll know I can also infiltrate her life as well as she has mine, but the difference is I plan on killing only her.

I help them move his body to the base of the tree and lay him out under a branch that Emmett and Vin break, making it look believable. Then we put some strategically placed branches on him before I smear dirt on his face and clothing. After we finish, I take a series of photos of him lying on the ground and the broken branch.

"We should get going," Emmett says while he grabs the duffel bag. "He'll wake up soon."

Vin and I follow Emmett out of the cluster of trees in the opposite direction I entered with Carlos. A blacked-out sedan is waiting, parked on the side of a service road, and I'm thankful Emmett thought about using this instead of Shelby. We pile in and Emmett takes us on a scenic route around the city until he's sure we don't have a tail. Once we're back at Vin's condo, I'm so exhausted I can barely lift my feet.

"Give me the phone." Emmett holds his hand out. "I'll send off the photos to the police and you guys can head to bed."

"Okay." I nod, too tired to object. "Don't tell Carm about our involvement in this."

"I won't." He shakes his head.

I hand over the phone and follow Vin into our bedroom. Once inside, he helps me out of the clothes I was wearing, dresses me in a sleep shirt and no underwear, then brushes out the knots in my hair.

"I'm proud of you, baby," he whispers, that sentence sending a chill down my spine. *You've made me proud.* I shake off the voice of my father as I rest my forehead on Vin's chest. "Your parents are proud of you too."

I really hope my parents can't see anything I have done with my life, that includes my mother as well. I truly believe if she's watching me now, she would find more of my father than herself in me, and I just can't live with that thought. Even knowing this, I can't stop what I've started until I have eliminated the threat to my family and the people I love most. So, I might as well have fun along the way.

Vin

The past week has been quiet, and as predicted, none of the suicide attempt was leaked to the media, but we are sure Jennifer got the message. Carm called to tell Ember it looked like Jennifer had taken her family on an impromptu vacation this past Tuesday and he didn't know where or for how long. Carm says he has his right-hand and best tracker, Trent, on the job.

Ember seems lighter and more carefree this week. Maybe it's because her brother is moving here, but I think it's because she doesn't have the weight of another murder on her shoulders. Emmett sent a moving van and it arrived today with most of his stuff. The fucking van was packed tight and I'm still wondering how the fuck a seventeen-year-old managed to accumulate this much.

"Is he a hoarder?" Em whispers as two guys unload his shit into her foyer. "Is this a sign for severe psychosis?"

I walk over to a stack of boxes and open the first one in front of me. It's filled with books and what looks to be manga. I open a few more boxes and find the same. Emmett must be an avid reader. You would never guess by his appearance, but then again, you'd never guess I was an aspiring actor by mine either. "He has a ton of books," I tell Em over my shoulder, "and some of these look hella expensive."

"Seriously?" she asks with shock while coming to stand beside me. "Emmett reads?"

"Yeah, unless he robbed a few bookstores for the fun of it." I step back as another three boxes are deposited beside us.

"That sounds more realistic." She nods as her brows crinkle

in thought. "This isn't going to all fit into his room. I wouldn't mind starting a library though."

"Library?" I echo as I look at her with surprise. "What room would you convert?"

"The only one in this house that remains empty." She can't mean her parents' room because she hasn't stepped foot inside since we received the news of their death. The door has been shut tight and no one is allowed to enter. "There's a large loft on the third floor. It's soundproofed too. Do you know of anyone that could build me a library?"

"We'll figure it out," I promise as I kiss the top of her head. "I'm going to stop by Travis' and find out if he's ready to go tomorrow."

"Okay." She grins at me and reaches up to kiss my cheek. She's happy that I'm trying to figure out how to salvage a relationship with my brother.

I leave her to the movers and hop into my Hummer to head over to Travis'. Danny is throwing another party when I pass by his house again, and I slow down and keep my eye on his front lawn. There looks to be some sort of fight going on with a few guys from our drama club and Danny himself is sitting on his front porch, spectating with pleasure. He spots my vehicle and jumps up from his seat.

"Hey! Vin!" I ease onto the brake as he jogs across the street. "Are you coming in?"

"Nah, I don't think so." I shake my head. "I was about to pick up Travis."

"Travis?" His nose turns up in disgust. "Why?"

"Probably because he's my brother," I retort, irritation

seeping through me.

"This shit is weird. I don't hear from you in weeks and suddenly you're best friends with your enemy?" he scoffs, his eyes rolling as if I've lost my fucking mind, and in a way, I have. I've grown a lot since the start of grade eleven.

"Sometimes we're mistaken on who's an enemy and who's a friend." I lean out my window. "Mind if I bring him by?"

"Whatever you want, man. As long as I actually get to chill with you this summer." He rubs his hands together in anticipation as I ease my foot off the brake.

I'm not sure how Travis will react about going to Danny's house for a party, but I'm hoping it'll take his mind off his homelife for a little while. He barely gets out as it is, and yeah, we're bringing him to New York with us this weekend, but the more time he's out of that house, the better.

I pull up to his driveway and find the gates open yet again. I take my time driving up to the house just in case something flies off the balcony in front of me. When the coast is clear, I park the Hummer and step out.

"Back again?" he asks from above me. I look up and find him smoking while leaning on the railing. "What's up? Are we leaving a day early?"

"Nah, I got bored watching movers unload Emmett's shit. Thought we could go chill. Danny is having a party," I suggest.

"You want to join the ranks of the delinquents today?" His brow raises, then a smile crawls along his mouth as he steps back. "I'm in."

"Yo! I used to chill with them." I cross my arms over my chest as I glare at him, his smug look making me want to smash my fist into it. For old times' sake, of course.

"Yeah, you did," he replies with a wink, hauling a snarl from my throat. "I gotta get dressed. Give me five minutes."

"Bastard," I mutter.

Sitting back in my vehicle, I wait a few minutes before the front door opens, but it's not Travis, it's his mother, Christina. She stands in the doorway with what looks to be a martini glass and a cigarette. She continues to stare at me, so I climb back out and go to lean on the front of the Hummer.

"Hi, Mrs. Greene. How are you doing?" I aim for polite, but my muscles tense as she continues to scrutinize me.

"Don't you just look delectable," she purrs, her tongue snaking out along her lower lip as she assesses me. "You have his eyes and his body build."

"You doing good?" I ignore her comparisons to the man I hate, fighting the urge to recoil.

"I am now." She takes a drink of her martini as her robe opens to reveal she has nothing on underneath. I turn away with a disgusted huff as she chuckles and says, "I could always be better. Want to come in for a drink?"

Before I can reply, she gasps, making me turn to find her being pulled by her arm back into the house. I push off the Hummer and start for the front door when Travis appears.

"Are you sick?" Travis' voice thunders out onto the front porch. "He's my brother! Get the fuck upstairs. You're embarrassing."

"That is a *man* in our driveway, and a handsome one at that," his mother croons, unaffected by Travis' words and actions. "I can show him what a real woman's like."

"Go pop some pills and put your ass to bed."

I stop snooping and head back to my Hummer, quickly jumping inside. Clearly, his mother is drunk and not herself right now. Travis comes out a few moments later and gets into the passenger side.

"Sorry about that." He avoids my eyes as he puts on his seat belt. "She's out of it."

"It's all good." I shrug. "You need to piss before we leave?" I grin at him.

"You asking to see my dick again? You realize we're related and incest is illegal?" He finally turns to look at me, his grin not quite meeting his eyes.

"Fuck, you're nasty, dude."

"That's what she said." He nods.

I chuckle as I pull out of his driveway, and we make our way over to Danny's. The music is still pretty loud and someone's already out front puking into a flower pot. So, the party has been going for a while clearly. I park on the road and we both walk up Danny's front drive. Travis lights another smoke and stops to check out two females slapping the shit out of each other.

"Those things are going to kill you." I point at his cigarette as he side-eyes me, exhaling the smoke in front of him.

He shrugs while pulling his hat lower over his eyes.

"Vin?" Marlana's voice sounds from the doorway. I figured she would probably be here, and maybe I wanted her to be. I would like to give her the closure she obviously needs for whatever the fuck we were.

Travis throws down his smoke and steps on it. "I'm gonna go find a drink." He brushes by Marlana and nods.

"Hey." She comes over to me, her eyes wary as she glances around. "Where's Ember?"

"At home." I take a step back to put a bit more distance between us, making it clear I want nothing to do with her.

"Oh, that's cool." She slips her hands in her jeans pockets and gives me a concerned look. "Is everything okay with you guys?" Hope flares in her eyes, but I need to squash that right now and make sure it sticks forever.

"I'm going to marry Ember, but I do owe you an apology because I used you for many years. I knew how you felt, and I continued to use you because it was easy." Her face falls and she grows a few shades redder. "I should have never continued to sleep with you because I never, ever intended to have a relationship with you. A relationship was never going to happen with you, Marlana, even if Ember hadn't moved here."

"Wow." She shakes her head and her purple hair billows around her face. "Don't hold back or anything."

"I'm telling you as a warning. Ember is not to be fucked with and if you keep up with the shit you were pulling last year and this summer, she will not hesitate to fuck you up. So just move on already. Stop approaching me like we're friends because we're not. What we had was never a friendship. We were fucking and that ended a long time ago." I pity her but I keep my tone firm and maintain the distance between us.

A tear escapes and rolls down her cheek as her face crumples. I can never tell what's real and what's not with this bitch, so I have a hard time not being apathetic toward her. "Okay, I got it." She nods and starts walking into the house. Then she turns when she gets to the front door and says, "It's over." *Duh, bitch.* I breathe a sigh of relief when she finally disappears into the house. It's as though a weight has been lifted from my shoulders.

Approaching the front of the house, I look for Travis and instead find Marlana sitting on the lap of a drama club dude and they're devouring each other's mouths. Perfect. I head toward the backyard and to the sounds of people splashing in the pool. That's where Danny and I would be during these things, drinking and watching the girls strip off their clothing. I do indeed find Danny, and surprisingly, I also find Travis with him. They have a line of shots in front of them and my brother is downing most of them in quick succession. Again, I would be impressed with his drinking skills if I wasn't so worried about how often he's doing it.

"Vin! Shots!" Danny yells out. Travis turns after downing the last shot and grabs his beer.

"Nah, dude. I'm driving, but I'll grab a beer." I take a beer from a nearby cooler and raise an eyebrow at Travis.

"What?"

"You good?" His eyes flick over to the right where Adri is sitting with Shay. She's wearing a barely there pink bikini and laughing at something a guy that's standing around them says. "Never mind," I state and clasp my hand on his shoulder. Then Adri notices us and she stands, stunned to find Travis and me here together. She moves away from Shay and the group of admirers to approach us.

"Hey, guys," she mutters, looking around us. "Is Ember here?"

"Nah," I reply. "She's home organizing all of Emmett's shit."

"Cool." She nods and looks at Travis. "Hey, Trav." He nods in response without making eye contact and then turns his back to head inside. "Fuck, I really don't know what I did wrong," she groans as her shoulders deflate with rejection.

"His dad died and his house is a shithole right now. His mother is out of her mind and he has no one. That's what's wrong." Her obtuse attitude toward Travis is grating on my nerves. I turn my back on her as well and head inside to look for my brother. He's leaving through the front door and I follow him. Suddenly, I'm stopped by Adri's hand on my arm.

"I'm not ignoring the issues he's going through. I'd help him if he would just let me," she whispers as tears fill her eyes. My heart squeezes for the confusion swimming in their depths, but Travis needs me more and Adri isn't high on my priority list to be honest.

"Don't wait for him to let you, just force him, like I've been doing," I tell her gently and pull my arm away. "I need to go find him."

He's on the porch lighting another cigarette and leaning against the side of the house. "Want to head out?" I ask him. He looks at me and shrugs, trying to look unbothered, but the muscle in his jaw tics with whatever he's suppressing. "Want to talk about her?"

"Nope." He pops his P then takes a drag of his smoke, blowing o's out in front of him.

"Alright."

I lean against the house beside him and finish my beer while he smokes. It's not an awkward silence and I make it a point to have a conversation with him this weekend. He needs to off-load because the look in his eyes is the same one I used to have until Em came and coaxed me off the ledge.

While we're driving back to his house, Travis scrolls through his phone, and I glance over to see Adri's IG page. I pull into his driveway and put the Hummer in park.

"Hey," I say to him, "open that glove box." He reaches forward and opens it, the lid falling forward. "Reach in and pull out what's in there." Slipping his hand inside, his eyes widen the moment he touches it.

"What the fuck, Vin!" he yells, pulling his hand back out as if he was burned. "Why do you have that?" Travis' eyes look about ready to pop from his skull as he stares at me like I've lost my mind.

"Because life is never predictable." I look deep into his eyes, forcing him to hear the truth in my words. The truth he's already lived through. "And I wanted to always be prepared. Now, I want you to take it."

"I..." His head drops forward, his chin hitting his chest. "I hate guns." The despair in his tone tugs on my heart.

"Look, I don't think our father was involved with the best of people and I need to make sure you can protect yourself." I can't delve too deep into what Ember has uncovered about Robert Greene, but he needs to at least keep his eyes and ears open in his surroundings.

He turns to look at me with his eyes wide. "How do you know who Dad was involved with?"

"I wasn't always sure, just a hunch, but seeing your reaction now proves I was correct. Take it, please." I purposely leave out the fact that Ember has looked into our father's past because it'll only lead to more questions I wouldn't be able to answer. He reaches back in and hesitantly pulls out the gun, then tucks it into the waistband of his jeans. I don't like forcing it on him, but I'd dislike it even more if something happened to him and he had no one around to help. "Hide it in a safe place, okay?"

His face becomes serious as he nods and gets out of the Hummer. "See you tomorrow."

Chapter Twenty-Three

Vin

When we finally arrive at the condo, it's late Friday evening. The drive was easier this time with the three of us rotating and I was able to rest. This place is beginning to feel like home since we're here every weekend, although that could just be because Ember is my home whether we're here or in Whitsborough. This weekend though, I want to have some fun and try to get Travis' mind off the bullshit he's dealing with hours away in Whitsborough.

"I haven't been here in so long," Travis says with a nostalgic tone, dropping his bag to the floor. "Nice view." He walks over to the windows, pressing his hand to the pane, and overlooks the busy city below.

"I love it here," Ember breathes out, her eyes becoming glossy as she looks at the view. "New York will always be home to me." I'll have to remind her later that I'm her home, no matter where the fuck we are. She heads into the kitchen and pulls open the fridge. We have little in the way of food because we don't want it to spoil in the fridge during the week when we're not here. "Fuck, I'm starving."

"Let's order some Chinese. Travis and I will take a walk to pick it up while you go take a shower and relax," I suggest as I lean in to kiss her softly.

"You're too good to me." She smiles against my lips.

"Is this what I have to deal with all weekend?" Travis asks with his arms crossed over his chest and a smirk on his face.

"Wear earphones while you sleep." I wink at him as I pull away from Ember. "We can be loud."

"Gross." He shudders and turns back to the window as Ember chuckles, her hands wrapping around my waist.

"I'm gonna call Emmett and tell him we're here. You guys order whatever." She gives me a squeeze, then heads into our bedroom and closes the door.

"I'll order," Travis says as he walks into the kitchen, finding a few menus scattered on the counter from our last few visits.

"Cool."

About ten minutes later, we exit the condo and walk a few blocks up the street to the Chinese restaurant. Travis has been quiet, but I'm planning on having a chat with him later, after dinner. Here in New York, you can't see a star in the sky. In Whitsborough, on a clear night, they twinkle brightly overhead.

The Chinese restaurant's entrance is a little way down a sketchy-looking alleyway, but Ember says this is the best one around and I'm excited to try it. We enter the alley and Travis takes a quick look over his shoulder, his face a mask of apprehension. Unease slips down my spine, like someone is following or watching us. I reach into the back of my jeans for the gun Travis returned to me, then look back as a hooded figure comes up quickly and hits me on the side of my head, making me drop to my knees. My sight grows hazy as I drop the gun, the guy making a jump for Travis, his shout the last thing I hear as everything goes black.

The sound of metal sliding open pulls me from my unconsciousness, and I open my eyes as two guys drag in a moaning Travis before dropping him on the floor. I don't have time to survey my surroundings as the two men approach me and roughly lift me to my feet.

"Who are you?" I slur out as I fight to stay conscious, my head pounding with agony.

They don't answer me and instead, drag me down a hallway to an open door. They pull me into a room and strap my arms to a chair with zip ties. "Hey!" I finally struggle against the bonds as my senses come back to me, only to have them cut into my skin, making me stop. "Where are we?" They exit the room without responding and then shut the door.

The room is the size of Ember's walk-in closet with concrete walls and floors. There are no windows, giving the space a dank, musty scent, and besides the chair I'm sitting in, there's only a metal table and another chair on the other side.

A few minutes later, I have blood oozing out of my wrists from trying to break the ties and my hands have gone numb because those bastards strapped me in too tight. The door bangs open, and my jaw drops from shock as I recognize the guy who enters. He walks straight up to the table and takes a seat in the chair across from me, smirking at the shock on my face while drumming out a beat on top of the table.

"You guys really thought you had me, huh?" He chuckles. "I'll admit, that pretty little girlfriend of yours is smart."

"I hope you know you've just signed your death certificate," I grit out as the numbness spreads up my arms. "We saved you once. It won't happen again."

"How did you guys find me?" Carlos leans his elbows on the table, his dark eyes manically flicking over me. "I don't even have the Talia last name." His words are filled with curiosity. Ember did all the digging, but even if I had the answer, I wouldn't tell him a thing. "I kissed her, you know? Ran my tongue along those luscious lips of hers. I even grabbed a handful of tit and squeezed. After we kill you and that other guy you're with, I'm going to head over to that condo of yours and rape her multiple times." Ember told me he surprised her with a kiss that night as soon as we got back to the condo, but he's lying about the tit grab. I school my features and put on a mask of boredom, but inside, I'm a blazing inferno. His eyebrow flicks upward. "Nothing? Fine."

He stands up from the chair and comes around to my side of the table. I keep eye contact with him because the little bitch doesn't scare me. He bends down into my face and opens his mouth to speak when I spit into it. His fist immediately connects with my right eye and my head snaps to the side as he retches and spits onto the floor. He hits like a little pussy too. When I laugh, he punches me again in the same spot and then on the side of my head before kicking me in the chest. My chair falls back and my head hits the concrete floor with a sickening thud, the edges of my vision becoming foggy and black. It's a fucking miracle I am staying conscious right now. He calls for a guard to come in and pull me back up to sitting, but only after he stomps on my chest twice more. Pain tears through me but I refuse to give him anything more than a grunt in response.

"You pull that shit again and I'll kill your buddy in that cell with you. I'll bring him in here and you'll watch as I torture him. Do you understand?" Until recently, I would've laughed in this motherfucker's face if he threatened Travis' life. I would've been noncompliant just to ensure his threats came to fruition. A lot has changed since then, and right now, I'm feeling very protective of my little brother. So I nod and he walks back over to sit in the seat across from me.

"How did you guys find me?" he asks again, his arms crossing on the tabletop as his fingers dance along the wood. He's nervous, and that tells me he knows just what he's up against.

"That had nothing to do with me. Ember found you." My voice cracks as my vision swirls, the throbbing in my head intensifying. It's time he knew just how fucking badass my girl is.

"Why did she come after me?" His mouth turns down as his brows crash together. It's hard to believe that he doesn't know about the feud between Ember and Jennifer Talia.

"You need to ask your mother why," I sneer as I try to fist my numb hands, the fingers barely curling.

"I'm asking you!" he screams and rips his hand through his hair, looking frustrated and confused with my answer.

"Your mother killed her parents and she wanted to kill you as revenge," I reveal, hoping he doesn't scream again because my head is about to explode.

"Why didn't she?" His brows crinkle in thought as his voice drops and his hand lands back at his side.

"Because she realized she didn't want you to pay for your mother's decisions. That's all I have. I know nothing else." I suck in a deep breath, the pain in my chest radiating outward. He must've fractured a few ribs.

"What about Emmett and Carmelo Torres? What can you tell me about them?" He leans forward, his eyes searching my face for clues he won't find. Even if I'm wondering how the hell he knows about them to begin with.

"Again, not much." I shrug, and the movement causes pain to slice through my chest as I release a breath through clenched teeth.

"Do you expect me to believe you know nothing about your girlfriend's twin brother and her older brother?" His sarcastic laugh fills the small room, the noise bouncing off the walls and smacking into my skull.

"You probably have more information than I do." It's not a lie. Emmett and Carm are still strangers to me, Carm more so.

"Is it not strange that Carmelo kidnaps his sister, stands complicit as she fights to the death, but somehow he's earned her full trust?" What is he trying to say? Is Carm against us? Dread pools in my gut, but I keep my face as neutral as I can.

"They had a common enemy," I provide, the words sounding empty, without conviction.

He throws his head back and laughs heartily this time, the sound like cymbals inside my head. "Common enemy? Tell me you're not talking about Raphael Torres?" I don't reply. What the fuck is he trying to tell me right now? How does this guy know about all this? Is Ember in danger with Carm? "Raphael was grooming the apple of his eye to run his entire organization. Carmelo had everything he ever wanted from that man." My heart pounds inside my chest and breathing is becoming difficult. "Shock looks good on your face. That just tells me you don't know shit." He reaches behind him before laying a gun on the table, spinning it around. "I should just kill you and get it over with."

"Go ahead." I grin, not an ounce of fear inside of me. "She's coming for you, regardless."

"I'm not afraid of her." He visibly swallows. *Liar.*

"That's your first mistake."

He gets up from his seat and saunters over to the metal door, then he raps on it three times before the guard on the outside opens it up. "Take him back to the cell and bring me the other one."

"You don't need him; he knows less than me. He wasn't even with us for what we did to you." Panic laces every word, but I don't give a shit. Carlos doesn't answer me as two guards come into the room and release me from the chair. I struggle, trying to get out of their grasp.

"Stop fighting us," one guard grunts as he gets my elbow to his ribs.

Before I can say anything else, Carlos steps forward and hits me on the side of the head with the gun, and finally, the unconsciousness I was fighting takes hold.

Mold and piss wafts through my nostrils and I swear I can fucking taste it. I tamp down the urge to vomit and try to get a clear view of where the fuck I am. My right eye is swollen shut and the left is blurry from the pain still throbbing through my head. That little bitch, Carlos, fucked it up real good. I pull myself up to sit, wincing as a sharp pain slices through my right side. I'm pretty sure my rib is at least fractured, fucking piece of shit. Why the fuck did I ever convince Ember not to kill him?

"Shit," a voice sounds to my right across the room. "Where the fuck am I?"

"Trav?" My head whips toward the sound and my heart

crashes through my rib cage as pain flares hotter.

"Vin?" he croaks out, not sounding any better than me.

"Yeah, bro. I'm here." My eye slowly adjusts, revealing some sort of cell, like a jail with bars and all. "Tell me you saw something when they brought us here." It's our only chance of getting out of here alive.

"Nah, just the inside of a black bag." His voice is rough, the gravelly sound echoing in the space around us.

"Fuck!" I snap and suck in a breath from the pain. "Are you hurt? Did they knock you out too?"

"No, that's why I had the bag over my head. I've had worse," he grunts and pulls himself to his feet. Guilt consumes me for a few minutes, and I lean my head back against the concrete wall. "I'm not talking about from you. That shit was child's play."

"From whom then?" I ask as I stare at him, surprise overtaking the pain for a few moments. Who else hurt him?

"I can make you a list, but I really don't have time to go through them all right now." He shuffles to the bars and tries pulling on the door. "Fuck. If that dude comes back here… I don't even care if he has a gun, I'm swinging."

"What were they asking you?" Travis has been kept safely on the outside of Ember's life. Her need to protect him meant not telling him anything.

"Shit about Ember and our father," he mumbles as he looks at me over his shoulder. "I didn't say a word to them though. They thought after a beating I'd change my mind. They thought wrong." He pats down his pockets and curses. "Fuck, I need a smoke."

They didn't ask me shit about my father. It was all about

Ember and her brothers. "What shit were they asking you about Robert?"

"If I was certain he took his own life." A ringing filters through my ears as my mouth runs dry. Something isn't adding up.

"What? That's fucked up." I shake my head, trying to clear the pain that's fogging my thoughts. "The man didn't want to die an invalid. He was too fucking proud for that."

"No." Travis runs his hand down his face. "You're wrong. Our father was still hoping to be cured. He thought the more money he paid doctors, the more they would be motivated to cure him. So, do I think he killed himself? The answer is no."

"So, you think someone murdered him?" Pins and needles rush along my arms as my fingers slowly begin to curl into my palms, my breath coming in heavy pants.

Robert Greene murdered.

Ember hating everything I told her about the man.

Her certain skills making her a deadly assassin.

"Yes. Someone broke into my house, made Father slice his wrists, and then wiped my security footage for the entire day." He leans against the concrete wall before sliding down to sit. "I just haven't figured out what for. To be honest, I thought it might've been you because he signed over the fucking condo we were talking about before that, but then I thought about it, and I figured you would've done it a lot sooner if you wanted the fucker dead."

"It wasn't me." But I think I know exactly who it was. I had just confided in Ember the weekend before about my father and how my hatred started. She also wiped Marlana's computer that one time and I was surprised she knew anything about technology on that level.

"I know," he agrees, his head tipping back against the concrete. "I already have my suspicions of who did it."

"Who?" I ask as my lungs refuse to expand and my chest screams in agony while I pray it's not Ember he suspects.

"I'd rather confront them to their face, and if you want to be there, you can be." He sounds so nonchalant, as if the death of his father is nothing more than an inconvenience.

"Alright." I nod, knowing this isn't the time or place to discuss it anyway.

"How the fuck are we getting out of here?" he grinds out as he looks at the bars.

"Ember and Emmett will find us." I don't have a single doubt about that statement. My girl would burn the entire world to the ground to find me, and her brothers will be right there to protect her if need be. Carm has a fucking mob behind him and he better fucking use it or else I'll fucking kill him myself once I'm free from this shithole.

"What? Are they like secret agents or something?" Travis' head tips to the side as his brow strikes upward. I won't reveal Ember's secrets. He'll find out soon enough because I know what he means to Ember and it's only a matter of time before she tells him. Especially after today.

"Or something," I say as my head rolls to the side against the wall behind me. There isn't much light inside our cell so I can't tell how injured he is, making guilt rush through me at bringing him to New York in the first place.

I can't ignore the pit of dread in my stomach about Carm. Ember would've gone straight to him once she realized we weren't coming back and this would be his chance to fuck her over, if that's what he wants to do. I just pray that she keeps her head clear and her emotions packed down like usual. That way, she'll notice the signs if he's double-crossing her. I really hope he's not and that this weird feeling I'm having is nothing but an overreaction.

"Why are you so quiet suddenly? You good?" Travis asks, breaking the surrounding silence. I understand his need to keep talking. Dark thoughts live inside darkened spaces.

"Yeah, I'll live. Just worried about Ember." I continue to open and close my fists, working my blood back into each finger and splitting the cuts on my knuckles further.

"Why? Doesn't she have her brothers?"

"Yeah, but I'm not sure about the older one and whose side he's on." I run my eye over the ceiling, seeing the blackened concrete layered in mold.

"Shit," he grits out.

"Yeah. Some of the shit that asshole was spewing in that room was making too much sense. Like he knew things that maybe Ember didn't." The thought has my stomach twisting with dread as I imagine Ember putting her life in Carm's hands to find me. She won't be able to endure another loss.

"Ember has been through some dark shit," he mutters. "Her eyes have always been filled with demons, right from the very beginning."

"She has." I nod, my throat sealing as I think of how many more she'll face if she discovers us too late.

"You have them too," he continues, his words hitting a part of me I've always tried to hide. "When you came back to Whitsborough, I was so scared for you."

I don't answer him right away as I keep my head back against the concrete. I went through a lot in Toronto and I came back a completely different person, especially to Travis. "You have it too."

"You think I've had a glorious life, living in luxury and getting everything I wanted,"—he coughs, the sound wet and deep, causing panic to rush through my chest—"but it wasn't like that."

"What was it like?" I lift my head and stare at him across the room, his eyes downcast to the floor.

"Father was practically insane. He had impossible rules, and as a child, I always broke them. He enjoyed doling out the punishment, which usually had a beating tied to it. Sometimes he used a paddle, a fire poker, or one time, a hammer." He chuckles, the sound deep and sarcastic. "He went through my emails a few years ago and discovered I had a guy as a new-age pen pal. Some emails were flirty, and he lost it, beating me within an inch of my life and leaving my mother to take me to the hospital. They told my doctor I was a victim of a hit-and-run. That's how bad it was, and all because he found out I'm bisexual."

"What the fuck…" I breathe out, shock tearing through me at his confession.

"It gets better…" I can sense he's lost his control and everything is just pouring out of him, needing to be released. "He had a close circle of friends, some of the wealthiest in Whitsborough, and one of them was Coach Halbert."

"Your baseball coach?" Dread curls around my throat and skates down my spine.

"*Former* baseball coach. He was forced into retirement last year… by me." I strain to hear him as his voice drops to low decibels.

"Why? How?"

"Coach Halbert had been teaching me baseball since I was

ten years old. He told my father I had a talent and that I should really focus on it. Even offered to coach me solo." He clears his throat, and I can sense he's struggling with how much to tell me. "My father practically handed me over to him and I never understood why. The man was a perv through and through. He sexually assaulted me for years. Grade nine was the worst year, and finally, I had grown strong enough to fight him off. Fuck… I don't know why I'm telling you all of this." He stabs his fingers through his hair, grabbing the strands and tugging on them as his voice breaks.

"Because you can trust me," I answer him as my stomach rolls with nausea at the news. "Let it all out, Travis."

"If he did it to anybody else on the team, they're not talking, but I have my suspicions. So, last year I took the gun my father hid in his office and paid the coach a late-night visit. I told him to retire for good and not to touch another kid or I would come back and kill him. He believed me and did as I asked. I wish I had the balls to go through with it and just kill him then, but I was so fucking scared." His voice shakes as he drops his hand, his palm meeting the concrete with a smack.

"Not all of us can be killers," I whisper. Travis is good, no matter the blood running through his veins. He's not tainted like me.

"Could you have done it?" he asks me, his glassy eyes meeting mine.

"Yeah." I nod. "I could've. I lived a different life than you though, and I've seen people killed right in front of me. I ran with a pretty rough gang in Toronto and that's why we ended up coming back to Whitsborough."

"When we get out of here…" he pauses and coughs, the sound still wet and pained. "I want you to tell me everything."

"When we get out of here," I repeat, "you, me, and Ember will have a chat."

"Deal," he answers quietly. Then he straightens and turns his head toward the bars, his head cocked. "Did you hear that?"

"Hear what?" I say as I struggle to my feet.

"Sounds like popping. Like someone shooting guns." Travis gets up and walks back over to the bars. "Footsteps are headed this way." Tensing, I begin to push myself to my feet. If there's going to be a fight, I won't be doing it on my ass.

As soon as the last word leaves his mouth, Carlos and a guard appear on the other side of the bars, Carlos looking frantic and the guard twisting his head over his shoulder to look down the corridor. "Get in there and line them up on their knees," he tells the guard.

"We won't do shit," I grit out as I hobble to the middle of the cell. Travis backs up to stand beside me as the door is unlocked and they step inside.

Carlos lifts his gun, cocks it, and then aims it at Travis' head. "You will or I'll kill him right now." Fuck, he's caught on that Travis is my weakness. We both gradually fall to our knees and Carlos comes to stand in front of us, his gun still trained on my brother. "Do it!" Carlos turns and screams at the guard by the door. "Shoot them! I want it done before they get here. I want her to see the—" His arm drops and his sentence is cut off as the guard falls forward, his face smacking off the concrete with a sickening crunch. A knife protrudes from the back of his neck, and I can't describe the immense relief that runs through me when I see that it's one of Emmett's knives.

Carlos' hand shakes as he tries to aim the gun at Travis' forehead. He doesn't have the time to shoot though because Carm rounds the corner into the cell and shoots him point-blank in the back of the head. Both mine and Travis' face is splattered with blood and God knows what else as Carlos falls forward and lands in a pile in front of us. It doesn't matter; we are both alive. I look up at Carm and he crouches down to look us in the eyes.

"Are you guys okay?" The panic in his voice and the worried look on his face tells me he's being genuine. He was always on our side, and I throw my earlier thoughts of betrayal away. He came here and helped Ember to find us.

"Yeah, we're okay," Travis answers as he turns his head toward me. "We're okay." He's sounding like he's reassuring himself as I give him a nod.

Carm helps us up as Emmett comes walking into the cell with an arrogant swagger. His face is covered in blood and his clothes look like he's showered in it. "Shit, you guys look worked over." He grins as he pulls his knife out of the back of the guard's neck. "Don't worry, you're both still pretty though."

"Fuck off." I grin back at him, just the sight of him making the pain worth it. "Where's Ember?" Carm gets me to my feet while patting me on the back, and I give him a nod before offering him a smile.

"She's disemboweling a man that said she was a worthless female." He chuckles, pride heavy in his tone.

"I bet she is…" Travis mutters as I turn to look at him with surprise. He doesn't sound shocked at all and his face remains neutral.

Just then, her voice floats from down the long hallway. She's screaming my and Travis' names as I shuffle toward the door of the cell. Suddenly, she's standing in front of me, her bright turquoise eyes wide with frantic worry.

"Hey," I groan out and try to reach my hand to touch her hair, but her face crumples and she falls to her knees as a sob escapes her throat. "Em?" I croak.

"I couldn't do it again…" she moans and wails, her body jarring forward as her hands hit the concrete, her knife hitting the floor and skating away from her. "I can't lose anyone else." Her head falls forward as the force of her sobbing wracks her body. "I'm… so… sorry…" she says between wails.

I've never seen her like this, like she's completely let loose all the grief she's ever bundled up tight inside her. I fall to my knees in front of her and wrap my arms around her shaking body as my stomach flips with fear. She grabs onto me roughly and I hiss through the pain of her compressing my sore ribs.

"It's okay, Em. We're okay. You saved us," I murmur into her hair. "You saved us."

Chapter Twenty-Four

Travis

"Get me the fucking vodka!" my drunk mother yells at Sonja. Usually, this is where I would step in and refuse her, but after the week I've had, I couldn't fucking care less. She can drink herself to death.

I step out onto my balcony and light a smoke. My ribs still hurt when I inhale too deep, and the gashes on my face still look nasty, but I'm thankful to be alive. I still don't know what made me spill my secrets to Vin, but my view on life has changed because of it. From now on, no one comes above me or my family and that doesn't include the woman I call Mother. My family is Vin and Ember. Finally, they've given me what I've always been looking for, an actual fucking family.

After Vin and I were found in that cell, we headed back to the condo. Ember had completely broken down and was inconsolable for a few days. Emmett wandered the condo anxiously and Vin was getting a desperate look in his eyes because he just wasn't getting through to her. So, I braved the room she was in and found her curled into a fetal position with her body shaking from how much pent-up emotion she'd released. I laid down on the bed beside her and told her everything. I detailed my abuse at home at the hands of both my parents, the sexual abuse I endured at the hands of someone I trusted, and the heartache I felt when I realized I was unable to love conventionally.

She finally moved and turned to wrap her arms around me and cried, and I shocked myself by crying along with her. It was cathartic, and in that moment, I knew we couldn't force her to come out of it. This just had to run its course so the healing could begin.

On the third day, she emerged, and even though she looked like she'd been through hell, she had finished her first step in grieving. Ember sat me down at the table and began telling me about her life in New York. About how she fought in illegal fights for money to help feed herself and her mother, about the circumstances of her mother's death, and then the role her father had in it all.

Ember told me about her kidnapping and being forced to kill by her father's demand, and as soon as she had the chance, she tortured and killed him too. She then told me about the nightmares that haunted her, and how the only way she could keep them at bay was to kill. She took hits that involved corrupt individuals and took immense pleasure from watching them die. It was hard to accept what she was telling me and even harder to not let it change how I viewed her, but that's the way of unconditional love. It doesn't matter what they do, you love them regardless.

I confronted her with the one thing that has plagued my mind for months. Did she kill my father? She reluctantly confessed that she coerced him to take his life after making sure he provided for Vin and his mother. I don't care that she took his life—a small part of me wishes I would've done it—I care that she never told me, but I understand why she did what she did. He was my father and I'm sure she wanted to shield me from the pain of losing a parent. A pain she knows all too well.

Vin voiced the same sentiment, and I was shocked to learn

her killing our father was the one death he had no idea about. I've been sworn to secrecy and asked not to breathe a word of Ember's double life to Adrianna. I wouldn't have anyway. Adri is too soft for this life, and that's exactly why I fight my urges to claim her. She is so innocent and sweet, while I've spent most of my life sinking into darkness and holding on to the fear of never finding the light.

A crash of glass breaking comes from inside the house and I force myself to flick my cigarette over the railing before heading back in to find out what the fuck is going on. My mother is wailing at the top of her lungs—nothing unusual—and I leave my room to investigate further. I peer into her room and find her sitting on the floor in front of a broken mirror and her silk rope sprinkled with blood, the sight making me roll my eyes. Sonja rushes by me and bends down to help my mother up.

"I need Robert back," she whimpers into Sonja's shoulder.

"I know, Miss Christina, I know. You must be strong; he would want you strong." She pulls my mother's fists open, revealing a few superficial cuts. "Let's clean these up."

I leave them to it and head downstairs to the kitchen. I don't know what I would do without Sonja these days, and honestly, I have no clue why she's sticking around. My mother verbally assaults her every day and it continues to escalate. I've tried to fire her three times now, but she keeps showing back up the next day. So I gave her a raise instead and told her to accept it as hazard pay for what she's enduring here.

I'm also dealing with the board members of my father's company. Right now, they're running the day-to-day, but as soon as high school is done, I'm expected to take over my father's position and continue his vision for the company. It's stressful because I don't know anything about the Greene businesses or where our money comes from, but I will find out sooner rather than later. I don't have a choice now that I've inherited everything.

I can't stand this house any longer. Living here is slowly driving me insane and I fear I'll become just as fucked-up as my mother. How do I leave and not feel responsible for cutting the leash I have her on?

The purr of an engine sounds outside in the driveway, the familiarity of it bringing a smile to my face. He keeps showing up here unannounced to whisk me away so I can forget my life for a few hours at a time and I've been looking forward to it every day.

I open the front door to see the gunmetal Hummer idling in my driveway. "Let's go, dickhead!" Vin yells, waving his hand out the window as he winces from the cracked ribs that've been slowly healing. "Em has been trying to reach you all day." Shit. My phone died last night and I forgot to fucking charge it. Being on the receiving end of E's wrath is scary and I'm almost tempted to shut and lock the door instead. I'd do it if I was sure that would keep the fucker out, but it wouldn't. "Don't be a pussy. Let's go!"

I roll my eyes and step out of the house, closing the door behind me. Then I lean in through the passenger side window and raise a brow. "Why am I coming with you?"

"Because I'm your only friend and I'm also your brother. So… that makes you a loser." The green of his eyes twinkle with mischief as he slaps his hands to the steering wheel.

"Granted, but that doesn't answer why I'm coming with you," I prod, knowing it pisses him off. It has the desired effect as he glares at me, his irritation bleeding through. Vin hates to explain himself, but I can't help but pick on him for fun.

"Em has been trying to text and call you all day. She's having a barbeque and she's demanding your presence," he huffs, smacking his hand to the horn, the noise startling me.

"Well, if her highness commands…" I shake my head and open the door to jump into the seat.

"I'm telling her you said that." He points at me with a grin. "You're getting smacked."

"Tattletale," I mutter and fasten my seat belt.

We pull up to E's driveway as she stands on her front porch, arms crossed and tapping her foot. Great, I know that look and I'm about to get an earful. Without prolonging the inevitable, we get out of the Hummer and head toward her.

"Travis and I will be a minute," she tells Vin as he leans down to kiss her cheek. He nods and grins at me over his shoulder. Asshole.

I light a smoke and sit down on her front porch, letting the nicotine soothe my nerves. There's no avoiding Ember, I have to face this now or else she'll hunt me down and it'll be worse. "My phone died and I didn't bother to charge it. I'm sorry." Might as well get that out of the way before she berates me for not getting back to her.

With a grunt, she sits down beside me. "Are you ever going to quit that nasty shit?" She points at my smoke.

"One day." I shrug. When she says nothing, I turn my head and look at her. Frustration is clear in her features but her eyes are soft as she stares back at me. "What? You're not going to yell at me?" I tease with a smirk.

"I'm irritated, but that's not why I wanted you here." She looks down at her painted toes and exhales loudly. "I got a lead on Jennifer, and I need to go after her."

"What? Where?" I stress as I flick my butt onto her driveway.

"Spain." She runs her hands through her hair. "Carm will come and Vin too."

"And me," I retort with my finger to my chest, giving her a

no-nonsense look.

"I need you here." She shakes her head, her eyes filled with pleading. "I won't be back in time for school to start and Emmett needs someone to look out for him. He's been homeschooled his entire life. This is his first year at an actual school."

"Everything about him just makes sense now," I mutter as I rest my arms on my knees, hating that I have to stay behind to watch out for someone I don't care too much for.

"Why do you hate each other?" she asks as worry coats her words. She bites into her cheek as her eyes search mine. Ember wants us to be one big happy family, but I don't think that'll work out the way she wants. I can see Emmett and I clashing, especially with how annoying I find him without even knowing him that well.

"I don't hate him." Looking at her, I shrug my shoulders when she cocks a brow, knowing I'm not being truthful. "I don't know."

"Can you please do this for me? I trust you." It's an honor to have gained her trust because I know she doesn't give it easily, and even though I want to be in Spain with her and Vin, I'll do as she asks.

"Fine. I'll babysit the brat," I grumble.

"You can stay here." She puts her hand on my arm. "I was actually going to ask you to move in with us."

"I don't need pity, E. Plus, I can't leave *her* at the house alone." She smacks the back of my head and my cap flies off. "Hey! What was that for?" I stare at her with shock, my eyes wide as she glares at me.

"First off, I would never pity you. I'm asking you to move in here to be closer to your family. And second, that woman is an adult.

What she does with what's left of her shit existence is her problem, not yours." The disdain in her voice and the hatred reflected in her eyes makes my chest tighten with worry. If I let it go too far, my mother will find herself at the wrong end of Ember's blade. I don't want Ember living with the fact that she made me an orphan.

"Fine, I'll think about it, okay?" I relent as I run my fingers through my hair.

"You can still go check up on her, but you belong here with me, Trav," she persists, wanting nothing less than a yes.

I can't deny that her kind words stir feelings of warmth I have never felt before, and I find myself on the brink of tears. I suck it all back in though and will myself to keep it together. "Thanks, E." My voice cracks, but if she notices, she doesn't say anything.

"Okay, come inside, and just to warn you, Adri is here and she's already drunk." Fucking great, that's just what I need right now. Adri loves to cry and bring up old shit when she's drinking.

Grabbing my hat, I follow her through her house and out to the backyard. The scent of grilled meat hits me in the face and I try to remember when the last time I ate was. Maybe it'll be a good idea to stay here and try to turn my life around.

My thoughts escape me when her laugh forces its way through my carefully erected walls to penetrate my icy heart. When Adri is genuinely happy, she has these full belly cackles and they are so contagious that usually anyone around her will join in. It's been a while since I've laughed like that with her. I turn toward the sound before I can stop myself and find her playing dominoes with Emmett. He has his head thrown back as he laughs with her, his mahogany hair shining in the sunlight. I'm instantly jealous and I can't really figure out why. Maybe because he can give her a normal relationship like I can't? Or maybe it's because he's become closer to her in a few short months than I've ever been in over two years?

My brother sidles up beside me, his shoulder nudging mine. "Bro, when are you going to tell her?" Hearing Vin call me bro after all these years is something I still haven't gotten used to, but I'm liking this new dynamic between us.

"Tell her what?" I play coy as I reach into my pocket for my pack of smokes.

"That you bat for the other team." He snorts as I side-eye him. Funny, using baseball analogies with me.

"Technically, I don't." I shrug as I pull out a cigarette and pop it into my mouth. Then I light the tip and take a deep inhale, letting the nicotine ground me once again.

"Fine." He bumps his shoulder into mine. "When are you going to tell her you like to bat and catch?"

"Fuck off." I shake my head, unable to hold back my grin.

Epilogue

My decorative skull makeup reflects back at me from the darkened window beside his front door. It's been a while since I put this on and I thought tonight would be the perfect occasion. I look up and down the street, waiting for any signs that I'm being watched. I'm in central Whitsborough right now and it's quite different from where I live on the outskirts. The houses are smaller here and closer in proximity, meaning noise will be an issue. Good thing I scouted this motherfucker's life before I came, and that was difficult, considering I wanted to kill him the first night I learned about him.

My anger has been swirling hot for days now and the molten lava flowing through my veins leaves my insides scorched. My body is practically humming with the energy it's consuming just to keep itself together. I could've held this off until I got back from Spain, but I needed to do it now within hours of when I have to be on that plane. There's no way I could be overseas and concentrating on Talia when this piece of shit is still breathing here in Whitsborough. Closing my eyes, I take a few deep breaths. I really don't want this to be over quickly because I'll need to savor his blood and commit every detail to memory so I can look back on this for years to come.

I look back into the house. Every light is off, save for the dim glow emanating from the kitchen. He likes to keep the vent light on at night for when he wakes up and pads to the kitchen for a late-night drink, which he does often. Seems the man has demons that plague him when he shuts his eyes and I am about to send him to Hell for eternity.

I quickly go around to the side of his house toward a single door leading to his garage he never locks. I slip in and see his older model Chevy pickup truck parked inside. Bags of baseball equipment that look older than me line the far wall and he has his lawn equipment tucked into a corner. I creep around the truck, over the four gas cans he has behind it, and find the three steps up to the door that leads to the house, grabbing an aluminum baseball bat on my way. Seems a fitting weapon to use.

I swing open the door and step into a laundry room. The musky scent of sweat hits my nostrils and I turn to find an overflowing basket of dirty laundry. Leaving the laundry room, I turn right in the hallway, running my gloved hand along one wall and the bat along the other. Tobacco smoke hangs heavy in the air and I think of Travis, which only adds fuel to my fire. The cigarette smoke isn't fresh, but it was definitely smoked not too long ago.

There are no stairs in this house, just a single-floor bungalow, two bedrooms and two baths. I've been stopping by for visits each night this week, so the layout is practically imprinted in my brain. Like, for instance, I know as I pass the door on my right, it's a powder room with a filthy toilet and peeling linoleum floors. The next door on my left is some sort of office with a computer full of child pornography. He also had pictures of children, and among them, I found a picture of Travis and also a picture of Marlana with her group of bitches. I packed those all up last night and they sit safely in a locked briefcase inside Shelby's trunk, knowing he wouldn't notice them missing in all his junk.

The last door straight ahead is where I'm headed. It's the master bedroom and inside is the sleeping form of the pedophile, Coach Halbert. I slowly open the door and step into the room. He has yellowed lace curtains hanging from his window, his carpet is a brown shag—not sure if that's the original color—with large, round stains in it, and his double-sized bed has a single sheet on it that's currently wrapped around his fat body.

I walk up to the side of the bed, lean the bat against the edge, and look down into his red, pock-filled face while trying to simmer the rage. I want him to suffer and not let him die quickly by stabbing my blade through his eye, but the urge to do so is overwhelming. His beefy, red lips smack together in his sleep and I fight back against wanting to slice them off.

"Coach," I say into the room. He flies up into a sitting position in the middle of the bed and the sheet falls off his body. He's as naked as the day he was born and he's sporting a very unimpressive erection. "Which boy were you dreaming about?" I sneer and point at his little dick. He takes one look at my face and screams. I pick up his stinking, sweaty sheet and stuff it into his gaping mouth. "Shut the fuck up."

He reaches up with his fat sausage fingers and tries to pull it out, but I hold my knife up to his face and grin. "Please do that so I can free you of these pesky fingers." I poke my blade into his forefinger. He immediately drops his hand as his body trembles. "You know what's funny?" I muse as I look down at him. "Every male predator I've killed has cried and trembled before death. Why is that?" I bend over and look him in the eyes. "You prey on others, abuse them and intimidate them, but when it comes down to fighting to survive, you all fold like little bitches." I slap his cheek and grin. "Are you going to piss yourself too? Did any of the boys you fucked piss themselves from fear?"

He mumbles around the sheet in his mouth and I roll my eyes. "If I take it out and you scream, I'll shove my knife through your throat and watch it come out the other side. Are we clear?" He nods and I rip out the blanket. He coughs and holds his throat like my threat caused him actual pain.

"I can give you information if you leave me alone," he begs

as his eyes water. "I have so much dirt on important people in this town."

"Really?" I reply with mock interest. "Give me an idea of what you got so I can consider this trade."

"The Whitsborough police chief is corrupt and can be paid off to ignore certain things." He shakes as his hands curl into the sheet, his face covered in a sheen of sweat.

"Like you fucking young boys?" I ask, tilting my head to the side.

"Or for watching videos of it and having pictures." His mouth quakes. He's probably realizing he's not getting away with this.

"That's good and all, but not enough compensation to just walk away from a filthy animal like you." I shrug as I pick the blanket back up.

"Wait!" He puts his hands out. "There's a group of us."

"A group of who exactly?" I pause and raise a brow.

"A group who enjoys the same… ah… proclivities."

"You mean raping young boys who trust and look up to you?" I demand angrily, my eyes narrowed.

"Or just rape." He cringes with the admission, his tone filled with regret. I don't care if it's genuine or not. You reap what you sow.

What the fuck? Where the fuck am I living? Whitsborough looks like a Stepford town on the outside, but really, it's teeming with underground indiscretions.

"So, who do we have in this group?" I ask as I drop the blanket and stand straight, tapping the point of my blade to my mouth.

"There are quite a few. I have them all on a file."

"Give me an idea. Name a few."

"Okay… there's the elementary school principal, Andrew Cox, then there's fire chief Wilson McKay and Judge Joseph Watkins."

"Hmm, that is a pretty important group of individuals. Is there anyone else at Precious Blood Academy?"

"No." He shakes his head. Perfect.

"You're going to get out of bed and fetch me that file." When he doesn't move, I widen my eyes. "Now!" I growl.

He jumps up so fast that it's almost comical watching his fat belly bounce until he's standing, his large, hanging stomach covering his small penis. *Gross.* I follow him as he makes his way into the office, banging the bat on the floor with each step. The noise makes his walk a little jerky and his nervousness pisses me off even more.

Inside the office, he goes straight for the desk and opens the top drawer, then he pulls out a letter-sized envelope and gives it to me. Inside is a small, green USB.

"That has every name and information on every person in the group. It also has the name and list of victims belonging to the serial rapist of Whitsborough." He steeples his hands beneath his chin, the skin nearly engulfing the tips.

"Alright, let's head out to the living room. You can take a seat on the recliner." I smile wide as his chin wobbles.

"Can I put some clothes on?" he squeaks, his fear only inciting me further.

"I think not. This is the body of a rapist!" I proclaim, raising the bat in the air. "Why not show it off, huh?"

He walks back down the hallway and we enter his small living room that also couples as his dining room. When he gets to the chair, I swing out the bat and hit him hard on his left knee. He cries out and lands on the floor, clutching his leg. I pick up a dirty sock that's lying on the floor and stuff it so far into his mouth he gags and tears spill out onto his cheeks. He doesn't dare try to take it out, the fucking coward.

"Sit in the chair," I grit out between my teeth.

He slowly hobbles his way into the chair and sits like he's told. Then he shakes his head profusely and mumbles around the sock in his mouth, but I'm done delaying the inevitable. I hold the bat in both hands and butt it hard into his gut. His eyes go wide and his scream is muffled by the sock.

"You know, I was never good at baseball. It's really hard for me to hit such a small ball with a stick." I drop the envelope to the table and pull back the bat, butting it into his balls. Not too hard, just enough to cause pain. "I've gotten better though, clearly." I throw the bat aside and pull my knife out of my hoodie pocket. He's still grabbing his junk and crying as he rocks back and forth in his seat. When I haven't attacked in some time, he looks up at me and startles when he sees the knife in my hand. "You really didn't think I was leaving you alive, did you?" My mouth splits into a maniacal grin.

His mumbling increases and I pull the sock from his mouth. Both his hands come to his face as he cries. So I take advantage of his unprotected genitalia and press the point of my knife into it. As soon as he feels it, his body becomes completely still and he lowers his hands from his face slowly to hold them out in front of him.

"Any last words?" I ask him.

"You're here because of Travis." It's not a question, so I don't answer. However he's managed to put two-and-two together is none of my concern. He's a dead man anyway. "He knows more than you think."

"Why's that?"

"Because he knows the serial rapist of Whitsborough."

"And that is who?" I ask, losing my patience.

"It was Robert Greene," he rushes out. "Robert Greene was the Whitsborough rapist and Travis knew all about it."

I stuff the sock back into his mouth, then I grab a hold of his flaccid dick in my left hand and slice right through it with the knife in my right. His muffled screeching sounds like music to my ears as blood pours out from between his legs and over the recliner. He convulses and grabs between his legs as he's about to pass out from the pain and blood loss combined. I grab his balding head in my hand and run the blade across his throat, reveling in the sight of blood running down his chest and the gurgled sounds coming from his throat.

Then I head out to the garage, swiping a pack of matches from his dining table, and grab a gas can. I come back inside to douse his body in it, making sure the surrounding area is soaked as well. Then, with the USB tucked safely in my pocket, I light a match and throw it behind me. The *swoosh* as the fire catches hits my ears, and with my gloved hands, I raise the hood of my sweater and exit the house through the front door, letting it softly click shut behind me.

For all book updates and social platforms, check out my website

C.A. Rene lives in Toronto, Canada with her family, where
most of the year varies from chilly to frigid. Most days
you'll find her wrapped in her many blankets in bed while
reading or writing her next dark, twisted story.
Her stories boast of inclusivity and refusal to be conformed
in any small box. Writing across genres is a hobby and
drinking wine is a must... Or coffee ... with a splash of
Baileys.

Also by C.A. Rene

The Whitsborough Chronicles

Through the Pain

Into Darkness

Finding the Light

To Redemption

The Whitsborough Progenies

Ivy's Venom

Carmelo's Malice

Saxon's Distortion

Gabriel's Deception

Desecrated Duet

Desecrated Flesh

Desecrated Essence

The Reaped Series

The Reaper Incarnate

Hunting the Reaper

Claiming the Reaper

Hail Mary Duet

Blue 42

Red Zone

Fusion Core

Tension

Release

Steel Dragons MC

Dragon Slayer

Dragon Strife

Dragon Scorch

Hell's March MC Duet

Hell's Viper

TBA

Second Chance Standalones

Fighting the Tide

9 781990 675812